VIRTUOUS

A QUANTUM NOVEL

BY: M.S. FORCE

VIRTUOUS
A Quantum Novel
By: M.S. Force

Published by HTJB, Inc.
Copyright 2015. HTJB, Inc.
Cover Design by the Designing Women: Courtney Lopes and Ashley Lopez
Cover Models Zeb Ringle, Danielle Tedesco, Scott Hoover Photography
Interior Layout by Isabel Sullivan, E-book Formatting Fairies
ISBN: 978-1942295112

All characters in this book are fiction and figments of the author's imagination.

www.marieforce.com

The Quantum Trilogy
Book 1: Virtuous
Book 2: Valorous
Book 3: Victorious

AUTHOR'S NOTE

Welcome to my new Quantum Trilogy, written under the slightly modified name of M.S. Force. Over the last few months, I've been asked a lot of questions about this new trilogy, and I thought I'd take a moment to answer a few of them for you.

Why a new trilogy when I already have three successful series going?
Well, simply put, I wrote the Quantum trilogy because I wanted to. When you're a writer of genre fiction, one of the key ingredients to turning out successful stories that resonate with readers is having a story "call to you." It simply demands to be written. Flynn and Natalie's story called to me, and I couldn't ignore it. I didn't want to ignore it.

Why a new author name?
I'm publishing these books under the name M.S. Force because they are different from anything I've written before. They are earthier, more intense, sexier. They are written in first person, present tense, which is a first for me (and I LOVED it). The language is saltier, the situations grittier and there are cliffhangers. In short, I wanted to send the signal to my loyal readers that these books are a departure for me, so they'd know to expect something different than what they are used to

There's an element of sexual domination in this trilogy that makes us wonder if you were influenced by another successful trilogy...

I understand there's a natural inclination to compare these books to those books. Let me just say for the record that while I admire and appreciate the attention that successful trilogy has brought to the romance genre, I have not read it. I do not plan to read it. This trilogy is my own original work and wasn't influenced by any other books or authors. As you will see, this trilogy is driven, almost entirely, by the characters of Flynn and Natalie, who are all mine. By the time an author has written forty successful books, it's probably safe to say she doesn't lack for her own ideas!

Are you still writing your other series under the Marie Force name?

Absolutely! There will be more McCarthy, Green Mountain, and Fatal series stories this year. In fact, if everything goes according to plan, I will have eleven new ebook releases in 2015 and 10 print releases—the first seven Fatal books and three new Green Mountain books.

And now for the thank-yous! To my HTJB team: Julie Cupp, Lisa Cafferty, Holly Sullivan, Isabel Sullivan, Nikki Colquhoun and Cheryl Serra, thank you for all you do to make it possible for me to do almost nothing but write. And to my husband, Dan, who runs our lives so I am free to write as much as possible. To my kids, Emily and Jake, who are so endlessly supportive of my career—you guys are the light of my life, and I love you to the moon and back. Thank you to my son Jake, who was my car consultant for the Quantum Trilogy and chose all of Flynn's cars for the various occasions—without reading the books.

Thank you to my beta readers Anne Woodall, Ronlyn Howe and Kara Conrad. To my copy editor, Linda Ingmanson: thank you for always making time for me when I need you. And to my proofreader, Joyce Lamb, you're the best, and I love having your eagle eyes on my books before they go live. Joyce did an amazing job helping me to keep all the details straight, and I appreciate her so much! To Sarah Spate Morrison, family nurse practitioner, thank you for your assistance with medical details for this trilogy.

And to my lovely, wonderful, amazing readers who have changed my life so completely, thank you so much for taking this wild ride with me. I'd be nowhere without each and every one of you, and I appreciate you more than you'll ever know. Thank you from the bottom of my heart!

xoxo

Marie

CHAPTER 1

Natalie

Winter in New York City is dirty business. A nasty, grayish hue hangs over the city from November through late March. During my first winter in the city, I've experienced everything from slushy puddles that soak through even the most resilient boots to icy sidewalks to the delightful combo platter of fried onions from vendor carts melding with mystery steam from the underground, creating a smell that defies description.

I love every stinky, icy, frigid inch of it. While others hide out inside, I take to the streets with my dog, Fluff, on a leash. Her full name is Fluff-o-Nutter, but don't judge me. I was nine when I named her after my favorite food group at the time, and fourteen years later, she's still my most faithful companion and the one tie to my old life that I brought to my new life. She goes everywhere with me, except school.

I tried to get her in there—once—but was stopped at the door by stone-faced Mrs. Heffernan, who told me school is no place for animals. Even after I swore I'd keep her under my desk and out of the way all day, the answer was still no. She cited health codes and rulebooks, her spittle hitting me under my left eye. Taking Fluff home cost me a personal day, and I swear Mrs. Heffernan still checks under my desk every day when I'm on recess or dismissal duty, just to make sure Fluff isn't there.

Because I can't take my twenty-pound baby to school with me, I hired a dog walker to care for her during the day. That's working out well, except for the time Fluff bit one of the poodles. The dog walker was irked, but I'm certain poor Fluff was only defending herself. She was quite indignant and put out by the entire incident. I told her she has to behave herself or get stuck inside all day if the dog walker fires us.

Fluff has behaved admirably ever since.

I'm rewarding her good behavior today with a long walk through the Village. The wind is bitingly cold and snow flurries fill the air on this early January day. It's the kind of bitterly cold New York day that keeps even the hardiest of souls inside, so Fluff and I have Bleecker Street mostly to ourselves.

As I'm still somewhat new to the city, everything about it fascinates the girl from Nebraska. I love the architecture and the chaos as well as the taxicabs and the bikes that zigzag the streets on even the coldest of days. I love the stylish women who put together amazing outfits I'd never conceive of on my own, the handsome men, the diversity, the dreadlocks, the tattoos, the music, the theater, the piercings and the food. I despise the poverty, the homeless sleeping outside, the grime, the graffiti. Overall, I love a whole lot more than I hate.

My roommate made fun of me for weeks when I first arrived because I gave money to every poor person I encountered. She told me I'd be broke before Christmas if I kept that up. So I stopped, but my heart still breaks every time I walk by someone in need, because I wish I could help them all. Most of all, I love that I feel safe here. If you're someone who worries the city is dangerous, you'll think that sounds crazy. But when you've survived what I have, safety is relative. The way I look at it, for every one person who might hassle you on the street, there're a hundred good people nearby who'd come to your aid. I take comfort in that.

I window-shop my way from one end of Bleecker to the other, lingering outside Marc Jacobs before the cold forces me on my way. A first-year teacher can only dream about shopping at Marc Jacobs, so there's no point going inside, not to mention they'd freak about Fluff being in there.

Standing still is not an option today. My face is so cold at this point, it's gone numb, and I have the start of an ice-cream headache without the pleasure of the ice cream. I'm thinking about heading home to the cozy apartment I share with one of my colleagues when activity in the playground at the end of the street catches my attention.

"Let's see what's going on, Fluff." We head toward the park, Fluff pulling hard on her leash, though I can't tell whether she's hot on the trail of a scent or a sight. I've learned to let her investigate these things or put up with her pouting all day. She's freakishly strong for a little old dog, and I find myself nearly jogging to keep up with her.

I'm not quite sure how to describe what happens next. All I know is one minute we're trotting along until I slide on a patch of ice, teetering for a moment between disaster and recovery. By the time I regain my feet under me, Fluff has taken advantage of my momentary loss of balance to bust loose. Her leash goes flying out of my hand, and she takes off like a shot, making for the gate to the park on tiny legs that move with puppy-like speed.

Fears of her fragile body being crushed under the wheel of a taxi keep me running as fast as I can, calling her name as I go. She rounds a corner and disappears for a horrifying second before I make the turn into the park and bring her back into view. I'm laser-focused on her and terrified of her clearing the other side of the park and dashing into traffic.

"Fluff! Stop! *Stop!*" I run so hard my lungs are burning from the cold and the exertion. My eyes are tearing, also from the cold, as well as the sheer terror that my defenseless little dog is going to end up as roadkill if I don't get to her—fast. "Fluff!"

I hit something hard and go down harder, landing on my back. You know what it's like when you get the wind knocked out of you and for a whole minute— or even longer—you can't breathe? That's me, lying on the ground in the Bleecker Playground, staring up at the cloudy gray sky, unable to get air into my startled lungs.

I actually begin to wonder if I'm dead. Have I been hit by a bus or a cab or a bike or some other vehicle? Am I drifting between life and death? A crowd forms around me, numerous sets of eyes looking down at me. People are always so curious when bad things happen to other people. I hear angry voices. There's pushing, shoving and jostling around me.

A face appears above mine. A handsome male face. He seems concerned—and familiar. Do I know him from the neighborhood? Someone screams in the background, and I think it might be me.

Then Fluff is there, licking my face, full of concerned obedience. That's when I know I'm not dead—and neither is she. A flood of relief at realizing she's okay relaxes my chest, allowing in oxygen I desperately need. The cold air hitting my lungs snaps me out of the stupor I've slipped into. I look up at soft brown eyes, a kind face, brows knitted with concern.

"Shut *up*, Hayden!" the kind face says. He has really nice eyes and dark hair shot through with hints of silver. I want to reach up and push it back from his brow and see if it's as soft as it looks. His lips are perfectly formed, the kind of lips you want to kiss, and his face is arresting, captivating, lived in, if you know what I mean. "Can't you see she's hurt?"

That voice. Something about it is familiar. I want to ask if we've met before, but I can't seem to speak.

"She fucked up my shot!"

"I said to shut *up*!"

"You shut up! It's not your shot she fucked up!"

Looking down at me, the kind man rests his hand on my shoulder. "Do you think you could sit?"

I try because he asked me so nicely and because Fluff and I have obviously caused some considerable trouble for these people.

His strong arms come around me, helping me to sit up. He's so close I catch a hint of his cologne. He smells expensive, a thought that nearly makes me giggle. Except my chest hurts, and Fluff is making a scene, yipping and trying to get my rescuer's hands off me.

Did I mention she's a bit territorial when it comes to me?

My rescuer's eyes bug out of his head as he gasps. "Holy shit, that damned dog bit me!" He waves his arm around, trying to dislodge Fluff, whose tiny body jerks at the end of his arm. The jerking only makes her more determined to hold on. He lets out an ungodly howl.

The other guy, the one who's been screaming at me, comes rushing over to assist him.

"Don't hurt her!" My voice returns as they're about to hurl poor Fluff across the park in their haste to remove her from the arm of my rescuer.

"Get her off me!"

I scramble to my feet and reach for her, my legs wobbling and my head swimming from the rush of moving too fast.

Thankfully, Fluff sees me on my feet and comes willingly to me, dislodging her victim.

"You're fucking bleeding," the man named Hayden says. "He's *fucking bleeding!*"

I'm not sure who he's talking to until a team of people descends upon the nice guy, tending to his wounds.

"Does he need the ER?" Hayden asks. He's crazy handsome—tall, broad-shouldered, with dark hair and ice-blue eyes. He's also seriously pissed. "Please tell me he's not going to need the fucking ER. If we lose this entire fucking day—"

"*Hayden!*" The injured man waves the others away and dabs at the wound with some gauze. "Shut the fuck up! Walk away and take a deep breath."

"Easy for you to say, Flynn. It's not your ass on the line to deliver this thing on time and on budget."

"Walk. *Away.*"

Hayden storms off, barking orders at people as he goes.

I finally take a look around and see cameras, ladders, light poles, electric cords snaking along the ground, a tented area off to one side and a lot of people milling about looking uncertain. "I'm sorry. I didn't realize you all were here. Fluff... she got away from me, and I went after her." I venture a glance up at him, and that's when it hits me. My dog has bitten *Flynn Godfrey. The* Flynn Godfrey. Flynn *freaking* Godfrey.

"You're... Oh my God. I'm so sorry. I don't know what got into her. One minute we're walking down the street, and the next... She's biting Flynn Godfrey."

His appealing eyes twinkle with mirth.

"It's not funny!" I can't believe he's *laughing.*

"It's kind of funny."

"It's not fucking funny!" Hayden shouts across the park.

"Shut *up*, Hayden," Flynn says without taking his eyes off me.

"Are you all right? I'm so sorry. The biting is new. She's fourteen and more of a terror now than she was as a puppy. And I'm totally babbling. And you're Flynn Godfrey." I take a step back, wishing for a way to simply disappear before I die of embarrassment right in front of the biggest movie star in the known universe.

"Wait."

I halt, because what else does one do when Flynn Godfrey issues an order?

"Are *you* all right?" he asks, his own injury apparently forgotten.

Words fail me under the potent glow of his magnetic beauty, so I nod.

"You're sure?"

"Yes." I force words past the odd sensation in my chest and throat. "Are you?"

"It's a scratch. Nothing to worry about."

"Well, um… It was nice to meet you. I'm a huge fan of your work. Perhaps your biggest fan. But I'm not a stalker or anything." I'm doing it again. I'm babbling in front of the biggest movie star on the planet. "I'm going to stop talking now. I'm sorry again for interrupting your work. Tell *him* I'm sorry, too." I nod in Hayden's direction. He's still ranting and railing, and suddenly I want out of there because the guy is kind of scary pissed.

I tighten my arm around Fluff and make a hasty retreat, nearly tripping over a power cord on my way out of the park. That's when I see the gigantic signs posted on the gates. "Closed Today for Film Shoot." Great.

Acutely aware of everyone in the park watching me go—including Flynn Godfrey, the biggest movie star in the universe—I walk as fast as I can on rubbery legs.

Behind me, I hear male voices arguing, loudly. Then I hear his voice.

"Hey, wait. Don't go."

Is he talking to me? I'm afraid to stop to find out, so I walk faster. Fluff is squirming in my arms, wanting down so she can walk, too. "No way, missy. Your wings are officially clipped."

She whimpers and continues to fight my hold on her.

"Don't even think about biting me, do you hear me?"

"Wait!"

It's *him*, and he's calling out to *me*. While everything in me is telling me to run, to flee, something makes me stop and turn. Much later, I will look back upon the decision to turn around as one of those life-changing moments that you don't realize is changing your life as it happens, but with hindsight you can see how important it was.

Anyway…

He's running after me. Flynn Godfrey is chasing me.

The few people on Bleecker pause in what they're doing to watch him. Even in the frigid cold, the sight of the biggest movie star in the universe stops people in their tracks. His breath forms puffy clouds as he catches up to me. The intense look on his face disarms me.

"Don't tell me you've decided to sue poor Fluff." I go for witty over panicked. "Her net worth is a goose-down bed, a couple of chew toys and a very expensive—and apparently useless—leash."

His lips quiver slightly, but his eyes… His eyes are deep and dark and determined. "You didn't tell me your name."

"Why do you want to know my name? You *are* going to sue me, aren't you? Before you spend a ton of money on lawyers, you should know that Fluff's net worth is quite a bit more than mine."

"I'm not going to sue you," he says, chuckling. "I wouldn't mind some coffee, though. If you have time—and if you tell me your name."

"You… you want to have coffee. With me."

"If you have time, and if you tell me your name."

I'm stunned speechless, and people who know me will tell you that happens well… never. They call me Chatty Cathy at school because I like to talk to my colleagues at lunch when most of them would prefer a few minutes of quiet.

"You do have a name, don't you?"

"It's, um, Natalie."

"Natalie. That's a good name. Does it come with a last name?"

"Bryant." Sometimes my new name still feels funny coming off my lips, but the old name… The old name belongs to the old life, and neither has any place here in my perfect new life that's just gotten a lot more perfect.

"Natalie Bryant. And Fluff." He raises his hand as if to pet Fluff, but her growl makes him think better of it.

"Fluff-o-Nutter."

"Excuse me?"

"That's her full name. Fluff is her nickname." I don't know why I tell him that, but when he laughs—hard—my stomach feels all fluttery and strange. I made Flynn Godfrey laugh. As he wipes a laughter tear from the corner of his eye, I discover I quite like making Flynn Godfrey laugh.

Well, isn't this turning out to be a rather interesting day?

CHAPTER 2

Flynn

She's beautiful in the effortless, guileless manner of truly beautiful people who don't know they're beautiful. Her hair is a mass of dark curls, spilling from under a knit cap that looks homemade. The cold and the embarrassment of our encounter have heightened the color on her cheeks and make her full, lush mouth as red as a ripe strawberry.

I couldn't let her leave without at least knowing her name.

Hayden was apoplectic when I told him I needed half an hour. "We're all fucking freezing out here, Flynn. You're going to make us wait half an hour while you chase after a skirt?"

Only because we are the best of friends—most of the time—did I resist the urge to punch my director and business partner in the face. We've been grating on each other's nerves for weeks as this interminable shoot comes to an end with these final shots in Greenwich Village.

A half hour isn't going to make or break our budget, and Hayden's cozy trailer is nearby to keep everyone warm. That is, if the selfish bastard chooses to share it with the crew. In case he doesn't, I gave the key to my trailer to one of the grips, with orders to invite the crew inside for a break.

The dog named Fluff-o-Nutter growls at me as I contemplate her stunning owner, Natalie Bryant. "So, coffee? Yes?"

Her deep brown eyes take an assessing glance at the neighborhood. "We can go to Gorman's. They'll let me bring Fluff in."

I've never heard of Gorman's, but it's fine with me if it means I get to spend a few more minutes with her. "Lead the way."

We walk the short distance in awkward silence and step into a coffee shop where Natalie and Fluff are clearly regulars. The owner, a big woman named Cleo, makes a fuss over Fluff, who wriggles with delight at the chin scratch.

"How's school going?" Cleo asks Natalie as she serves up what looks to be a skinny latte with skim milk.

I'm guessing, because Natalie doesn't actually place an order.

I can feel Natalie's gaze darting between me and Cleo and can sense her trepidation as she carries on a conversation with Cleo, who either hasn't noticed me or hasn't recognized me. Yet.

"It's good," Natalie says. "I got the best possible class for my first year. I love them all, and even the parents are great."

"You're lucky. My daughter is a teacher uptown and got the exact opposite this year. Bunch a brats, and the parents are worse."

"Yikes. That's got to be tough."

"Does Fluff want a biscuit?"

"No, she's been naughty this morning. No treats today."

Fluff whines in protest.

"That's three twenty-five, honey."

"I've got this." I step up to the counter before Natalie can pull out her wallet. I invited her. I'm paying.

Cleo's eyes widen, and her mouth falls open. "You. You're. You're…"

"Flynn Godfrey. Nice to meet you."

She screams. Loudly. So loudly that Fluff starts barking frantically while squirming in Natalie's arms.

Cleo's scream brings the entire staff to the counter along with some of the patrons. By the time I sign autographs, kiss Cleo's quivering cheek while one of the staffers takes pictures, and get around to ordering a coffee for myself that she won't let me pay for, I've used up a big chunk of my precious thirty minutes.

Looking at Natalie, I point to a table in the corner. "Join me for a minute?"

She glances around at the prying eyes fixed on us, and I hate how uncomfortable she seems. "Um, sure, for a second." She settles into the chair I hold for her, adeptly managing the squiggling dog and her coffee.

This is the part of fame I absolutely hate. I've met a woman I find interesting, but I can't take her for coffee without causing a three-ring circus. In fact, I rarely go out in public anymore without security, but I've decided to risk it for a chance to talk to Natalie. By now she's probably convinced I'm far more interested in myself than I am in her.

I walk a fine line—how do I deny Cleo and her staff a few autographs and a couple of pictures without looking like a jerk? On the other hand, how do I indulge them without appearing self-centered to Natalie?

"Sorry about all that." I tip my head toward the counter where Cleo leans, her rapt attention fixed on us.

"Probably happens all the time, huh?"

I shrug, not wanting to talk about myself. I'm sick of myself and far more interested in her. "So you're a teacher?"

She seems surprised by the question. "That's right. Third grade at the Emerson School, one of the top charter schools in the city."

"Impressive."

"Sure, it is," she says with a laugh that makes my gut clench with desire. She is stunning. Fresh-faced and full of life and exuberance and passion.

"It's very impressive. I give you so much credit. I'd go crazy spending seven hours a day with seven-year-olds."

"My kids are eight, and it's six hours a day."

"I stand corrected," and captivated, which I don't share with her. She's young, I think, as I take a sip of my coffee. Far too young and fresh for me, and yet... I'm captivated. "Are you from the city?"

She shakes her head. "Nebraska. I applied for a special program that brings first-year teachers to the city. They help us find housing and roommates and get settled in exchange for a two-year commitment to the program. They also help with our student loans."

"You're a long way from home."

"And loving every minute of it."

Young and vanilla and from the heartland and so far removed from the kind of woman I normally pursue… I need to get out of here and get back to work before Hayden has me killed, but I can't bring myself to move. Not while the young and stunning Natalie Bryant sits across from me, looking slightly shell-shocked to be sharing coffee with me. I hate that part of fame, too. Right now, I wish to be just a man having coffee with a gorgeous woman, but I'm always FLYNN GODFREY, MOVIE STAR. It's as if the words "movie star" are part of my name, like Junior or Senior or Roman numerals.

She regards me with a glint of humor in her eyes that I find wildly attractive. "I'd ask you what you do, but I already know. Movie star. I'd ask where you're from, but I know that, too. Beverly Hills. I'd ask how old you are, but I know you're thirty-two—"

"Thirty-three," I say, amused by her recitation. "I'm surprised you don't know about the Christmas birthday."

"I know that superstar actor Max Godfrey married superstar singer Estelle Flynn, and when their son was born *on Christmas Day*, Flynn Godfrey was anointed Hollywood royalty. I could ask if you have siblings, but I know there're three sisters, all of them older. So what else should we talk about?" As she poses the question, she props her chin on her upturned hand and gives me a cheeky little smile that slays me.

I'm slain. I'm enchanted. And I'm late. "We could talk about dinner," I say before I give myself even two seconds to think about what I'm doing. I can't let her get away without knowing I'll see her again. I *need* to see her again.

"Dinner."

"Are you familiar with the third—and often final—meal of the day?"

"I've heard of it, but I've never had it with the biggest movie star in the world."

I grimace, because at this moment, I *hate* that I'm the biggest movie star in the world, especially if it's going to cost me the chance to spend more time with this incredible woman. "Is that a major turnoff?"

"Not a turnoff, per se, but you have to admit that for a school teacher from Nebraska spending her first year in New York City, this has been a rather surreal morning."

"I can see how it would be from your perspective, but from mine, it's been a rather refreshing kind of morning. I was hoping it could also be a refreshing sort of evening, too."

"I won't sleep with you."

I'm stunned speechless, which almost never happens. I can't recall the last time someone has surprised me so profoundly.

Her face flushes with color that only adds to her beauty. I want to feel the heat of her cheeks under my lips, and my cock stirs to life as that thought makes it to my addled brain.

"I'm sorry. That was rude. You weren't asking me to go to bed with you."

"No, I wasn't." I smile at her flustered state. "Not yet, anyway. I thought we could begin with dinner and go from there."

"As long as 'going from there' doesn't involve a bedroom, I'd consider having dinner with you."

I'm far more relieved than I should be to know I'll get to see her again. "I promise there'll be no mention of bedrooms."

"Or sofas or backseats or any other horizontal surfaces."

"You forgot walls, stairwells and shower stalls. I do some of my best work vertically."

Her eyes widen and her mouth forms an adorable O that makes me want her fiercely. "You're rather experienced at these things."

"It's more about imagination than experience."

"I, um, I should go and let you get back to work."

I want to kick myself for taking our flirtation a step too far and unsettling her to the point that she wants to get away from me. "I apologize for being forward. I was only teasing. You have my word I'll behave as a perfect gentleman while in your presence, and I'd be extremely honored if you would have dinner with me tonight."

"You... you'd be honored."

"That's what I said."

"Why?" She seems genuinely curious. "You could go out with any woman in the world. Why me? My dog bit you, made you bleed. I'd think you'd be furious with me, not asking me out."

Does she not have the first clue how adorable she is? "Why not you? I told you. It's just a scratch. I've already forgiven Fluff."

At the sound of her name, Fluff bares her teeth at me.

"That's nice of you. I haven't forgiven her yet."

"Could I have your address?" I withdraw my phone from my coat pocket so I can type it in as she hesitantly shares the information. "How about your phone number so I can call you if I'm running late?"

The area code is one I don't recognize, so I assume it's a Nebraska phone number. "Got it." I stand, reluctantly. "I'll text you so you'll have my number if you need to reach me." I wish I had nowhere to be on this cold-ass day. I'd like to spend more time with her. "Sorry to drink and run."

"Thank you for the coffee."

I don't mention that she should be thanking Cleo, who wouldn't accept payment for either drink. "I'll pick you up at seven?"

She rolls her plump bottom lip between her teeth. I'm instantly hard and grateful for the coat that covers the evidence of my arousal. Nodding, she says, "What should I wear?"

I think about that for a second. "A dress. Maybe a black dress. You're a New Yorker now. I assume you have a black dress?"

"I have a black dress," she says with a small, shy smile.

"Excellent. I'll see you soon. Fluff, it's been a pleasure. Take good care of your mom and behave on the way home."

Fluff again bares her tiny—and very sharp—teeth and growls.

"I'm so sorry. I don't know why she's behaving this way. It's not like her."

I wink at Natalie. "Not to worry. At least she didn't ask me for an autograph."

I leave her laughing, pleased with myself and with her and looking forward to this evening with far too much anticipation as I jog back to the park and Hayden's wrath, sending the text I promised her on the way.

He's pacing the length of the playground when I return. "What the *fuck*, Flynn? Are you all done seeing to your personal agenda? Can we get back to work?"

I ignore the first two questions. "Yep."

"What's the deal with the girl?"

"No deal." It's none of his fucking business, but unfortunately, he's known me forever and can tell I'm lying to his face.

"Dude... Seriously? She's an *infant*. You've got no business dragging a sweet girl like that into your world."

The sad part is, he's totally right. There's no place at all for a nice girl like Natalie in my world. No place at all. But I'm fascinated nonetheless and counting the hours until I can see her again.

CHAPTER 3

Natalie

Flynn Godfrey asked me to dinner. The sentence runs through my mind over and over and over again on the walk home. I've put Fluff down to walk because my arms are aching from holding her for so long. She's got a new pep to her step, probably because she thinks she's succeeded in running off Flynn.

It also occurs to me on the walk home that preparing for this evening is going to occupy my entire day. By the time I reach the three-story brownstone where I live with my roommate, Leah, I'm wishing I never agreed to go.

Fluff and I dash up the stairs to the front door and up one flight to our second-floor apartment. Inside, it takes me a full five minutes to remove all the layers I've worn for my walk. By then, Fluff is dancing around my feet, wanting her lunch.

I feed her and stand in the kitchen for a minute, feeling stunned and numb as I relive the events of the last hour. Reaching for my phone, I read and reread his text: *So nice to meet you, Natalie. Look forward to seeing you later. Flynn.*

Leah comes in, carrying a huge basket of laundry and bitching about the stink in the laundry room that seems to get worse with every passing day. She is tall and stick thin with long brown hair and blue eyes. I envy her ability to eat anything she wants. She envies my curves. Except for a couple of fundamental differences in philosophy, we get along well.

"Tell me the truth," she says, dropping the basket and coming over to me. "Do I smell like the laundry room?"

I lean in and take a whiff of her hair, but all I smell is the salon shampoo she's gotten me addicted to, even though neither of us can afford it. "You smell fine."

"Remember that episode of *Seinfeld*? When he picks up his car from the detailer and it smells like BO? Then he starts to smell like BO, and Elaine starts to smell, too, because she's been in the car?"

I wasn't allowed to watch TV growing up and I was too busy trying to survive in college, so I've gorged on television since moving to the city. Leah's obsession with *Seinfeld* reruns has worn off on me. "I love that episode."

"That's going to be us if they don't figure out what the fuck *stinks* in that laundry room. No one will want to be around us."

She swears like a sailor when she's home, getting it out of her system, she says, after a week on best behavior in the classroom with fourth-graders. She encourages me to swear, too, but the few times I tried resulted in hilarity on both our parts. Leah says if I live with her long enough, she'll eventually wear off on me.

"How was the walk?" she asks from the sofa where she's set up shop to fold the mountain of clean clothes.

"It was… You won't believe what happened." The story bursts out of me in a flurry of words and hand motions. When I'm done, Leah stares at me as if I've just told her I saw aliens in the park.

"You're making this up. You're fucking with me."

"No, I'm not. I swear to God it's true."

"You smashed into Flynn Godfrey in the park, Fluff *bit* his arm, you had coffee with him, *and* he asked you to dinner?"

"Yep."

"You're fucking *lying*."

"Leah," I say, beginning to feel exasperated, "*why* would I make that up?"

"You really met Flynn Godfrey."

"I really met Flynn Godfrey."

"*Holymotherfuckingshit!*" She's off the sofa and grabbing me. "Tell me everything. Don't leave out one single detail."

I go through the whole thing again, slowly this time, with as many details as I can recall—which is all of them, of course—and she hangs on my every word.

"And he's coming here? Tonight?"

I show her the text he sent me. "Seven o'clock."

"I'm calling in sick to work." She moonlights at a bar down the street and makes almost as much working Saturday night as she does in a full week at school.

"No, you're not. You can't afford to call in sick." I tutor nearly every day after school to supplement my income. Since Leah can't stand to spend one extra minute with her kids, she works at the bar on weekends.

"I'm not missing the chance to meet Flynn Godfrey."

"I'll bring him by the bar to meet you before we go wherever we're going."

"Where are you going?"

"I don't know. He didn't say."

She waves a hand frantically in front of her face. "I feel like I'm hyperventilating. Am I hyperventilating?"

Since she's still able to form sentences, I say, "I don't think so."

"You're really going out to dinner with Flynn Godfrey."

"I really am."

"You *soooo* have to do him."

"I am not *doing* him. I already told him that."

She moans loudly. "Natalie, honestly. You're going out with the hottest guy *on the fucking planet.* If you won't have sex with him, I will."

"You know my feelings about that." I made what I now know to be a mistake of epic proportions when I told my new friend and roommate I wouldn't have sex with any man unless I'm married to him. I haven't told her—or anyone—the reason for my vow. I have a good reason, but it's my business and mine alone. What she doesn't need to know is that by telling men I'm saving myself for marriage, I save myself the bother of sex, which is exactly the way I want it. She has mocked me endlessly, so much so that I finally told her to shut up about it or I would never tell her another thing ever.

She shut up about it, but she hasn't forgotten. "This is no time for rigid virtue, Nat. This is the time to cut loose and have some fun that you'll remember for the rest of your life."

"It's not happening. I know you find my beliefs ridiculous, but they're important to me."

"They're not ridiculous," Leah says with a sigh. "They're admirable."

I roll my eyes at her because I don't believe for a second she means that.

"They *are* admirable, and I'm not making fun of you. I swear I'm not. It's just… They might be slightly… unrealistic. That's all."

"Maybe so, but I'm not changing my mind or my values just because a famous actor asked me out. If I change who I am for one night, who will I be tomorrow?"

Leah puts her hands on my shoulders and looks me dead in the eye. "You'll still be you. You'll just be *you* having been *done* by *Flynn Godfrey*."

She's so sincere and so imploring that I bust up laughing, which she doesn't appreciate.

"Mark my words. You'll look back in ten years, when the cherry has been popped and you're stuck with the *one guy* you'll get to have sex with for your *whole* life, and say to yourself, 'I so should've listened to Leah and fucked Flynn Godfrey when I had the chance.'"

I put my hands over my ears, pretending I can't hear her.

"I'm writing the date down so I can remind you of this conversation in ten years."

"I'll look forward to that, but for now I need to figure out what I'm going to wear. Are you going to help me or what?"

"Will you please, for the love of God and all that's holy, wear 'just in case' underwear underneath?"

"Absolutely not."

"Ugh," she sighs, "you're ridiculous, but I'll help you anyway."

At four o'clock, the buzzer sounds from the lobby with a delivery that Leah goes down to get. She returns carrying the most incredibly gorgeous purple orchid in an equally beautiful ceramic pot.

She hands me the card. "As if there's any doubt, it's for you."

I feel foolish as I take the card from her, because my hands feel shaky as I open the envelope.

Enjoyed meeting you and Fluff this morning. Looking forward to dinner. FG

"What does it say?" Leah is jumping around trying to see over my shoulder, so I hand the card to her.

"Oh my God! That's so romantic!"

Granted, it's nice of him to send me such a beautiful plant—that I haven't the first clue how to care for—but romantic? I don't know if I'd go that far.

"Isn't it romantic?" Leah's excitement is starting to grate on my nerves. It's just dinner. I can't figure out why she's making such a big deal out of it.

"Sure," I reply, because it's easier than getting into another debate with Leah about why I'm not wired the way other women our age are. I stopped being like other people my age when I was fifteen. That's when someone I trusted stole my youth and innocence. But I'm not thinking about that today. If I allow myself to think about that, I'll never be able to get my act together in time for Flynn's arrival. I've made not thinking about that into an art form, and I've learned the hard way what happens when I allow the darkness to intrude on my new life.

By six thirty, I'm a total disaster. I've spent all afternoon with Leah, primping and preparing, and I hate the way my hair looks, my makeup is awful, and I'm almost out of time.

She's spraying more crap in my hair that now looks nothing like my hair. It actually resembles hair in a picture she found in *Vogue* that she said would be similar to what he'd expect. As if she somehow knows what he expects.

I don't know who I'm trying to be, but it's not me, and I can't do it. "Leah. Stop."

"What do you mean, stop? We're not done."

"Yes, we are." I pull the towel off my shoulders and turn to her in our cramped bathroom. "I look like a freak. It's all wrong."

"What're you doing? Natalie! He's going to be here in *half an hour!*"

I have just enough time to do this my way. "I need the bathroom, Leah."

Throwing up her hands, she storms out, and I move faster than I ever have in the shower to wash all the crap out of my hair and off my face. I dry my hair in record time, but don't bother to straighten it the way I normally would before a big event. A bit of mascara, a touch of lip gloss, and I'm done.

I emerge from the bathroom just as Leah is about to leave for work. She takes one look at me and shakes her head, her dismay apparent. "Don't forget to bring him by the bar."

"I won't."

"Have fun, Nat, and don't be a total prude. Let your hair down a little—for real."

"I can have fun without getting naked."

"Don't knock it till you've tried it, girlfriend. I'm out."

I want to tell her that virtuous and prudish are not synonymous, but she's gone before I can get the sentence out of my mouth. I'm not a prude. I don't judge others for their choices. I don't expect anyone to embrace my beliefs, nor do I try to inflict them on others. I've never said to Leah, for instance, "You shouldn't sleep with every guy you date," because that would be prudish and judgmental.

Yet she finds it perfectly acceptable to tell me I need to let loose and get naked with someone I don't even know. It's a double standard I could defend all day except I'm down to ten minutes until Flynn will be here. I still cannot believe I'm casually having that thought. *Flynn will be here.*

In my room, I put on the one black dress I own along with thigh-high hose and high-heeled black boots. I hope I don't regret the heels, but I'm also hoping we won't be outside for long, because the temperature has dropped into the teens. Feeling rushed and not at all ready for a date of this magnitude, I fill a small purse with the essentials, adorn my wrist with silver bangles and insert fake diamond stud earrings to complete my ensemble.

I take an assessing look in the mirror, and while I could never compete with the casual perfection of the women I see on the streets, at least I look like me—for better or worse. The buzzer sounds, and I jump a foot, which startles Fluff into a barking frenzy.

"Stop it." I bend down to pat her furry head and kiss her furry face. "I'll be back later. Behave yourself, and I might give you a treat."

At the word treat, she sits and looks at me expectantly.

"Oh, all right." I fear I'll be an awful mother to my future children, and it'll be Fluff's fault. Fully manipulated by the woeful eyes of a twenty-pound dog, I dole out a couple of treats and grab my coat and purse. Pushing the button on the intercom, I say, "I'll be right down" and end the connection before he can reply.

My hands are shaking again, and I hate that I'm so nervous. He's just a man. A man who puts his pants on one leg at a time, as my grandfather would say. On the stairs, my heel catches on one of the rubber treads, and I stave off disaster by grabbing the banister. I strain a muscle in my arm in the effort to keep from pitching down the stairs. That only adds to the remaining aches and pains from my fall in the park this morning.

Humbled by the near miss, I stop and take two very deep breaths. *Just a man. One leg at a time. Just a man. A person like anyone else. In through the nose, out through the mouth.* While I'm standing still, I finish buttoning my red wool coat and pull on my gloves. Holding on to my composure, I go slowly down the remaining stairs and open the door to Flynn Godfrey himself. He's wearing a black overcoat that he's left unbuttoned, which is how I can see a crisp white dress shirt that he's worn without a tie. I briefly home in on that triangle of exposed skin above his top button.

In that moment, I realize I expected him to have a driver. Movie stars don't drive themselves around the city, do they? Apparently this one does.

He stares at me for a long moment—long enough that I fear I forgot to wipe the toothpaste from my mouth or worse…

"You… You're stunning."

It's then I realize he's staring at me for all the best reasons, and my heart begins to do this weird galloping thing that quickly makes me feel light-headed. He extends his arm, and because I'm prone to disaster today, I take it gratefully.

As he helps me down the stone stairs, I notice the shiny black vehicle with tinted windows parked at the curb with hazard lights flashing. My hands go sweaty with nerves. I'm grateful for the gloves and the cold air whipping against my heated cheeks.

Flynn opens the passenger door and holds it for me until I'm settled. As I slide into a heated leather seat and breathe in the scent of the most appealing cologne I've ever encountered, it occurs to me that no one will know where I am tonight. Leah knows who I'm with but not where I'll be. She's working at the bar until two a.m., and she won't get home until after three—that is, unless she gets a better offer, and then she won't be home at all. These thoughts begin to make me feel panicky as he gets in next to me and closes the door.

"You are lovely," he says.

"Thank you." I look at him, still not quite believing I'm sitting in a fantastically expensive sports car next to Flynn Godfrey. "Could I ask a favor?"

"Of course."

"My roommate was very disappointed that she had to go to work before you picked me up. I wondered if you would mind—"

"Where does she work?"

I tell him where the bar is, and he considers it before turning his potent gaze on me, seeming troubled. "I hope you understand… I can't go in there without causing a circus. Perhaps you could ask her to come out to see us?"

"Sure. She can do that."

"What now?" he asks, studying me so intently that I feel unsettled and on display.

"I… I wondered if it would be all right if we told her where we're going tonight."

He raises a dark brow. "Are you scared of me?"

More like terrified, but I can't say that. "No, but I only met you this morning, and it would make me more comfortable if someone who cares about me knows where I am."

"I understand."

Despite what he says, I can't help but wonder if he really does understand what it's like to be a young woman, new to the city, navigating the many perils. If I'd been speaking to my parents, they would've tried to talk me out of coming here. They were afraid of everything, especially things they didn't know or understand. But I haven't talked to them in eight years, so they didn't get a say in my big decision. The second I got the letter of acceptance into the program, I knew there was nothing that would keep me from moving here to make my dreams come true.

I pull off my gloves and send a text to Leah, asking her to come outside to meet us. We pull up to the bar a few minutes later, and she is waiting in the cold without a coat on.

Flynn puts the passenger side window down, and leans over me without actually touching me, but I'm acutely aware of his nearness.

Leah's hand comes up to cover her mouth when she sees him.

I'm grateful she doesn't actually scream.

The words "shut up, shut up, *shut up*" are muffled by her hand.

"Leah, I presume?" Flynn says in the rough, sexy tone that made him a superstar.

With her hand still over her mouth, Leah nods.

He looks at me. "Is she always so talkative?"

That makes me laugh. "Give her a second to recover, and then she won't shut up." I look out at her. "Satisfied?"

"For now," Leah says.

"Natalie would like you to know where we'll be tonight. I'm going to use her phone to text the address to you, all right?"

"Um, yes," she says, her voice squeaky. "That's fine."

"If I don't come back, I expect you to *do* something about it," I add.

"I believe she's concerned I'm going to abscond with her and never bring her home. I have to confess, the thought crossed my mind, but I'm going to save the absconding for our second date."

Leah visibly swoons, fans her face and spins around in a complete circle. Then she leans in the car and points to me. "Remember what we talked about?"

I'm so petrified she's actually going to say it out loud that I refuse to even nod for fear of encouraging her.

"No time like the present, my friend. Mr. Godfrey, it was indeed a pleasure to meet you. If you abscond with my roommate, I won't call 911."

"Leah! *Yes, you will!*"

"Relax. Have some fun. Go a little *wild*." She waggles her brows and succeeds in infuriating me. I hope the look I give her makes it clear I'm going to kill her in her sleep.

"We can leave now," I say to Flynn, who seems to be settling into the conversation.

"But this is just getting interesting."

"Go to work, Leah."

"Go wild, Natalie."

"It was very nice to meet you, Leah," Flynn says, chuckling softly.

"You, too. Thanks for coming by. Come back again sometime when you can come in and I can impress all my coworkers because we're friends."

"I'd be happy to."

She waves and skips back inside, no doubt ready to spill the beans about who her roommate is out with.

"She's hilarious," he says, earning a glare from me. "What? She is."

"If you say so."

"May I borrow your phone to send her the text I promised?"

I find Leah's name on my list of contacts and hand him the phone with the text screen open.

He taps out a quick text and returns the phone to me.

"Do I get to know where we're going?"

"When we get there."

I don't like his answer. All of a sudden, I don't like this whole thing. His vague response to a legitimate question coupled with Leah's foolishness has put me in an unsettled mood. I wish I was at home with Fluff, eating takeout and watching movies on TV like I do every other Saturday night. What am I doing in this car with Flynn Godfrey?

"I'd like to go home, please."

CHAPTER 4

Flynn

For the second time, she has stunned me. I turn in my seat so I can see her face. She's staring straight ahead, refusing to look at me. "Excuse me?"

"I said I'd like to go home."

"Why?"

"Because I don't know why I'm here, and I no longer wish to be."

"You're here because I enjoyed your company this morning, and I'd like to get to know you. And I sort of hoped you felt the same about me."

She finally looks at me, and I discover she's even more stunning when she's angry. "Why me?"

It occurs to me that I should choose my words carefully. Any chance I have with her rides on what I say right now. "I found you to be a refreshing change of pace. Do you know how rare it is for me to meet someone who doesn't go all crazy about what I do and who I am?"

"I did that. A little."

"A little. And then you were… normal. I liked that. I *appreciate* that. I want to spend more time with that. With you. You're beautiful and sweet and unaffected and passionate about your job and your new city, and… I like you." I shrug off the unexpected swell of emotion that starts in my chest and threatens to close my throat. "I miss normal conversations with normal people. Do you know how long it's been since I met someone normal?"

"I appreciate that you think I'm normal, and I understand you mean that as a compliment."

"As the highest of compliments."

"But…"

"But what?"

"I don't know how to say this without hurting your feelings, and I don't want to do that."

She's adorable, and I want her with a desperation that stuns me. "Don't worry about me. I can take it. Lay it on me."

"I know things about you."

That frightens me, another emotion that catches me by surprise. "What things?" I notice her fingers are trembling when she brings them to her throat. "I know about your feelings in regard to women and relationships and marriage and commitment."

"You know what's been reported in the media."

"Yes, and it's not particularly flattering to women. I didn't take the time earlier to consider how I feel about those things. Now that I have, I don't see the point in spending time together when nothing can come of it."

"You have to know that much of what's reported about me is utter bullshit."

"Much but not all."

"No," I concede, "not all of it."

"Is the part about how you were so burned by your first marriage that you'd never marry again true?"

The question registers a direct hit to the gut, and I fight the need to squirm under her sharp gaze. "That part might be true."

"So then there really is no point at all to us spending more time together, because if you're like most men, and I suspect you are, the dating ritual is undertaken with one goal in mind—to get your flavor of the week into bed. Since I have not and will not sleep with anyone I'm not married to, and you have no intention of ever marrying again, I'd say we're at an impasse."

"So wait, you haven't… That's to say…"

"You heard me correctly."

For the third time, she has knocked the air out of my lungs. "Well…"

"Let's skip this whole thing, shall we? Would you mind taking me home?"

"I…" Suddenly, I'm panic-stricken at the thought of her escaping before I have the chance to know her. I realize I'm in deep, deep trouble when it occurs to me that it doesn't matter if she won't sleep with me. What I want from her, what I *need* from her, goes far beyond sex. "Please." My voice has been reduced to a mere whisper. "Give me tonight. If after that you don't want to see me again, I'll respect your wishes." I reach for her hand and bring it to my mouth, brushing my lips lightly over her knuckles.

She draws in a sharp breath that tells me she's not immune to me. Not at all. But as always, I have no idea if she's reacting to me or to the fact that a movie star kissed her hand. I'd like the opportunity to find out.

"Please."

She looks at me for the longest time, and I have the oddest feeling that my entire life and any chance I have to be truly happy depends on what she says next. It's a feeling I've never experienced before, and it shocks the living shit out of me.

"Okay," she says softly, making me feel as if she's given me a priceless gift.

Maybe she has. She's given me the pleasure of her company, which is suddenly the most important thing to me.

I turn the car toward our destination, and we drive uptown in silence. I'm not sure who's more nervous about how this night will go—me or her.

Natalie

I'm frightened by the attraction I feel for him. I've never felt such a strong pull toward another human being, and I don't know if I'm attracted to the man or the celebrity. Wouldn't any woman with a pulse feel tingly and breathless sitting next to the specimen known as Flynn Godfrey? Or does what I'm feeling have nothing to do with who he is to the rest of the world and everything to do with who he could be to me? How will I know?

We drive farther uptown, the cross-street numbers increasing with every block. Traffic slows us down in the theater district, where the bright lights of Broadway dazzle me. I haven't spent much time up here, haven't ventured beyond Times Square or the designer boutiques on Fifth Avenue. I've been where the tourists go. He's taking me somewhere else entirely.

"Have you been to any Broadway shows yet?" he asks.

"Not yet. The tickets are a little steep."

"Yes, I suppose they are."

He probably gets in for free, which is ironic. Those who can most afford admission don't have to pay.

"Which show would you like to see?" he asks.

"Either 'Book of Mormon' or 'Wicked'."

"They're both amazing."

"Of course you've probably seen everything."

"Not everything, but I try to catch a couple of shows whenever I spend time in New York. I love live theater."

"Have you performed in the theater?"

"A very long time ago. Back when I was just getting into the business. It's something I'd like to do again someday."

A few minutes later, we pull into an underground garage, and my nerves come back with a vengeance. I feel like I'm being taken into the bowels of Manhattan, and I may or may not ever be seen or heard from again. I share this thought with Flynn, who finds it hilarious.

"You have one hell of an imagination, Natalie Bryant."

My new name sounds right coming from him. It sounds like me—the new me. I like the new me. She's brave and bold and mostly fearless. That is until the biggest movie star on the planet decides he wants to spend time with her. Then she becomes nervous and fearful and riddled with the anxiety that nearly debilitated her in the past.

I don't want to be her anymore. I worked so hard to escape those shackles, to find my way out of the nightmare of my past into a future bright with promise. I can't let one night with an enigmatic man undo all that hard-won progress. I won't let that happen.

"I can hear you thinking," he says as the car descends ever deeper into the garage.

"How can you hear someone thinking?"

"Your thoughts are so loud they permeate the silence."

"All right. I'll bite. What am I thinking?"

"Wait. You bite? Really?"

I roll my eyes at his shameless flirtation. He's incredibly gifted in that regard. A master, if you will. I am woefully out of my element, and we both know it.

He pulls into a parking space and turns off the engine. "You're thinking this is the craziest, most impulsive, most ridiculously unsafe thing you've ever done in your life and…" He tips his head and studies me in that intent, knowing way that has become familiar to me in the short time we've spent together. "You're wishing you were home sharing Chinese takeout with Fluff rather than wasting your time with a man who wants things you aren't interested in."

I'm stunned, shredded, exposed and reminded of how broken I truly am. I have no business being interested in him or wondering what it would have been like to meet him as a whole and healthy woman who could give him what he wants.

"How close was I?"

"Startlingly."

He sticks out his lip in a pout that is naturally adorable coming from him. "I've never been so jealous of a twenty-pound ball of fur in my life. I bet she even gets to sleep snuggled up to you, right?"

"Of course she does."

"What about the goose-down bed that was listed among her assets earlier?"

"It's all for show. We don't want people talking about us sleeping together."

The pout morphs into a smile so potent, my panties feel too tight all of a sudden. I'm constricted and tingling in places I've never tingled before. It is the smile that has landed him twice on *People* magazine's Sexiest Man Alive cover. It's the smile that opens movies and makes women do crazy things like climb the security fence at his home and send him photos in the mail that no one but their husbands should ever see. Yes, I've read every word that's ever been printed about him, so I have an unfair advantage.

I know everything about him. He knows nothing about me, and if I have my way, he never will.

Flynn

I want to know everything about her—if she requires coffee to function in the morning, what her favorite song is, her favorite color, what she likes to sleep in. The possibility that she prefers to sleep in nothing at all is one I can't afford to entertain at the moment. Not when I'm trying to keep her from running away. She's like a skittish colt being introduced to a saddle—always ready to bolt. I've known her less than twelve hours, and I already understand that if I let her run, if I let her get away, the memory of her will haunt me forever.

"What kind of car is this? It's nice."

Yes, it's nice and worth more than one-point-five million dollars, not that I'd ever tell her that. "It's a Bugatti Veyron."

"I've never heard of that."

"Cars are one of my vices." I gesture to the white Range Rover SUV and the red Ducati motorcycle, which is my preferred means of transport in the city. I decided earlier that the Range Rover is too pedestrian for such an important evening, and the Ducati would scare her away for sure. I'll save that for the second date, if I get that lucky.

The thought gives me pause as I get out of the car and go around to help her. It's not often that I worry about getting a second date. I've become complacent where women are concerned. It's been a long-ass time since anyone made me work for a second date the way I already know I'll have to with Natalie.

She takes the hand I offer to help her out of the car, and the impact of her skin brushing against mine travels through my body like a live wire. When she glances up at me, eyes wide and lips parted, I know for certain my touch had the same effect on her.

I watch as her sleek legs propel her up and out of the car, my mouth going dry at the thought of touching those well-defined muscles.

When she runs a hand over her skirt, I discover I'm staring and force myself to look at her face and not at the rest of her. I close the door and lock the car out of habit, not out of fear of it being stolen from a garage only I have access to. As I lead her to the elevator, I continue to hold her hand and consider it a small victory that she doesn't pull away from me.

In the elevator, I insert the keycard that takes us to the top floor. She's quiet on the short ride, but observant, her gaze darting around to take in the details of the well-appointed elevator but steering clear of me. For some reason, I find her reaction to me amusing and endearing and more than a little refreshing. Women tend to be silly around me. They talk constantly. They fill every silence with chatter, as if they fear I'll lose interest if they aren't endlessly entertaining and charming.

Natalie fills the silence with more silence, and I find myself desperately trying to think of something to say that will engage *her* and keep *her* interested in *me*. I'm humbled to admit I'm way out of my league with this woman, which only makes me more determined to know her.

Before I can be charming or witty, the elevator dings, and we arrive at my top-floor apartment. The doors open, and I lead Natalie into the foyer.

"Can I take your coat?"

"Sure, thanks."

I release her hand to help with her coat.

"May I?" She gestures to the rooms beyond the foyer.

"Of course. Make yourself at home."

She wanders into the living room and gravitates toward the floor-to-ceiling windows that overlook Central Park and Fifth Avenue. "This view is incredible. You can see the skating rink and the boathouse."

"The view sold me on the place."

She turns away from the window to take a look at the rest of the apartment, which consists of a spacious living room, a kitchen I rarely use, an office where I spend most of my time when I'm in New York, and the bedroom and master bathroom.

"Want to see the rest?"

"I'd love to."

I take her into my office, where she spends a few minutes looking at the photos of family and friends I've put up on the wall over my desk, which is covered with scripts that threaten to avalanche onto my laptop. I need to clean this place up one of these days.

When she's looked her fill, we cross the hall to the bedroom, and she surprises me when she steps inside for a better look at my king-size bed and the photos of my nieces and nephews on the bedside table. "Bathroom is in there."

As she opens the door to take a peek, I'm grateful I took the time this afternoon to make the bed and pick up the towels from the floor.

"I love your tub," she says when she rejoins me in the bedroom. "If I had a tub like that, I'd take bubble baths every night."

The image of her in my tub surrounded by bubbles has me swallowing hard and forcing thoughts of anything other than her naked body into my mind, so I don't embarrass myself—and her—with a predictable reaction. "Feel free to come over and take a soak any time you want to."

"Sure," she says with a laugh. "I'll just pop over for a bubble bath."

"My tub is your tub."

"Be careful making promises you have no intention of keeping."

I'm surprisingly wounded by her certainty that I'm being insincere. I cross the room to my dresser and return to her with a keycard that I hand to her. "Any time you want."

"I was joking," she says as a flush of color overtakes her cheeks.

"I wasn't." Nothing about the way I feel when she's in the room is a joke to me. I've lived long enough, dated enough women, slept with more of them than I probably should have, to know when something is different, special and unique. Natalie is all those things.

She tries to give the key back to me. "You shouldn't give someone you barely know a key to your home. Don't you have security people to tell you things like that?"

Her indignant reply makes me laugh, which seems to annoy her. "Are you telling me you can't be trusted with my key?"

"I'm telling you that you shouldn't be so cavalier with your security. How do you know I'm not a crazy stalker fan girl?"

"Are you?" I ask with mock concern. Somehow I already know I can trust this woman with everything I have.

"No, but you have no way to know whether I'm lying to you."

"Do you believe in instinct? Gut checks?"

"I guess. Sort of."

"My instincts are telling me you can be trusted with that key. My gut is telling me I won't regret sharing my bathtub with you, since I never use it, and it's a shame to let it go to waste if it could bring you pleasure."

Once again her cheeks flush, this time at the word "pleasure."

"You never use that tub? Seriously?"

"I'm ashamed to confess I've never used it."

"And how long have you owned this place?"

I have to think about that for a second. "It'll be ten years in March."

"That's tragic."

"What can I say? I'm a shower kind of guy."

All at once, she seems to realize we're having a somewhat intimate conversation within the confines of my bedroom. "Does this place have a kitchen?"

"Right this way."

I turn on the lights in the kitchen as a smile stretches across her face. "Wow. Now I have kitchen envy, too."

"You have the key. Feel free to use it. This is another room that gets very little attention from me, other than the fridge where you can always find a cold beer."

"Such a guy."

"Guilty as charged. Speaking of my utter inability to cook, I thought about hiring a woman I know who cooks for our production team whenever we're in town to come over and make something for us tonight, but that seemed too pretentious." I open a drawer, withdraw a stack of takeout menus and lay them out on the counter before her.

She presses two fingers to her lips, seeming to suppress a laugh.

"Are you laughing at me?" I ask her, mocking outrage.

Pinching her index finger and thumb together, she says, "Just a little."

"That's not very nice of you. Here I am, laying myself bare, admitting my failings, and you're laughing at me." I shake my head, delighted when a gurgle of laughter erupts from her, making me feel like I've won something precious. My stomach lets out a loud growl, which only makes her laugh harder. "Yes, I'm starving, so if you wouldn't mind telling me what you'd like to eat, I'll make the call."

She rolls her lips adorably and studies the menus with the same intensity I suspect she gives everything. It's a little unsettling to admit how much I want to be on the receiving end of that intensity.

"This," she says, handing over the menu for a nearby Italian place that delivers. "My favorite. What's your pleasure?"

"Chicken piccata and a Caesar salad, please."

I stare at her for a brief moment. "You won't believe me when I tell you this, but that's my regular order."

"You're right. I don't believe you."

Shaking my head in amusement, I withdraw my phone from my pocket and dial the number from memory. "This is Flynn Godfrey. Two of my regular, please." I smile at her as I place the order. "Thanks."

"That doesn't prove anything, you know," she says after I end the call.

"Yes, because I really could've set that up in advance." She laughs, and I'm captivated all over again. She's adorable and sassy and funny and easy to be with. I'm Flynn Godfrey, regular Joe, with her, and I like how that feels. I get so fucking tired of being FLYNN GODFREY, MOVIE STAR, with other women.

"You surprise me," she says.

I'd been reaching for wineglasses, but I stop to turn to her. She's taken a seat at the bar that separates the living area from the kitchen. "How so?"

"I figured you'd have... people. Driving you, cooking for you, tending to you."

"Are you disappointed that I don't?"

"To the contrary. I'm pleasantly surprised."

"You can't believe everything you read, you know." I hold up a bottle of pinot noir and another of chardonnay.

She points to the white, and I get busy uncorking it.

"I can believe some of it, though, right?"

"Very little. Most of it is utter bullshit."

"If they print lies, why don't you sue them?"

Shrugging, I tell her, "Because I have better uses for my time and money. If I sued over every lie they publish, that's all I'd do."

"But if you sue every time they lie, maybe they'd stop lying."

"As long as their lies sell papers and magazines and bring people to their websites and TV shows, they'll keep doing it."

"I can't imagine what that must be like, to constantly have to read lies about yourself in the media." She takes a sip of the wine and makes a satisfied noise that has everything male in me standing up to take notice. "Wow, that's good."

"I'm glad you like it." I don't mention that my partners and I own the vineyard. It had better be good. "And as for the lies, I mostly ignore them. I have lawyers on retainer to keep an eye out for particularly egregious lies, but for the most part, I don't give them any of my time or energy."

"What counts as a particularly egregious lie?"

"Last year, I sued a tabloid in the UK for insinuating that my nephew—my sister's son—is actually my child because he looks like I did as a kid."

She stares at me, her mouth agape. "Are you *serious?*"

"Afraid so."

"I hope you sued their asses off."

I laugh at her indignant reply and fall a little deeper into what's happening between us. "I sued them and so did my sister and her husband. It was ugly, but we made it go away before Ian, my nephew, ever caught wind of it. Thank God for small favors. The settlement will pay his way to any college he wishes to attend."

"It's so disgusting and invasive. I'm sorry that happened to you and your family."

"Thank you. I hate to say that we're sort of used to it, but when you grow up with parents like ours, it seems to come with the territory. It's gotten a lot worse in recent years. My mom says all the time that she would've lost her mind if it had been like it is now when she was starting out in the business."

Natalie props her chin on her upturned fist. "Is she as fabulous as she seems?"

"More so." My smile is genuine when I think of my feisty, funny, wonderful mother. "She'd like you."

That seems to please her. "Really? How come?"

I take a seat on the stool beside hers, careful to make sure that no part of me is touching any part of her. "Because you're passionate about your work and you have true purpose. She appreciates those qualities in people."

"I do love my work. I wasn't sure I would, but it's amazing to feel like I'm really making a difference for my kids. At times I wonder how I'll ever let them go when the school year ends. I've gotten rather attached."

"They're lucky to have such a devoted teacher."

"I'm the lucky one. So many of the teachers I was in college with have gotten awful kids and worse parents. Mine are all so great. I'm told to enjoy it because no one gets that every year, but for now, there's nothing not to love."

"I bet all the little boys have mad crushes on Miss Bryant."

"*Whatever*," she says, rolling her eyes.

"I had the worst crush on my second-grade teacher, Mrs. Carole. She was so hot."

"You've been a ladies' man since you were seven, huh?"

"I like to think I have discerning taste," I say with a wink that makes her laugh.

The intercom buzzing stops me from staring at her. I like when she laughs. I like it a lot. "Excuse me." I cross the room to the elevator, where the intercom is located. "Yes?"

"Sorry to disturb you, Mr. Godfrey. We have a delivery downstairs for you."

"Send it up. Thank you."

"Thank you, sir."

While I wait by the elevator, I catch her looking at me. She seems embarrassed to have been caught and diverts her gaze. The elevator dings and opens to reveal a delivery woman I haven't seen before. She must be new. She stares at me, agape, until I reach for the bags she's carrying. I hand her a twenty-dollar tip and step back, letting the elevator close before she has time to recover.

The episode amuses me, but not as much as it amuses Natalie.

"That poor girl had no idea what hit her when those doors opened and you were standing there."

"It happens." I have absolutely no desire to talk about my fame or the weirdness that goes with it. In the kitchen, I plate the food and serve it to her at the bar. On a whim, I light a couple of candles and place them between our plates. "There. Almost as good as a five-star restaurant, but without the inevitable disruptions."

"It's very nice. Thank you."

"Thank you for not making me eat alone."

"Like you don't have a million people you could call on a moment's notice."

"There you go believing everything you read again." I refill our wineglasses before I settle on the stool next to hers. "Just because I know a lot of people doesn't mean I want to eat dinner with them."

"I don't mean to make assumptions." She takes a sip of her wine. "On the surface, your life seems so… glamorous and exciting."

"It can be at times. And I'd never want anyone to think I'm complaining about what's been an embarrassment of riches, but it's also a lot of twenty-hour days in less than ideal circumstances. I once spent eight hours in freezing water while filming and ended up in the hospital with hypothermia. It took two days to feel warm again. Another time, our entire crew got hit with food poisoning in Mexico. That was fun. I've broken bones while filming. I've torn ligaments and blown out my knee—twice. Best of all was spending two days, all but naked, in bed filming a love scene with the woman who cheated on me and ruined our marriage. That was *awesome*." Of course, that's not the full story, but the rest isn't something I wish to share with Natalie.

She stares at me, her eyes wide. "Wow."

"Sorry. Didn't mean to go off on a rant. My life is extremely fun and often very exciting and sometimes even glamorous. But there are times when it's bloody miserable, too. The press doesn't report on that part of it, because who wants to hear about food poisoning?"

She takes a delicate bite of her chicken and winces. "Not me."

"Exactly. It's much more fun to show us in tuxedos and ball gowns, going to one award show after another where we pat ourselves on the back for jobs spectacularly well done."

"You are awfully good at that, as an industry."

I howl with laughter. "Yes, we are. We're brilliant at it."

"I'm ashamed to admit I've never once considered what you go through to make the movies."

"Don't be ashamed. If you're not in the business, how would you be expected to know what it's like? And again, I want to say emphatically I'm not complaining.

I've been blessed beyond all imagination with the career I've been lucky enough to have. It's just that sometimes I wish the public at large knew there's a lot more to it than tuxedos and champagne."

I put down my fork and take a sip of my wine, surprised to discover I'm nervous about what I want to say next. "Speaking of tuxedos and champagne, next weekend is the Golden Globes, and I seem to be a nominee. I'd love to take you with me if you're not busy." I wish I'd had the forethought to record her reaction to my invitation. It's priceless and precious.

"You... You want..."

I cover her hand with mine and wait for her to look at me. "I'd like to take you to California as my date to the Golden Globes. If you'd like to come."

"I... That's very nice of you, but I have work. School. I... I have nothing to wear."

"We can fix you up with something. The designers would go crazy over you. You'd have them standing in line to outfit you. And you might have to take one day away from school. Do you have any personal days?"

"Three, but..."

"Maybe you could take one? We could fly out on Friday night and get you a dress on Saturday. See some sights, visit my parents and the rest of the family. The show is on Sunday, so we'd fly home on Monday. Back to school on Tuesday."

"You're serious."

If only she knew how serious I am about her. "Very much so."

"You just met me today! You can't give me the key to your apartment and invite me to the Golden Globes after knowing me for twelve hours!"

I glance at my watch. "Is that all? Seems like I've known you longer than that." More like forever. She's blown into my life and my soul like a tornado and left me permanently changed. Why and how that's possible, I can't say. It just is. "Think about the trip. You don't have to decide anything tonight." I nudge her and redirect her attention to the food. "Finish your dinner."

"I don't know if I can eat any more."

"Did I upset you?"

"No. You surprised me."

"I'm two for two on the surprise front."

"What I don't understand..." She shakes her head as if she's reconsidering what she'd planned to say.

"What don't you understand, Natalie?" I'm desperate to know, but I keep my expression neutral, hoping she'll tell me without me having to beg her.

"I... I said I won't sleep with you."

"And?"

"And nothing. Why do you want to take me away for the weekend when you know nothing will happen?"

"How can you say nothing will happen? I'll get to spend three whole days with you. I'll have the chance to introduce you to my family and show you the house where I grew up as well as my home in LA. I'll get to take you to one of the most exciting events of the year in Hollywood. I'll see your eyes light up with delight every time you meet someone you've admired from afar for years. I'll have you by my side to talk to when the show gets long and boring, which it always does. Maybe you'll hold my hand when my category is announced? And afterward, I'll have the most beautiful date at all the parties. How can you call that nothing?"

After a long pause, she says, "Why me?"

"Why not you? I like you, Natalie. I like being with you and talking to you. I'm not asking for anything other than the pleasure of your company for three days, during which you'll have your own room with a lock on the door to keep me out. And I fully intend to see you as often as you'll allow me to before we go anywhere together. I asked you now because tomorrow is the last day I can request an additional seat at the awards ceremony, and because I need some time to make arrangements."

"Oh. I see."

"What do you see?"

"You aren't rushing things between us. You're being practical."

"Yes," I say, once again dazzled and amused, "I suppose I am."

"So if I ask for some time to think about it, you won't be able to get an extra seat."

"Right. And if I ask for an extra seat and then you tell me you can't make it, I'll look like a loser who couldn't get a date on national television when the seat next to me is empty. You wouldn't want that for me, would you?"

"You're making that up! You could get a date in two seconds flat if I can't go."

"It's you or no one. I'm not going to ask anyone else."

"This is a lot of pressure for a first date."

"I know, and I'm sorry about that. I really am."

"Somehow I don't think you're sorry at all."

I laugh again. I've laughed more with her in the little time I've spent with her than I did in the first month with the last woman I dated, a model obsessed with her looks and her weight and her work. I lasted six weeks with her before I ended it. Unfortunately, it took a restraining order to make her go away. I shake off those unpleasant thoughts to concentrate on the lovely Natalie.

"How do you feel about dessert?" I ask her.

"Generally or specifically?"

"Both."

"In general, I'm a big fan of dessert, but I have rules."

"Oh do tell."

"First of all, there must not be fruit or vegetables of any kind involved."

"That excludes the entire carrot cake family of desserts as well as strawberry shortcake, a personal favorite."

"Carrot cake is disgusting. Carrots have no business in cake. However, I will make an occasional exception for strawberry shortcake, as long as it's covered in whipped cream."

The thought of Natalie and whipped cream does crazy things to my raging libido. Figures I'm wildly attracted to a woman for the first time in longer than I can remember, and she's already let me know there's no chance of sex. I'm fairly confident I could convince her to change her mind. I'm almost certain I could. But I won't. I'd rather know why a sweet, gorgeous woman would make such rigid rules for herself. There has to be a reason, and I want to know what it is. Of course it could be a religious thing, but I sense it's more complicated than that.

"Earth to Flynn."

Her comment draws me out of my thoughts. "Sorry."

"Where'd you go?"

"Whipped cream. It gave me ideas."

Her blush is nearly as adorable as the rest of her. "What are your rules in the area of ice cream?"

"What kind are we talking?"

"I have coffee chocolate chip, strawberry, which is probably out due to your rules, and French vanilla."

"Coffee chocolate chip is my favorite."

"You're making that up," I say, echoing her earlier claim.

She laughs. "No, I'm not!"

"Whatever you say." I take our plates to the sink and leave them to deal with later. I don't want to waste one second of the time I have with her doing dishes. I make bowls of coffee chocolate chip for both of us and return to the bar where I get to enjoy the supreme pleasure of watching Natalie enjoy ice cream.

"Mmm, so good."

My throat tightens around the cold blast of ice cream as I wonder if she might react similarly to my hands on her skin. I quash those thoughts before they can lead to an embarrassing reaction. I take another bite, hoping the ice cream will cool me off.

She lifts the spoon to her mouth, and I'm transfixed by the slide of her lips on the metal. "Did you really ask me to go to the Golden Globes with you?"

"I really did."

"You're crazy. You know that, don't you?"

"I've been called worse things."

"You can't take someone you just met *today* to one of your most important events of the year."

"Why not?"

"Because."

I tip my head and raise my brows, letting her know she'll have to do better.

"It's not done."

"Sweetheart, let me tell you the upside of celebrity. *Everything* is done. We're a bunch of self-indulgent sloths. I'd think, with all the reading you do, you'd know that about my people. If I want to take someone I just met to the Golden Globes, no one is going to stop me. Except you, of course."

She shakes her head. "This whole thing is nuts. I feel like the clock is going to strike midnight and your Bugatti will turn into a pumpkin."

I stare at her, horrified. "If my Bugatti turns into a pumpkin, I'll never forgive you. I *love* that car."

"You know what I mean. This entire day is right out of *Cinderella* or something."

"Do you have an awful stepmother? Terrible stepsisters?"

She pauses long enough for me to wonder what she's thinking. "No."

I put down my spoon, push my bowl aside and reach for her hand. "It may be hard for you to believe this, but underneath all the hoopla and attention, I'm just a guy. I eat and sleep and breathe the same way everyone else does. I'm just a guy who met a woman who interests him. I'd like to spend more time with her. I'd like to take her with me when I go to LA for the Globes because I'm kind of nervous. They're saying I'm going to win this time, and if I do, I want to celebrate with you. If I don't, I want you to make me feel better just by being there. That's why I asked you to come."

"You're totally serious."

"Dead serious."

CHAPTER 5

Natalie

Nothing about this night has gone the way I expected it to. I've been surprised and caught off guard from the minute he picked me up in a car he drove himself and brought me to his lovely but small apartment where he clearly gets by without household help.

And when he asked me to go with him to LA for the Golden Globes, he blew my mind. It's all I can think about... What would it be like to walk the red carpet on the arm of the biggest movie star in the world? It's right out of a fantasy, thus my correlation to Cinderella.

Strangely enough, I want to go. I want to be part of his big night. I want to see Los Angeles and Hollywood for the first time with him as my tour guide. The thought of meeting Max Godfrey and Estelle Flynn nearly makes me swoon, but not nearly as much as the idea of spending three days with this charming, handsome, utterly beguiling man who says he's just a regular guy and enjoys the same food I do.

"I'd like to go," I say tentatively, "but nothing has changed in regard to how I feel about a relationship with you."

"I understand that, and I respect it."

"So you, who could have any woman on the planet, are choosing to spend time with the one woman who won't fall into bed with you at the snap of your fingers?"

He goes strangely still as he contemplates my question. "Yes."

"Why?"

"Why what?"

"Why would you want to be with me when you could have anyone? Why would any sane man want to be with a woman who won't sleep with him when he could have his pick of women who would?"

"Despite what you may believe, not every guy lets his little brain do the thinking for his big brain."

"Really. Hmm, that hasn't been my experience."

"Then you've been hanging out with the wrong guys." Once again he takes hold of my hand. Every time he does that, my skin tingles and my nipples tighten. I've never had that kind of reaction to anyone else. Not that I've let any other man get close enough to test my reactions. "Let's take care of this concern of yours once and for all, okay?"

"Okay..."

"I like you. From the first minute I laid eyes on you, on the ground, the wind knocked out of you, your adorable little beast of a dog hovering over you, I wanted to know you. My first thoughts about you weren't, 'Damn, I need to get this woman in my bed.' They were more along the lines of, 'Don't be an idiot and let this incredible woman walk away without getting to know her.'"

I'm finding it difficult to swallow all of a sudden. I clear my throat and meet his intense gaze. "So you don't think... that way... about me?"

"What way?"

"You know."

Suddenly he gets exactly what I mean. "Oh! *That* way... Yes, I've definitely had a few thoughts about what it would be like to get you naked and into my bed. I won't lie to you about that. I think it would be amazing, unbelievable, off the charts, spectacular—"

Smiling, I press my fingers to his lips to make him stop talking.

His eyes light up with silent laughter. He brings his free hand up to cover the fingers I've placed on his lips, and the next thing I know, he's nibbling on my finger. The charge of heat that travels through my body sears me and collects in an insistent throb between my legs.

Overwhelmed by my reaction, I pull my hand free.

"Sorry," he says, "I couldn't resist."

I'm undone and confused by the way my body responds to him. I've never experienced these particular reactions before, and I'm not sure what they mean. Am I reacting to Flynn the man, or Flynn the movie star? Even as I ask myself the question, I know it's the former, and I'd be lying to myself if I said otherwise.

He has my full attention again when he runs his finger over the furrow between my brows. "Don't overthink it, sweetheart."

That makes me want to laugh. I overthink *everything*. I haven't had a choice about that. When you leave your home and family at fifteen, overthinking becomes a way of life.

"I should go home—"

"Do you want to watch a movie?" he asks at the same time.

"Oh, um…" I check my watch. It's only nine, and I don't really want to leave, but I need a moment to get my emotions under control without his overpowering presence distracting me. "May I use your restroom?"

"By all means. You know where it is. Feel free to also use the tub, if you'd like."

I laugh at that. "Thanks, but I'll pass tonight."

"The offer stands."

"I'll be right back."

"I'll be here."

In the bathroom, I take a moment to practice the deep-breathing techniques my court-appointed counselor taught me. Any time I find myself out of balance or off-kilter, I breathe my way through it. I've been off-kilter since the moment I realized I'd crashed into Flynn Godfrey. And now… Now he's asking me to go to California with him, to attend the Golden Globes, to meet his family. It's too much.

I look in the mirror, and I'm shocked by what I see. My cheeks are flushed with color, my lips are slightly swollen as if I've been passionately kissed, and my eyes… My eyes are wide and somehow brighter. The rest of my body fairly vibrates with sensation, especially my nipples and between my legs.

Gazing at my reflection, I can't deny that what I'm feeling—and seeing—is desire. It's all new to me, so I can barely process the cascade of emotions that go along with this startling realization. After what happened to me when I was fifteen, I tamped down that part of me, the part that's a young, healthy woman. Since then, I've avoided men and relationships and sex and all the things other young women seek out with unfettered abandon.

I can't afford unfettered abandon. I survive by being in control at all times, and right now, I'm certainly not in control of my body's reaction to Flynn. I use the facilities and then take a moment to run my hands under cool water. I bring my cold hands to my neck and face, hoping to regain the control that's so critical to my new life.

I can enjoy the company of a handsome, charming, interesting man and hold it together. Maybe if I keep telling myself that, it'll actually be true. It's probably time to go home, but I don't want to leave yet. I don't want this evening to be over. I just need to keep things in the proper perspective and not allow my puzzling reactions to govern my actions.

I'm in control at all times. I'll never forget the excruciating journey that led me to this precious new life. I won't let one handsome, charismatic man undo the hard work that allowed me to reclaim my sanity.

"Never forget," I whisper to my reflection before I leave the bathroom to rejoin him.

"What's the verdict?" he asks. "Movie or call it a night?"

Because he seems amenable to either option, I decide to stay awhile longer. "What do you have in the category of chick flick?"

He groans and makes me laugh with the look of agony he sends my way. "For real?"

"You asked. If it weren't for you, I'd be home with Fluff well into a Lifetime movie by now."

"Lifetime, huh? Wow, not sure I can compete with that."

"Give it your best shot."

He goes to the built-in entertainment center and opens a deep drawer that is completely full of DVDs. "Lady's choice."

"Do you have every movie ever made in there?"

"Only half of them. The other half is at my place in LA."

"And you still buy the DVDs when you can stream most of these movies?"

"I like to own them. I'm a bit of a collector."

"I see that."

"Actually, you see a fraction of it. It's a bit of an obsession. Film, VHS, DVD, Blu-ray. I have it all."

"I suppose your obsession makes sense when you consider what you do for a living."

"If that's how you want to justify it. My sisters say I need a twelve-step program for this and my addiction to cars."

"Better to be addicted to movies and cars than to some of the other things celebrities get hooked on."

"See? That's what I say, too, but they give me no quarter. Until their kids want an advance viewing of the next big movie. Then Uncle Flynn comes in *awfully* handy."

"It's not easy being you in your family, huh?"

"And you wonder why I like you so much. You feel my pain."

I feel a lot more than his pain, and despite the talking-to I gave myself in the bathroom, I'm already spinning out of control again. It takes mere minutes in his presence to forget my vows, to be drawn in by his effortless charm and self-deprecating humor. There's something incredibly attractive about a man who can laugh at himself, especially when the rest of the world holds him up as a deity of sorts.

Anxious for something to do with all the energy zinging around inside me, I squat for a closer look at the wide array of movies in the drawer. I home in instantly on my favorite movie of all time. Removing it from the drawer, I raise it for him to see.

His agony is immediately apparent. "*Really?*"

"Really. Lady's choice and all."

Crossing his arms and shaking his head, he says, "Well, I knew you were too good to be true. No one is perfect."

"If you don't like it, why do you have it?"

"It's my mom's favorite. My parents stay here when they're in the city, so I keep some of their favorites on hand."

I smile widely at him. "Your mom has excellent taste in movies."

"If you say so. I'll watch it on one condition."

"Name it."

"You have to sing all the songs to me."

"Done." He has no idea what he's in for. I know every word to every song in the movie.

"Crap, I figured you'd say no way to that."

Laughing at the disgusted face he makes, I say, "Guess you haven't got me totally figured out yet."

"Maybe not, but I'm definitely making headway."

Flynn

She knows every word to every song in *The Sound of Music*, and her voice is crystal clear, angelic even. Singing about how she must've done something right to find the love of her life, she can't bring herself to look at me. Her color is high, and I detect the slightest tremble in her hands. It's all I can do to refrain from pulling her into my arms and kissing her senseless. I've never wanted to kiss anyone more desperately than I want to kiss her right now.

We've engaged in a spirited debate about what exactly constitutes schnitzel with noodle, and I want to send her something inside a brown paper package tied up with string. Perhaps some schnitzel with noodle? My mother and sisters *love* this movie. I've always considered it saccharine torture, but watching it with Natalie and witnessing her love for all things Von Trapp, I'm even more captivated than I was before.

Who am I kidding? It's not the movie. It's *her*. She's sweet and unaffected and adorable. And I have absolutely no business spending time with her, let alone allowing myself to wonder what might be possible. She's too pure for my world. Being with me would ruin her, but knowing that doesn't stop me from wanting her like I haven't wanted anyone in longer than I can remember. Perhaps ever…

I have to hold myself back so I won't give in to the urge to run my fingers through her long dark hair, to stroke the sweet heat that floods her cheeks whenever she looks my way, to press my body against hers to show her what she does to me just by sitting next to me singing silly songs with such unabashed glee.

She's far, *far* too good for me, and if I weren't such a selfish asshole, I'd take her home and forget I ever met her. That would be best for her. But I already know I won't do that. I *can't* do that. She hasn't yet left my home and I'm already craving more of her and making plans to see her again—hopefully tomorrow.

Her lips move in time with "Edelweiss" as the captain performs at the music festival, and I notice her eyes are suddenly bright with unshed tears.

"Natalie?"

"Hmm?"

"Are you okay?"

She nods. "It's this song… It gets me every time. Makes me homesick."

"When was the last time you were home?"

She seems to consider her answer carefully, which I find odd. "It's been a while. A long while."

"You didn't go home for Christmas?"

She shakes her head. "Not this year."

"You miss your family." I pose it as a statement rather than a question, eager to see how she replies.

Without taking her gaze off the TV, she nods. "Yeah."

I have a sudden, powerful feeling that there is much more to her story than what she's let on.

"This is my favorite part," she says of the nuns holding up parts from the Nazis' cars.

"You gotta love a clever nun."

She smiles at me, and I'm slayed, ruined, destroyed. Though it would be best for her—and probably for me, too—if I call it a night and try to forget about her, I won't do that. I can't do that. I want to know why she hasn't seen her family in a long time. I want to know everything there is to know about her.

But she must never, ever find out everything there is to know about me.

The movie ends with the Von Trapps crossing the mountains on foot, and I offer to take her home. I hope she'll ask to stay a little longer, but she agrees it's time to call it a night. I retrieve her coat and hold it for her, again fighting the powerful need to touch her in any way I can. But I don't. She's made her feelings clear, and I want to respect them even if I don't agree with them.

We take the elevator to the garage, and I help her into the Bugatti. The ride downtown is quiet, even as my mind races with things I'd like to say to her. *I want to see you again. I want to be with you. I want to know you. Please come to California with me. I'll show you my life, introduce you to the people I love.* I want to beg her to tell me what she's thinking. Did she enjoy herself tonight? Does she want to see me again? Will she come to the Globes with me?

Christ, Flynn. Act like you've been here before, will you? Yeah, I'm a mess over this woman, and I like how it feels. I like how I feel when I'm with her. I want to continue to feel this way for as long as I possibly can. These thoughts are reckless in light of who I am—not who I am to the public, but who I am in private. I have no business or right becoming involved with someone like Natalie. Yet I'm already involved with her. I've been involved with her since the moment she crashed into me and her little beast of a dog bit me.

I pull up to the curb in front of her building and kill the engine. Before she can tell me not to bother, I'm out of the car and going around to help her from the low-slung vehicle. She takes hold of the hand I offer, and I give a pull. Maybe I pull a little too hard on purpose so she'll tumble into my arms, so I have no choice but to catch her, to bring her body in tight against mine.

"That was graceful," she mutters against my chest, drawing a low rumble of laughter from me that belies my immediate reaction to the feel of her in my arms.

"I might've pulled a little harder than necessary."

"Now the truth comes out."

"Sorry." I reluctantly release her, but she surprises me once again when she doesn't immediately let go of my coat.

"I had a really nice time tonight. Thank you."

I look down at her looking up at me, and the desire to kiss her is primal. But I don't act on the urge. I exercise more self-control than I ever would've suspected I possess and take hold of her hand to walk her up the stairs to the door. "I had a really nice time, too. Thanks for giving me a chance."

"Thanks for sitting through *The Sound of Music*."

"It wasn't as torturous as I remembered."

She smiles again, and I feel like I've won something priceless because I made her smile. "I'd better go in before Fluff blows a gasket."

Now that she mentions it, I can hear the little beast howling. "We can't have that. Sleep well, Natalie."

"You, too."

Not likely, I think as I wait for her to use her key and step inside the vestibule. "Good night."

"Night." The door clicks shut behind her, and I have to tell myself to move, to go down the stairs to my car when every fiber of my being wants to be inside that building with her. Leaving her feels wrong, as if I've left something essential behind. Astounded by the way she has tipped my entire existence so precariously out of balance in the scope of one day, I pull away from the curb and head back uptown.

With my body alive with unspent desire and frustration and other emotions that defy easy definition, I know there's no way I'll sleep. Rather than go home, I head for the Park and East 65th building that houses the Quantum offices, among other things. It's the other things I'm interested in tonight.

I take the ramp to the underground parking garage and place my hand on the palm scanner. The metal doors slide open, and I drive into the garage and park between Hayden's black Porsche 911 and Jasper's silver Audi A-8. I also notice Marlowe's sleek white Bentley and Kristian's gaudy red Lamborghini Aventador. I hate that car, but he loves it, so I keep my opinion to myself.

The whole gang is here tonight, and I'm eager for some time with my closest friends and business partners. We came up together in Hollywood. Hayden is a director, Jasper a cinematographer, Kristian one of the top producers in the business, Marlowe and myself the token actors who have starred together often enough that the paparazzi love to speculate on our personal relationship. Despite the drooling lust of the Hollywood press, since a brief romantic relationship ended years ago, there's been nothing but close friendship between us. She's like a fourth sister to me—the one who doesn't report directly to my parents.

Thanks to the extreme secrecy and security in effect at Quantum, no one knows much of anything about the five of us or our sexual "predilections." Beside the elevator, I place my palm on yet another scanner, and the doors open for me.

Inside, I'm faced with a decision—go upstairs to the offices or downstairs to the playground, as we call it. I'm too wound up to concentrate on work, and I'm *way* too wound up for the playground, but I know I'll find my friends there at this hour on a Saturday night, so down I go.

The doors open into what might be mistaken, at first glance, for a nightclub. It is that, but it's so much more, too. While music thumps a low and sexy beat through the sound system, Jasper stands over a naked woman strapped to a St. Andrew's cross. Flogger in hand, he speaks directly into her ear.

Dressed in leather from breasts to thighs, Marlowe is berating her naked sub for some infraction that will require stiff punishment. The man, president of one of the biggest banks on Wall Street, weeps from the pain of Marlowe's stilettos cutting into his back. She's a harsh Dominatrix with a line of subs waiting for a chance to experience her brand of punishment.

At the bar, I drop onto a stool, and Gabriel, the bartender who is also our head of security and club manager, puts a glass of my favorite Scottish single malt in front of me. "Thanks, Gabe."

"Rough night?"

"No, a good night." *A great night. A fantastic, life-changing night.* I take a sip of my drink, and the Bowmore burns its way through me. "How are things here?" I spot Kristian on one of the sofas, fully clothed and speaking with a woman I don't recognize.

"Same as always."

"Who's that with Kristian?"

"A new member."

Though Gabriel knows the full story on everyone who steps foot into the club, he's good about staying out of the personal business of the five celebrities he works for. When Kristian wants me to know more about the new member he's brought in, he'll tell me himself.

"Is Hayden around?"

"In the dungeon with Cresley."

"This I've got to see." I take my drink with me when I cross the room, waving to several other members of our exclusive club who are making use of the sofas and sitting areas to get to know each other. Perhaps they're negotiating the terms of a Dominant/submissive relationship or maybe they're talking shop. The Hollywood lifestyle is as present here as the BDSM lifestyle is. Both are a big part of my life, which is why I have no business starting anything with Natalie.

"I won't sleep with any man unless I'm married to him."

What would she think of this place? The thought, which I would normally find amusing, saddens me. I've been a part of this lifestyle for most of my adult life, and have long ago stopped feeling like I have to explain myself to anyone. My need for sexual domination is as much a part of me as my parents' DNA or the chin that comes straight from my paternal grandfather.

I lay my hand flat against another palm scanner and gain entry to the stairwell that leads to the dungeon in the basement. This area is available only to the five principals and their guests, all of whom are subjected to the same in-depth background checks and medical testing that prospective members endure. The difference being that full members are required to pay million-dollar initiation fees and sign confidentiality agreements that make it clear we'll ruin them if they ever speak of what goes on here. Guests are only required to sign the confidentiality agreement, and we let them know we'll enforce every word of it without hesitation.

Our chief counsel, Emmett Burke, drafted airtight language that has kept our clubs here and in LA the best-kept secrets in show business for more than a decade now. The five of us approve every member, all of whom come to us via referrals from existing members, and we admit only people who have something to lose. Case in point—the supermodel currently being vigorously fucked by Hayden.

Cresley Dane, one of the most famous faces in the world, a dynamic, aggressive businesswoman who rules the runways from New York to Paris and everywhere in between, is a true sexual submissive. Tonight, the gorgeous blonde is trussed up in an elaborate web of rope with her arms tied above her head, her spectacular breasts and torso tightly wrapped and her legs hoisted up and apart. Hayden is a master of Kinbaku, the Japanese art of erotic tying.

Standing in the shadows of the dungeon, I sip my drink and watch my friends, thinking of the many threesomes we've enjoyed in the past. Cresley is always up for an adventure, as she calls the scenarios Hayden and I have dreamed up over the years. We think of it as harmless fun among consenting adults who like to stretch their boundaries. We've only recently brought her into the club as a member, thus the formal training process she's embarked upon with Hayden as her Dom. A year ago, Cresley won a hard-fought battle with her vindictive ex-boyfriend for custody of their three-year-old son. She has a lot to lose, thus we trust her implicitly.

Hayden catches my eye, nodding slightly to acknowledge me without losing his focus.

He's also a master of delayed gratification, a skill he taught me after making me aware of the BDSM lifestyle. An actor he met on a film set when we were twenty-one introduced it to Hayden. He introduced it to me, and we were both instantly hooked. It was like we'd found the missing piece to a puzzle. I like to watch him in action, though I'm not attracted to him or to men in general. I'm objective enough to admit that my best friend is an extraordinarily good-looking man. He has dark hair and blue eyes that women go nuts over. Watching usually turns me on. Not tonight, however. Tonight, I'm stuck in a weird never-never land thanks to Natalie.

Thinking about her, I realize just how long it's been since I spent time with a woman outside the lifestyle. A "vanilla," as we call people who prefer their sex straight up with no embellishments. The term, which implies blandness, doesn't do her justice. There's absolutely nothing bland about Natalie, except perhaps her thoughts on sex, which make her extremely vanilla by my usual standards.

I already know that nothing about her or how she makes me feel can be classified as "usual."

Hayden and Cresley interrupt my musings with their sharp, high-pitched cries of fulfillment as they finally let go and give in to the desire that's probably been building between them for hours at this point, if I know Hayden. Their releases are epic and loud, and under normal circumstances, I'd be hard as a rock watching Cresley get off. Not tonight. Tonight I feel nothing but confusion, agitation and anxious desire to see Natalie again—as soon as possible. As if she might slip through my fingers if I don't act quickly. I'm unaccustomed to feeling desperate when it comes to women.

Hayden slowly unties Cresley, wraps her in a blanket and holds a bottle of cold water to her lips.

She drinks greedily. "Thank you." Her voice is hoarse from hours of screaming.

"We've got company." Hayden nods in my direction.

She's not at all surprised to see me. "Oh hey, Flynn. How long have you been there?"

I step out of the shadows to join them in the middle of the enormous room. "I got here just in time for the big finish."

"It was a big finish," Cresley agrees.

"You know me," Hayden says with a cocky, satisfied smile, "go big or go home."

"You've certainly got the *big* part covered. I may never walk properly again." Cresley gathers the blanket around her and stands on trembling legs.

"Why thank you, darlin'." Hayden reaches out to steady her, and I step closer out of habit. Protecting and caring for subs, especially after a scene, is essential to who we are as Doms.

"I'm okay," she says, waving us off. "I've got to get home. My sitter can't spend the night." She leans in to kiss Hayden's cheek. "Thanks for the lesson."

"Any time."

She pats me on the chest. "Flynn, nice to see you as always."

"You, too, Cresley. Say hi to my little buddy for me."

"I will."

Her son, Ty, is one of my favorite kids, right up there with my own nieces and nephews.

As she heads to the elevator, Hayden pulls on a pair of sweatpants and gets busy cleaning the equipment and coiling his ropes. "I wondered if we'd see you tonight."

"I had a thing."

"A thing." Hayden glances at me disdainfully. "With the *child* you met earlier?"

I love Hayden. He's the closest thing I have to a brother, but damn, he pisses me off sometimes, mostly because he knows me better than anyone on earth— and never fails to remind me of that. "She's hardly a child." I make my way over to the bar in the corner and refill my glass. Arguing with Hayden requires reinforcements.

"You can't be seriously considering starting something with her."

"So what if I am?"

"Flynn, for the love of God and all that's holy, *what the fuck are you thinking?*"

I nearly snort whisky out my nose at his choice of words. Only he can mix religion and fucking with such powerful effect. "I like her. She's different."

"You're goddamned right she's different. I took one look at her and could tell she's pure as the driven snow. How do you plan to tell her about all this?" His wide gesture takes in the dungeon, the implements hanging from the wall, the hooks and cables extended from the ceiling, the spanking bench, the St. Andrew's cross and the cabinet that contains every sex toy known to mankind.

"I don't plan to tell her. We're not about that."

"You're not about what? Sex? Since when are you not about sex?"

Since about ten o'clock this morning. I wisely decide to keep the thought to myself. Hayden is right. Everything he's saying is true, but none of it changes how I already feel about Natalie.

Hayden stores his ropes in a cabinet that he locks with the only key. Then he turns to me, hands on his hips, the muscular chest and abs that make the ladies drool on full display. "You need to stop this before it goes any further. Didn't you learn anything from what happened with Val?"

The mention of her name is a flashpoint for me, as he well knows. "Don't bring her into this. She has nothing to do with it."

"She has *everything* to do with it! And you know it."

I do know it, but I don't want to think about her now or ever. I especially don't want to think about her in relation to Natalie.

Hayden crosses the room and takes the seat next to mine. "I don't mean to piss on your parade."

"Sure you do," I say with a gruff laugh. He and I go all the way back to childhood in Hollywood with four parents in the business. Whereas mine stayed together and thrived through all the madness of fame and fortune, his self-destructed in spectacular—and very public—fashion. Hayden and I graduated together from Beverly Hills High School and often tell people we were the real-life inspiration for the show *Beverly Hills, 90210*. That we were eleven when the show debuted is of little consequence. We've never believed in letting the truth get in the way of a good story.

"Seriously, Flynn. For once I'm not trying to be a flaming asshole. I saw the way you reacted to her, and I had a bad feeling about it from the get-go."

"Funny, I've had a good feeling about it from the second she barreled into me."

He raises an eyebrow that conveys a full dose of skepticism. "Even when her dog was taking a piece out of your ass?"

"It was my arm, not my ass, and yes, even then."

"Make me understand, because I'm really struggling to get how someone as self-aware and intelligent as you are would willingly go down this road—*again*—after being so badly burned once before."

His words strike a chord with me, even as I try to convince myself they don't. "She's normal, unaffected, passionate about her work, and she doesn't give a flying fuck about who I am. Do you have any idea how refreshing that is?"

"Of course she gives a flying fuck about who you are. There's not a woman alive who could spend five minutes with you and not be completely tuned in to who and what you are—or the parts of yourself you've given the world. The rest, the part you keep private, is what worries me the most—and it should worry you, too."

"She's no threat to me, Hayden. Shit, Cresley is a bigger threat to me than Natalie will ever be."

"Cresley, and all the others we let in here, poses a threat to your *reputation*. Natalie is a threat to your *mental health*. Big difference."

Did I mention Hayden knows me better than anyone?

In a low, soft tone, he says, "She's a mouse, Flynn. A young, inexperienced, albeit strikingly gorgeous, *mouse*. She has no place in this life. It'll swallow her whole and spit her out utterly changed. Is that what you want for her? You gotta stop this while you still can."

Fuck, I hate his guts, because every word he says is true, and I can't deny he's one hundred percent right. I don't dare mention that I asked her to go to the Globes with me, but then again, she never gave me an answer, so there's really nothing to tell. And then I remember the key I gave her to my apartment.

"Don't you ever want more?" I ask him.

"More than what?" He throws his arms out wide. "Who has it better than we do? Look at this place we built together, and not just down here. Upstairs, too." Our production company is one of the most successful in the business, and we have the awards to prove it. We long ago dispelled the notion that we're riding on the coattails of our successful parents. We've proven ourselves over and over again, until all talk of nepotism and favoritism has been erased by results.

We live by our own rules and have life by the balls. What more could we possibly want indeed? Except, sometimes... Sometimes I want more. I want the connection my parents have, that ability to catch an eye across the room and to know without a shadow of a doubt what the other half of me is thinking in that given moment. As I get further into my thirties, I've also begun to think, occasionally, about one day having kids of my own.

"Flynn."

Hayden brings me back to the present, to the stark realities of this life I've chosen. After growing up in the shadow of my famous parents, I certainly knew what I was signing on for, although I never could've predicted that my fame would eclipse theirs a thousand times over. At times like this, I resent the fame, the notoriety and everything that goes with it. I also resent the needs that drive me, that have made it impossible for me to have a long-term, satisfying sexual relationship that doesn't include domination. Those needs played a big part in the disaster my marriage became, so Hayden's point is well taken.

"You know what you have to do."

"Yeah." The detour with Natalie was just that. A detour. A diversion. A night away from reality. My life is here, in the basement of Quantum, with hooks hanging from the ceiling, a willing sub bent over a spanking bench as I fuck her up the ass that I turned bright pink with my hands and paddles. Not in my wildest dreams can I ever picture Natalie as that willing sub.

Hayden is right. It's better to stop this thing with her before it gets started. But damn, it would've been nice.

"You need to get laid, man. Want me to set something up for you?"

"Not tonight. I'm going home." The thought of touching any woman who isn't Natalie makes me sick. I hope that will pass before too long, because I need sex the way other men need air.

"Are you okay?"

"Yeah, I'm fine." I tell him what he wants to hear, but I know it'll be a while before I forget about Natalie and what could've been if I was someone different. I take the elevator from the dungeon straight to the parking garage, and when I get in the car, I'm greeted with the lingering remnants of her scent. I take greedy breaths on the short ride home.

When the elevator opens into my apartment, I'm again assailed by her scent, and the desire for more of her nearly brings me to my knees. Then I imagine her horror and disgust if she discovers who I really am, and I know I'm doing the right thing calling a stop to it now, while I still can.

It's only when I toss my keys on the dresser in my bedroom that I see the keycard I gave her. Any hope I had that she might seek me out evaporates in a cloud of profound disappointment and bitter regret. In that moment, I actually hate my life for the first time ever.

CHAPTER 6

Natalie

Snuggled into bed with Fluff at my side, I'm unable to sleep as I relive every minute of the evening I spent with Flynn. Nothing about our time together was what I'd expected. He's right—I have to stop believing everything I read about him and other celebrities. He picked me up himself, took me to his lovely but somewhat humble home where he offered me takeout and a movie.

After what I went through early in my life, I tend to view new people with an air of cynicism. I'm very rarely surprised by anyone the way I was tonight by Flynn. I was all set to bail out of our date and come home without giving him a chance. Now I'm glad I went, and I'm looking forward to seeing him again. I'll be on pins and needles until I hear from him.

I feel silly for expecting to actually hear from him after I was so blunt about my position on sex and relationships. Maybe I should've held that info back for a while. But if I had, I might've had to fend off an unwelcome advance, and where I'm untested in dealing with such things, I'd rather not experiment with someone like him.

He was a perfect gentleman. He respected my wishes and my feelings by keeping his distance all evening. So why am I lying awake wishing he hadn't been such a gentleman? What might it have been like to kiss him? The thought of it makes my heart beat fast and my body tingle in ways it has never tingled before.

After tossing and turning for hours, I wake with a start when Leah comes home from work. It's after three in the morning.

"Oh my God," she says from my doorway. "*What* are you doing here?"

Groggy and out of sorts from being woken so suddenly, I rub my eyes as Fluff gives off a low growl. She hates being disturbed. "Um, I live here?"

"Only you would go out with Flynn Fucking Godfrey and come home to sleep in your own bed."

"I don't know why this surprises you. I told you I wasn't going to sleep with him."

"And I told you you're an idiot."

"Go away. I was sleeping."

"Well, now you're not." She comes in and flops down on the other side of my queen-size bed. "Tell me every single thing that happened and leave nothing out."

"It's three o'clock in the morning, Leah!"

"So what? You got somewhere to be tomorrow?"

As Fluff continues to growl at Leah, I stroke her ears, which calms her. I resign myself to dealing with Leah, who shows no sign of going away. I tell her about my night with Flynn, from the moment he picked me up until the moment he brought me home.

"*He seriously asked you to go to the Golden Globes with him?*" Her voice is so high-pitched that Fluff whimpers from the frequency.

"Yes," I say, laughing at her reaction. "He did."

"What did you say?"

"We left it open-ended for the moment. I said I'd think about it."

Groaning, Leah falls to the bed and covers her face with one of my pillows. Then she lets out a scream that makes me jolt and Fluff bark. "You are freaking *insane*, Natalie. *Insane!*"

"Why does being cautious and reasonable make me insane?"

"Because the hottest man in the *world* asked you to go to one of the biggest events in Hollywood, and you said you have to *think about it? What's there to think about?*"

"To start with, do I want to use one of my precious personal days to spend three days with a man I barely know?"

"Yes, you do want to use one of your precious personal days—what better use will you ever have for them? And it's three days with *Flynn Freaking Godfrey!*"

"Will you please stop screaming before the neighbors call the cops?"

"If I told the neighbors *Flynn Godfrey* asked you to the *Golden Globes* and you told him you have to *think about it*, they'd call the cops on *you*, not me."

"You're being ridiculous! I just met him. How do I know if I want to spend three days in California with him?"

"I honestly don't know what to do with you, Natalie." Leah looks at me with what appears to be genuine concern. "I know there's shit in your past that you don't talk about, and I respect that. It's just… If you don't do this, if you don't go with him and have this amazing adventure, you'll always regret it."

"I can't jump in with both feet the way you do. I have to take my time and think about it. That's just the way I'm wired. I'm sorry if that annoys you."

"It doesn't annoy me. Most of the time. But this is *Flynn Godfrey. Flynn Godfrey!*"

I can't help but laugh at the faces she's making to go along with her pleading tone. "Yes, I know his name."

"Every single woman in America would like to be you right now. Hell, most of the married ones would like to be you, too. You know that, don't you?"

"I'm aware that women find him appealing, yes."

Leah snorts with laughter. "*Appealing.* You crack me up! He's fucking sexy as all hell, and I'd do him in a New York minute, as would most women. I bet most men would, too."

I take my pillow and stuff it into her face, hoping to shut her up.

She pushes it aside and throws it back at me. "You have to go."

"No, I don't."

"Yes! You do!"

"No! I don't."

She moans as if she's in severe pain. "If you don't go, can I?"

"Shut *up*, Leah! Go away and let me sleep, will you?"

"When are you going to see him again?"

"I don't know."

"*You let him get away without making plans for another date?* What am I going to *do* with you?"

"Go away and let me sleep?"

"Fine, but we're going to continue this conversation tomorrow, and you *are* going to LA if I have to take you there myself."

"Good to know. Nighty night."

She makes a big dramatic production of getting up and out of my bed. At the doorway, she pauses and then turns to me, her face serious. "I'd hate to see you have regrets, Nat. Something like this… It's right out of a fairy tale. I don't know what happened to you, but whatever it was… You have a right to be happy just like everyone else."

"Thanks for caring, Leah." I mean that sincerely. She's been an incredible friend to me in the short time I've known her. And she makes me laugh even though she can be a pain in the ass.

"I do care. I really do."

"Likewise. Now go to bed."

I hear her in the kitchen, fixing a late-night snack that she takes to her room, closing the door.

In the quiet that follows, I have to admit that Leah is probably right. I'm crazy not to jump at the chance to have my very own Cinderella moment with an amazing, handsome, sexy man who makes me feel things I've never felt before. But in the back of my mind, always, are the memories of another man who took everything from me long before I should've had to face such a horror. I've spent a long time—years—putting the pieces back together without ever letting another man get close to me.

Until tonight. Until Flynn Godfrey.

And now he's offering me things right out of a fairy tale while making me laugh and *feel* for the first time in what seems like forever. I just wish I had Leah's daring and her courage. What I wouldn't give for even a small bit of her ballsy approach to life and men and dating and sex.

Hoping I'll fall back to sleep, I turn on my side, snuggle up to Fluff, who's already snoring like a buzz saw. I let my mind wander again through the memories of my hours with Flynn, smiling as I drift peacefully before dropping off into sleep.

By Tuesday, I'm convinced the date with Flynn was a figment of my overactive imagination, not the magical fairy tale I turned it into with more than a little help from Leah. She blabbed the whole thing in the teachers' room at our school, making me the center of attention all day Monday. She has no way to know how much I hate that kind of attention, so I kept a smile on my face, nodded in all the right places and answered all their foolish questions about what he is *really* like. It occurred to me late Monday afternoon that they all think I slept with him. Of course I did.

The school buzzes with my Flynn Godfrey news until noon on Tuesday when Mrs. Heffernan's husband is caught driving drunk in New Jersey with a woman who isn't his wife in the passenger seat. That news takes precedence over my brief flirtation with Hollywood, which is over now as far as I'm concerned.

Two days without a word from him sends a rather straightforward message.

A few minutes before dismissal on Tuesday, one of my favorite students, Logan Gifford, comes up to my desk.

"Miss Bryant?" He's always so polite and solemn, and I adore him. His mother is fighting an awful battle with breast cancer, and the whole school has rallied around their family with fundraisers and meal deliveries and anything else we can do for them. I make sure to hug Logan at least once a day to let him know I care.

"What's up, Logan?"

He glances over his shoulder to make sure none of his friends are listening to our conversation, but they are taking full advantage of the ten minutes I give them at the end of every day to talk freely to each other. "I was wondering..." His dark hair falls over his forehead, and he has a slight lisp thanks to his missing front teeth. He's utterly adorable.

"What were you wondering about, honey?"

"When we went to art class, I heard Mrs. Drake say that you met that movie star, Flynn Goffy."

"Flynn Godfrey. Yes, I did."

After another glance over his shoulder, Logan says, "He's my mom's favorite. She loves him and all his movies. I was just wondering if he could come over to my house to see her."

I feel as if all the air has been sucked from my lungs—for two reasons. First, what Logan is asking would require me to reach out to Flynn, and I have no plans to do that—ever. And second, how sweet is he to think of his mom this way? It nearly brings me to tears. Then the bell rings, and all hell breaks loose as the kids bound for the door.

"I'll try," I say to Logan, drawing a small smile from him.

"Thanks, Miss Bryant." He gives me an impulsive little hug before he too bolts from the room.

I grab my coat and follow behind my class, making sure each of them gets to where they're supposed to be before heading back to my classroom to straighten up. I clean the surfaces with disinfectant wipes, prepare my lesson plans for tomorrow and correct the stack of papers the children completed that day.

As I work, Logan's request weighs heavily on my mind. The cute little guy has been so stoic and brave as his mother wages war with cancer. Single mom Aileen Gifford is an incredible person, so upbeat and positive despite a rather grim prognosis. I like her as much as I like her son, and there's nothing I wouldn't do for either of them. I've even given Aileen my number and offered to stay with Logan and his younger sister if she ever needs me. I haven't told Leah or any of my other colleagues how involved I've gotten with their family, but you'd have to be awfully coldhearted not to be drawn in by their plight.

The thought of being able to brighten her world for a brief moment with one simple phone call or text is tempting, to say the least. I pick up my phone from the desktop, open the text screen and scroll back to the one text he sent me Saturday when he was still looking forward to seeing me again.

I stare at the screen for a long time. My insides are twisted up in knots. All day Sunday, I waited to hear from him. I was *sure* I would hear from him after the evening we spent together. Leah pestered me endlessly, asking if he'd called. After the twentieth time, I snapped at her, and she stopped asking. Then Sunday became Monday, and Monday became Tuesday. I might be new to dating and men, but I recognize a blow-off when I see one.

Still... I can't get Logan's little face out of my mind or the way he screwed up the courage to ask me to set this up for his mother. Finding my own courage, I blow out a deep breath and begin to type.

So I know the mother of the dog who bit you and made you bleed has no right to ask for a huge, enormous, massively inconvenient favor... However, there's this adorable kid in my class whose mother has breast cancer. You won't believe who her favorite movie star is...

I read the text at least a hundred times, debating, dithering and actively sweating before I close my eyes, take another deep breath, open my eyes and press send. Then I put down the phone and dive into the stack of correcting so I won't be tempted to stare at the phone until he replies—or until he doesn't.

Did I strike the right tone between friendly and witty and noncommittal? Did I give him an easy way out if he can't do it? No! I didn't. I groan and drop my head into my hands. I'm agonizing over what he must be thinking when my phone chimes with a text.

I nearly drop it on the floor in my haste to handle it with the aforementioned sweaty hands.

Three words: *When and where?*

"Holy crap," I whisper. In that moment of uncertainty, I realize I hadn't expected him to reply, which is why I'm woefully unprepared to answer his question.

I write back with hands that are now trembling as well as sweaty. *Possibly tomorrow after school if you are available then? Could I let you know?*

I hold my breath until he writes back. *Sure, no problem. I'm available any time tomorrow.*

Thank you so much for this. I'll get back to you.

Sounds good.

I'm left with more questions than I had before, if that's possible. If he's available all day tomorrow and has time to text with me today, why haven't I heard from him since Saturday? Why didn't he say anything about getting together again during our exchange of texts? I know I didn't dream the crackle of attraction that simmered between us during both our encounters on Saturday.

"Face the facts," I say out loud, "when you tell a guy there's no chance of sex without a wedding ring, he's hardly going to be planning the second date."

The thought deflates and disappoints me. Leah is right—I'm my own worst enemy. Though my heart is heavy in regard to my near miss with Flynn, I pick up the phone again and dial Aileen's cell number, hoping I'm not waking or otherwise disturbing her.

"Hello?" Her voice is strong, and I'm relieved.

"Hi there, Aileen. It's Natalie." We've been on a first-name basis since parent-teacher conferences when we chatted like long-lost girlfriends, rather than a parent and teacher. Perhaps I have a ways to go in mastering the professional distance most teachers put between themselves and the parents of their students, but I genuinely like Aileen.

"Hey, Natalie. How's it going? Is everything okay with Logan?"

"He's doing great. And he's always so polite."

"I love to hear that. He knows better than to misbehave."

"I was wondering if you'll be home tomorrow after school. I'd like to stop by for a quick visit if that's convenient for you. I have some new books I thought you and the kids would enjoy, and I wanted to drop them off."

"I'd love to see you. It's very nice of you to think of us."

"Great, I'll see you then."

"Look forward to it."

I end the call and switch over to the text screen. *Tomorrow works for her. Would you mind meeting me outside my school around 3:30?* I include the address and set the time for more than half an hour after school ends in the hope that most of my colleagues will be long gone by then. I can only hope.

His reply arrives less than a minute later. *No problem. I'll be there.*

Thanks. See you then.

Now if someone could tell me how I'm supposed to function between now and then, I'd really appreciate it.

The next twenty-four hours feel like a week rather than a single day. I'm out of sorts, nervous, anxious, eager… In short, I'm a hot mess, and my kids take their cues from me. It's a long, trying day for all of us. I catch a moment with Logan and tell him the plan for later. His eyes light up with a kind of unfettered glee that I've never seen on him before. No matter what this might be costing me personally, I'd do it again—a thousand times over—to witness his joyful response.

"Thank you so much," he whispers.

"You're welcome." I squeeze his shoulder and send him to the coatroom to get his lunchbox. His smile never dims all afternoon, and his joy is contagious. By the time the bell rings, I feel like I'm going to spontaneously combust from both the excitement of surprising Aileen and from knowing I'm going to see Flynn again.

I wink and wave to Logan as he heads out. "See you soon."

His smile is so wide, I worry about his face breaking as he scurries out of the room. I follow the kids, as I always do, to watch them get on buses or be signed out by the parents, grandparents and guardians who pick them up.

I spend the next thirty minutes cleaning my classroom and preparing for tomorrow, while trying not to think about what's about to happen. At exactly three thirty, I run a brush through my hair, apply lip gloss and put on my red wool coat that leaves only a small portion of my tights uncovered between the coat and knee-high leather boots. I'll confess to having dressed for him today, not that it will matter. After he does this enormous favor for me, I don't expect to ever see him again. I tell myself I'm fine with that.

Slinging my satchel filled with work I'll do at home later over my shoulder, I head out of school, nodding to a few of my colleagues who I encounter in the hallway. I haven't heard a word about Flynn all day today thanks to the unfolding scandal involving Mrs. Heffernan's husband that has everyone's attention. While I wouldn't wish that on anyone, she was nasty to me about Fluff, so there's no love lost between us.

The cold air hits me like a slap to the face as I emerge from the building and head down the stone steps, looking around for him as I go but careful not to trip over my own feet. I stop short when I see him, across the street, arms crossed as he leans against the red motorcycle I saw the other night in his garage.

He's wearing a black leather jacket and well-faded jeans. His face is red from the cold and his hair mussed, maybe from the helmet that's propped on the seat next to him. He's stunningly gorgeous, and I can't do anything but stare at him for what feels like five minutes, though it's probably much less than that. At least I hope so.

He stares right back, his expression unreadable as I finally snap out of it and cross the street to where he's parked.

"Hi." *Wow, Natalie... Way to bowl him over with your opening volley.*

"Hi there. You look beautiful as always."

"Funny, I was thinking the same thing about you."

He offers a small smile that's tinged with sadness that wasn't there Saturday night. It makes me desperate to know what he's thinking and why he didn't call me. I was so sure he would.

"It's really nice of you to do this for someone you don't even know."

His intense gaze devours me. "I'm doing it for someone I know."

His meaning isn't lost on me, and if I wasn't so breathless from being near him, I might've acknowledged it.

"So where are we going?"

I give him the address a few blocks away.

"Hop on. I'll give you a lift."

I eye the motorcycle with trepidation. I've never been on one, and I'm not even sure how to get on, especially while wearing a skirt. "I'm, um, not really dressed for a motorcycle."

"You'll be fine. No one will see a thing."

Before I can formulate further protest, he's putting the helmet on me, straddling the bike and holding out his hand to help me get on behind him. I guess I'm going for my first ride on a motorcycle. Too bad it's freezing out and I won't be able to truly enjoy it. I want to ask about a helmet for him, but before I can pose the question, the bike roars to life and we take off like a shot.

I have no choice but to hold on tight to him if I want to survive this— not that holding on tight to him is any sort of imposition. I expect to be cold and uncomfortable, but I'm neither of those things. Rather, I'm exhilarated and thrilled to be pressed up against him for the all too short ride to the Giffords' home.

Flynn pulls right up to the building and squeezes the bike into a parking space on the street. He gets off the bike and then helps me with the helmet.

He studies me intently, but then I've come to expect that from him.

"Did I say thank you for this?"

"A few times."

"Is it okay to say it again?"

"Sure."

"I appreciate it more than you'll ever know. She's an amazing person, a single mom fighting an awful battle. Her son, Logan, is in my class and he told me you're her favorite."

"How did he find out you know me?"

"Um, well, yesterday, the whole school was talking about how I met you over the weekend."

He cocks his head and raises a brow, two things I've seen him do before when he is amused. "How did they know?"

"Leah told everyone. I didn't say a word. I promise you."

"I wouldn't have cared if you did."

"Oh. Well, I didn't."

"Anyway, your friend…"

"Aileen Gifford."

"What's the prognosis?"

"I'm not really sure. It's stage three, and she's been in treatment since before the school year started. I don't ask too many questions, but I like her. We've become friends."

"How about we go pay her a visit?" He helps me off the motorcycle. Or I should say he basically lifts me off and sets me on my feet in a move so unexpected and oddly thrilling that my knees nearly buckle under me. "You okay?"

"Yeah, sure." Other than a racing heart and sweating palms, I'm just fine. "You know she's going to freak out, right?"

"Believe it or not, that's happened before."

"Still, I don't want to drag you into an ambush without proper warning."

"Do I need to be worried that she'll jump me?"

"If she does, I'll protect you."

"Then I hope she does."

Is he flirting with me? After two days of total silence following what I considered a rather amazing date? I'm sure my definition of amazing and his are vastly different. That thought depresses me profoundly, so I try to push it aside as we head up the stairs to the wall of buttons for each apartment. I press the one for 3C and wait for an answer.

When the buzzer sounds, I say, "Hi, it's Natalie."

"Come on up." The buzzer sounds again, and we enter through the main door.

As I trudge up the stairs, I'm acutely aware of Flynn behind me. I can almost feel his eyes on me, watching my every move in that all-consuming way of his.

On the third-floor landing, he stops me with his hand to my arm. I feel the heat of his touch through two layers of clothing, but before I can wonder how that's possible, he releases me. "How do we want to play this?"

"What do you mean?"

"Am I just going to be standing there when she answers the door?"

"Good point. How about I say I brought a friend to meet her and then you come into view?"

"I can do that."

I begin to feel really excited for what we're about to do for someone who so deserves a little pleasure. With one last glance at Flynn to make sure he's in place, I knock on the door.

Aileen answers, and I'm immediately taken aback by how diminished she is from the last time I saw her. A funky scarf covers her head, her eyes are sunken into her face, and she's lost weight she didn't have to lose. I give her a hug. "So good to see you."

"You, too. Come in."

"I hope you don't mind, but I brought a friend who wants to meet you."

Her hand goes immediately to the scarf, and I'm heartbroken to realize I've made her feel self-conscious about her appearance.

"You look great," I whisper as I signal to Flynn.

When he steps into view, Aileen's eyes nearly pop out of her head, and her hand over her mouth suppresses her shriek. "Oh my God. *Shut up.* No way."

Behind her, Logan and his sister, Madison, giggle madly at her reaction.

"You must be Aileen." Flynn extends his hand to her. "It's great to meet you."

"Stop it," she says even as she shakes his hand, still in near-swoon mode. "What in the name of hell is Flynn Godfrey doing on my doorstep?"

"It was all Logan's doing." I love the way the little boy beams with pleasure at what he's done for his mother.

"Logan? You knew about this?"

"Yep," he says proudly. "You should invite them in, Mom."

"Oh God, of course. Please. Come in."

As we follow Aileen into the apartment, I share a smile with Flynn, who seems genuinely pleased. I'm sure he's done stuff like this a million times, and maybe it's nothing to him, but it's everything to Aileen and her children.

"Have a seat," she says when we gather in her cozy living room. "Can I get you anything?"

"Not a thing," Flynn says, glancing at me.

I shake my head. "No, thanks."

Logan and Madison take up residence on their mother's lap. "How did you keep this a secret?" Aileen asks her son, giving him a squeeze that makes him giggle.

It's so nice to hear him laugh. He's always so somber and quiet.

"It wasn't easy," he says. "I just told Maddie today so she wouldn't mess up and tell you."

"I kept the secret," Maddie says.

"You did great." Aileen glances tentatively at the love seat where Flynn is sitting so close to me I can feel the heat of his leg against mine. "You have to tell me how you two know each other."

I look at him, and he nods for me to go ahead and tell her. So I relay the story of how we met in the park, how Fluff bit him, and how we had coffee and then dinner together Saturday.

"*So you guys are dating?*" she asks, her squeal reminiscent of Leah's.

I answer quickly. "Oh, I don't think so."

He shocks me when he reaches for my hand and links our fingers. "Yeah, we are."

Aileen fans her face. "Holy shit."

Logan pounces. "Mom!"

"Sorry, honey, but really, you have to admit this situation calls for a swear word or two."

Madison giggles while Logan stares at his mother like he's never met her before. I get a glimpse of what Aileen was like as a younger, healthier woman, and I'm saddened all over again for the battle she's waging.

"I've seen all your movies," Aileen says almost shyly to Flynn. "Most of them at least five times."

"I'm so glad you enjoy them. That's great to hear."

"You must hear it all the time," she says.

"Never gets old to know that what we're doing is connecting with people."

"It's connecting all right." The dirty double meaning isn't lost on us, and we laugh.

"Which one is your favorite?" I ask.

"Oh gosh, do I have to pick just one?"

"You can pick as many as you want," Flynn says, making Aileen giggle.

I love seeing her laugh. We spend an hour with them, talking movies and Hollywood. Flynn is amazing. He answers all her question about his friends and what they're really like and how much of what is printed about all of them is utter crap. Aileen hangs on his every word, as do I, because I feel like I'm learning more about him listening to him talk about his work.

When I see her begin to tire, I suggest we should go and let her rest.

"Not before we take some pictures," Flynn says. "Aileen will want to brag to her friends about this, and she can't do that without pictures."

In that moment, I absolutely adore him. It no longer matters that he didn't call me. I feel like I'm seeing his heart right now, and I like what I see. I like it very much. He poses for no fewer than fifty photos with Aileen and the kids, some of them silly, some of them ridiculous and a few that will give her something to keep her warm on cold winter nights. He is endlessly patient with her and the children.

"I will never, ever forget this," she tells him when he gives her a final hug to say good-bye.

He kisses her forehead and then pulls back to look her in the eye. "If there's ever anything I can do for you or the kids, here's my card. Call me. I mean it."

Aileen's eyes fill with tears. "You've already done more than you'll ever know." She turns to me. "And you, you sneaky devil! Thank you. Thank you so much."

"My pleasure. Feel good and keep in touch, okay?"

"I will."

After we say good-bye to the kids and I receive a very tight, very emotional hug from Logan, we take our leave. We are quiet as we descend the stairs and head outside into encroaching darkness. The days are so short this time of year, something I normally find depressing. But I'm so exhilarated by what we just did there's no space for depression.

"That was so fun," I say to him when we reach the bike. "Thank you again." I look up at him and note that he seems tense.

"What can I do for them? How can I make this easier for her?"

"What you just gave her—"

"Is a small thrill that'll last a day or two until reality sets in again. How can I help her in some more meaningful way?"

I stare up at him, not sure how to reply.

"How do I give her money?"

"You, um, you don't have to do that."

"I know I don't. I want to. That would make me happy. Is there a fundraising effort or anything?"

"Yes, through the school, but you don't have to—"

He taps his finger against my lips and smiles. "I know I don't. I truly want to."

"That's very nice of you. All of this… Really, I can't begin to tell you how much it meant to her—and to me."

"It was a pleasure."

"I'm sure you have somewhere to be, so I, um, I'll let you get going."

"That's it?" He fixes that gaze on me, and I feel like the proverbial deer trapped in headlights. It's that potent.

"I'm not sure what you mean."

"You're going to walk away and that's that?"

"I know how busy you are, and I've already taken a good chunk of your time."

"I'm actually enjoying a rare bit of time off before I leave for LA and then begin postproduction on the film we just wrapped."

"Oh." I'm not sure what else to say. Hearing he's been enjoying time off that didn't include calling me annoys me, even if I wish it didn't. "Well, I hope you enjoy your time off."

"Thank you."

Suddenly I need to know. I have to know. It's the last thing I want to ask and the only thing I need to know. "Were you going to call me? If I hadn't texted about Aileen, would I have ever heard from you again?"

He looks down at me for a long, intense moment. "No."

"Good to know." I begin to walk away, but he follows, grasping my arm in a grip loose enough that it doesn't trigger any of my well-honed defense mechanisms but tight enough that I can't get away without a fight.

"Let me explain."

I attempt to pull my arm free of his grip. "No need. I get it. You could have anyone."

He gives a gentle tug that throws me off balance, and before I know what's happening, I'm pressed against his chest and his arms are around me. "I don't want just anyone. I want *you*."

I'm so busy trying to catch my breath from the events of the last two minutes that I can barely process what he's said. And then he's kissing me. His hands frame my face as his lips move softly over mine. The kiss is sweet and undemanding, but I feel its impact everywhere. I lean into him, wanting to be closer, and raise my arms to encircle his neck.

I forget we're on a city street where anyone can see us. I forget who he is and that photographers stalk him. I forget that it's freezing or that I was about to walk away. I forget that he had no plans to call me. I can only think of what it feels like to be surrounded by his rich, masculine scent as his lips destroy my resistance.

He breaks the kiss and turns his attention to my neck. "I wasn't going to call because of me, not because of you. Not because I didn't want to see you again, because I did. I *do*. You're all I've thought about since I saw you last. When I got your text yesterday, I was so happy to hear from you."

I'm not sure which is having a greater impact on me—what he's saying or what he's doing to my neck as he speaks. His breath is warm against my cold skin. I'm one big goose bump as I hang on his every word. I'm breathless as I wait to hear what else he has to say.

But he withdraws from me, so suddenly I stumble. He's right there to catch me, his hands on my shoulders steadying me. "Will you come with me so we can talk some more?"

I know I should decline. I should walk away from him while I still can. This whole thing is nothing more than a fantasy that can't possibly go anywhere. I already know he has the power to hurt me, perhaps worse than I've been hurt in the past, and I can't bear the thought of that. "I… I don't know what to say."

"Please?" He bends his head to the side and smiles at me. He's cute, and he knows it.

Maybe if he hadn't kissed me, I'd be able to resist that adorable grin and the equally adorable plea. He who could have anyone wants to spend more time with me. It's hard not to be flattered by that. What's another hour with him at this point?

"Okay."

He raises his arm and flags down a cab. "You'll freeze on the bike. I'll come back for it later."

Only when we're ensconced in the back of a toasty warm cab do I realize how cold I am. How long were we outside? I have no idea. Could've been five minutes or an hour. My brain is still scrambled from the Kiss with a capital K. It's been a very long time since I've been kissed. The last time, I was fifteen, before my life changed forever.

Two boys kissed me that year, but what a difference it is to kiss a *man* rather than a *boy*. There'd been no overabundance of spit or awkward tongue thrusting with Flynn. No, his kiss was sublime and skilled, even if it included only the touch of lips and nothing more. He knows what he's doing. And the spontaneous way in which it happened… I'll be thinking about that long after this interlude with him is a distant memory.

CHAPTER 7

Natalie

In the backseat of the cab, he puts his arm around me and nuzzles my hair.

I lean into him, wanting to be closer to him.

"Did I fuck up by kissing you?" he asks, his voice gruff.

I raise my head off his shoulder to meet his gaze. He seems genuinely worried. "What? No. You didn't."

"Are you sure?"

I nod because the words I wish to say are stuck in my throat. I can't look away from him. He draws me in with his magnetic appeal, and the closer I get to the heat, the more enthralled I seem to be. His kindness to Aileen and her children makes him even more attractive to me than he was before.

I need to be careful. I know that. I can't afford the kind of disruption he could be in my well-planned and well-ordered life. But right now, in this moment, with his arm around me, his scent filling my senses and his nearness making me want so much more, being careful isn't my top priority for the first time in eight years.

We ride uptown in silence, until the cab stops outside a high-rise.

Flynn releases a low curse. "Can we go around the block?" He rattles off a new address, and the cab merges into traffic again.

"What's wrong?"

"Paparazzi camped out front waiting for me."

"How could you tell?"

"I recognize them. They're paid to follow me."

"Paid to follow you… What that must be like…"

"It's no fun, especially when you value your privacy and that of your friends." He asks the driver to pull into a driveway that slopes downward to a metal door. "Stay here for a sec."

I watch him get out of the car and punch a code into a number pad that opens the metal doors. Then he gets back into the car. Handing a fifty-dollar bill to the cab driver, he says, "Will you take us in please?"

"Will I be able to get out of here?" the cabbie asks.

"Yeah."

We descend into the parking garage we were in the other night. The cabbie lets out a low whistle at the sight of the Bugatti.

Flynn directs him to turn around on the other side of the garage, well away from the priceless vehicle. He gets out and reaches for me. "Thanks for the lift. The door will open for you."

"Could I bother you for a photo with the car?" the driver asks in broken English.

"Sure," Flynn says, even though I can see he's impatient and not really in the mood for pictures. Still, he stands with the driver, smiles for the photo I take of them with the driver's camera. We wait to make sure he actually leaves the garage before we head up to his place.

"That was nice of you," I say in the elevator.

"What was?"

"Taking a photo with him."

He shrugs off the compliment. "It was no big deal."

I like him all the more for his humility. "It was to him and to Aileen."

"My dad likes to say it doesn't cost anything to be nice to people."

"I think I'd like your dad."

"I know he'd like you." He reaches for my hand and leads me into his apartment. "Can I take your coat?"

Still processing what he said about his dad liking me, I unwrap my scarf and hand it and my coat to him.

"I could go for some hot chocolate," he says. "You?"

"I never say no to that."

"Come help me. I'm lost in the kitchen."

"Can you boil water?"

"It's best if I don't do that on my own."

I roll my eyes at him because I can tell he's being outrageous on purpose, but since he's also being adorable again, I go into the kitchen to help.

"I'm going to be really bummed if I offered you hot chocolate and I don't have any," he says as he roots through cabinets.

I spot the box of instant hot chocolate mix and reach over his head for it. When I start to lose my balance, he steadies me with his hands on my hips. That's all it takes for my entire body to feel like it's encountered a live wire. The current travels through me, waking up all the parts that make me a woman. "Here," I say as I hand him the box.

"Thanks." He seems reluctant to let me go, but he does so he can get mugs.

We sit at the bar, and he produces whipped cream that he applies to both mugs of steaming hot chocolate.

"You know what this needs?" He stands and goes back into the kitchen, returning with a bottle. "Bailey's." Holding up the bottle, he says, "Yes?"

"Sure. I'll try a little." After he pours the liquor into my mug, I take a sip and feel the warming burn of the Bailey's deep inside. "That's good."

He tucks a strand of my hair behind my ear and traces my cheekbone with his finger. His touch starts an all-new burn inside me that has nothing to do with liquor or hot chocolate.

I glance at him. "You wanted to talk?"

Seeming reluctant, he drops his hand from my face and looks down at the floor.

I hold my breath, waiting to hear what he will say.

"I was convinced, by a friend, that there's no place in my life for someone as sweet and lovely as you."

"What does that mean?"

"It means," he says with a deep sigh, "I'm an idiot because I let someone tell me this is a bad idea when every cell in my body is telling me you're the best idea I've had in years. Perhaps the best idea ever."

"Oh." I don't know what to say to that.

He takes my hand again, bringing it to his mouth and running his lips over my knuckles. "My life isn't for everyone. You just got a small demonstration of how the paps camp outside my building hoping for a glimpse of me so they can sell a picture to a tabloid. They pursue me relentlessly."

"And that's why your friend doesn't think it's a good idea for you to see me?"

"That's part of it." He twirls his finger through the dollop of whipped cream in his mug. "The thing is, though, since Saturday, you're all I think about. I've relived every second we spent together probably a hundred times since then."

"So have I."

"Yeah?" He looks so hopeful that I can't help but smile.

"Yeah."

"You've cast some sort of spell on me, haven't you?"

"That's it exactly. You've figured me out."

"It's the only possible explanation for the way my heart nearly jumped out of my chest when you texted me yesterday."

"It did not."

"Yes, it did."

I focus on my drink because I don't know where else to look. His confession has me reeling.

"Natalie... Look at me."

I summon the courage to let my gaze meet his, and I'm astounded by what I see—affection, amusement, desire.

"You're very satisfied in your life. You love your job, your kids, your roommate and your new life in the city. If you get involved with me, your life will change in ways you can't imagine."

"What sort of ways?" I ask, genuinely curious.

"For one thing, the paparazzi will stalk you, and when I say stalk you, I mean they will be *relentless*. They'll take photos and print lies about you. They'll tear apart your clothes, your hair, your past."

I take a sip of my drink, and we both notice the tremble of my hand. My past is buried so deep, it'll never be uncovered, but that doesn't mean the thought of being pursued doesn't terrify me, because it does. I didn't do anything wrong in that situation, so it's not like I have something to be ashamed of. But I'm ashamed nonetheless, and I'd hate for him or any of my other new friends to know about my past.

"What else?" I ask.

"That's not enough to scare you away?"

"I'd like to have all the information before I decide."

He tips his head again, something I'm coming to recognize as one of his charming characteristics. It conveys interest and a sense that I'm the only person in his universe, even when I know that's so far from true. "There're women who will say things, do things, *infer* things… You'll always be wondering. Is what he says true? Is he leading me on? Is he lying? She has pictures… She must know something I don't know."

"That's a tough one."

"It was a deal breaker for the last woman I cared about. She believed everything that was said and written about me. I got tired of defending myself."

"I can see how that would get old fast."

"It does. I like to think I'm a trustworthy person."

"Have you ever done something while in a relationship that you're not proud of?"

After a long pause, he says, "Yes. When I was married. I told you she cheated on me."

I nod.

He blows out a deep breath. "I was so furious and hurt and embarrassed. People tried to warn me away from her, but I was blind and in love and stupid. So stupid. I cheated on her after she did it to me."

"Did you feel better after?"

Laughing, he says, "No. I felt worse because I let her make me into someone I didn't even recognize, but what I did is on me, not her. I did it. I knew what I was doing. And it was all about revenge. I slept with her friend and made sure she found out about it."

"Ouch."

"Not my finest moment."

"How old were you?"

"Twenty-four."

"And this is why you've said you never want to be married again?"

"Part of it. Yeah." He tightens his grip on my hand. "I want to say something here, but I'm so afraid it'll sound insincere or ridiculous or even counterproductive to my effort to warn you off me."

"That was quite an intro."

I love the deep grooves in his cheeks that form when he gifts me with one of those genuine smiles that made him a superstar.

"What do you want to say?"

"Remember I'm being totally sincere here."

"Got it."

"Since I met you and spent time with you and then tried—unsuccessfully, it seems—to walk away from you, I don't feel so... certain... that I'll never get married again."

"You sure know how to make a girl all fluttery inside, Flynn."

He raises a brow. "Are you fluttery?"

"On the inside."

Leaning in to close the distance between us, he says, "I'd really like to kiss you again."

"I'd really like you to kiss me again."

"Right now?"

"Now would be good." I wonder who this confident, adventuresome person is. She's been gone such a long time, I barely recognize her.

With his hands on my face, he draws me into another of those sizzling kisses that make my head spin. I love the way his hands feel on my face, the tender, cautious way he kisses me, as if I'm something precious and priceless. This kiss is more intense than the first one, maybe because we're alone and not standing on a public street.

Then I feel the press of his tongue against my lips, and I can't think about anything other than how amazing it feels to be held and kissed by him. He stands and brings me with him, my arms curling around his neck as I lean into him and the kiss. I can't seem to get close enough.

"Natalie," he whispers.

It takes a second for his words to permeate the fog I'm in after kissing him.

He takes my hand and leads me to the sofa. We sit close to each other, and he kisses me again. "Is this okay?"

"Yes."

"How about this?" He slips his tongue between my lips and rubs it against mine, making me moan. "Is that a yes?"

"Mmm."

"I need the word."

"Yes, Flynn. *Yes!*"

When he smiles, his eyes light up. "I need to be sure in light of your… previously stated…limitations."

"I said no sex. I never said a word about kissing."

"So kissing is good?" His lips touch mine as he speaks.

"Kissing is very, *very* good." It might be the best thing ever.

"I couldn't agree more."

I can't get close enough to him. I want to be absorbed by him, consumed. I've never wanted that before. If anything, I've kept my distance for reasons that are mine and mine alone. Then he breaks the kiss and moves to my neck, his lips setting me on fire.

"So I haven't succeeded in warning you away," he says.

"I'd say you've failed miserably."

"Thank God." He kisses me again with deep sweeps of his tongue that have me on the verge of begging for something I said I didn't want. "Come to LA with me, Natalie. Come be with me. I want you next to me, holding my hand when they read my name."

"Flynn…" I'm tempted. So very, very tempted.

"I told them I'm bringing a date." His teeth close over my earlobe, and I feel it in every nerve ending. "You aren't going to leave me high and dry, are you?"

I draw back from him so I can see his face. "You said you weren't going to call me, and yet you still planned to take me to the Golden Globes?"

"What can I say? I'm a hopeful person. And then when I got your text yesterday and knew I would see you again, I hoped I could talk you into coming. I saw that text as a sign."

"So even as you try to warn me off you, you're scheming to get me to LA."

"Yes, I'm guilty as charged. I figure if you have all the facts, you can make an informed decision."

"And I have all the facts now?"

"Except for one."

"What's that?"

"I'm sorry I didn't call you after our very special evening on Saturday. I'm sorry I let someone else's opinion sway me when the only thing that should've mattered is what I know to be true—you're special, and I want a chance with you."

CHAPTER 8

Flynn

I hold my breath while I wait for her to answer me. I wouldn't blame her for saying no after what I've told her about my life and what to expect if she spends time with me.

"Tell me the truth," she says.

"Always." I ignore the alarm bells from my brain, reminding me of the secrets I am keeping from her.

"The thing with the media… How bad will it be?"

"It could get pretty bad. They'll dig for dirt, and if they don't find any, they'll make it up. You're apt to have problems with your job if they decide the attention is too much of a distraction. You'll be defending yourself against accusations that aren't even true."

"All that from one night out with you?"

"All that and maybe more." I wish I didn't have to make her aware of these things, but I have to be fair. They're the realities I live with every day. Celebrity is a dicey business in the age of the twenty-four-hour news cycle. It's my life. I'm used to it, but I won't expose her without making her aware of the potential fallout.

"You make it sound like I'd be crazy to go with you."

"You would be, but I still hope you'll come anyway."

"There are things… about me… that I don't talk about. Ever. To anyone."

"Are these things that would come out if the press were to dig into your life?"

She shakes her head. "I was someone else then. I'm not that person anymore."

I want to ask her to explain. I want to be the one she tells, but I'd never ask her for more than she's willing to give. I've already figured out that pushing her outside her comfort zone is the fastest way to push her away.

"Then other than the potential for a huge distraction and massive hubbub that I'll do everything in my power to protect you from, it'll be like any other date."

She tosses her head back and laughs, and I fall in love with the sound of her laughter. It's lusty and genuine and gorgeous, just like her. I want to make her laugh every day just so I can enjoy the delightful sound. "Like any other date, huh?"

"Like any other date that includes designer attire, a few camera flashes, a couple of celebrities here and there, lots of parties." He shrugs. "No biggie."

"Just another night in Tinseltown for you."

"It won't be like any other night if you're with me."

"You're good. I've got to give you that."

"Is that a 'Yes, Flynn, I'd love to go to LA with you and be your date to the Golden Globes'?"

"That's a yes, Flynn, I'd really like to go to LA, but—"

I groan loudly and throw myself back against the sofa. I'm being silly and dramatic. "I hate the word *but*. I've never hated a word more than I hate that one."

"*But*," she says, smiling, "I want to make sure I can get the time off before I commit."

"Ugh, you're *killing* me. When will you know?"

"I'll ask tomorrow."

"How will I survive until then?"

"You weren't going to call me, which means you were going to survive the whole rest of your life without me in it. Remember that?"

"We're going to forget all about that." After two hours with her, I understand I was crazy to follow Hayden's advice. The more time I spend with her, the more I want her. I want her to be mine. It doesn't matter that I might not be good for her.

I can be someone different for her. I'll be anyone she needs me to be if it means I get to have her in my life.

I've never had these sorts of thoughts about any woman. Ever. I ought to be scared shitless, but I'm not. I'm exhilarated by her and determined to show her the time of her life in Hollywood.

She leans her head against the back of the sofa and studies me intently.

"Do I have something on my face?"

"No," she says, releasing that husky, sexy laugh that makes me hard every damned time. That laugh is dangerous and potent.

I'm thinking about kissing her again when my stomach lets out an obnoxious growl.

"Someone is hungry," she says.

"We need food. What do you feel like tonight?"

"You don't have to feed me. I need to get home to let Fluff out anyway."

"We could go to your place, take Fluff for a walk and then grab something in your neighborhood."

She seems incredulous. "You want to take Fluff for a walk."

"Well, I want to spend more time with you, and she's part of the package, so yes, I'd like to take Fluff for a walk."

"What if she bites you again?"

"I'm willing to take my chances. It's important that Fluff get used to me, because I'm going to be around. A lot."

"Are you?"

"If you'll have me." I reach for her hand, and she curls her fingers around mine. "Shall we go?"

"How do we get out of here without the photographers seeing us?"

"I'll show you."

Natalie

When he emerges from his bedroom wearing dark sunglasses and one of those fur hats that Soviet KGB officers were known for during the Cold War, I laugh so hard that tears run down my face. "*I* want a picture of *that*."

"Not happening. There's a Russian diplomat in the building. He's about twenty years older than me, but his build is somewhat similar to mine. The hat hides his gray hair. Every time I leave the building wearing this, they think I'm him and they leave me alone."

"Does he know you've stolen his identity?"

"Shhh, no. Don't tell." He holds my coat for me and then pulls the hood up and over my head, enveloping me in a cave of obscurity. "That ought to do it." Then he goes to the phone by the elevator and asks the doorman to get us a cab. The whole thing is handled so smoothly and competently that I begin to see the advantage of celebrity. People do things for you simply because you ask them to.

We make a clean escape from the building into a waiting cab. The photographers camped outside the main door are too busy smoking and bullshitting to notice their prey has escaped undetected.

"That was awesome, Mr. Gorbachev. Well played."

"Avoiding them is a game I've gotten rather good at over the years." He removes the hat and waggles his brows. "Wait until you see my other disguises."

"I look forward to that." I look forward to everything now that I know I'll see him again after today, now that I've committed to what promises to be a magical weekend in LA. Excitement courses through my body, making my nerves hum with anticipation. I've never felt more alive in my life than I do with him sitting next to me, holding my hand. I wonder if he'll kiss me again before the evening is over.

I hope so.

After a slow trek through rush-hour traffic, we arrive at my place. As we head up the stairs, I wonder if Leah is home and what sort of scene she'll make when she sees Flynn. I can hear Fluff going nuts in the apartment. "Are you ready for this?" I ask him.

"As ready as I'll ever be."

"Here goes." I open the door, and Fluff goes into her usual tizzy at the sight of me, but when Flynn comes in behind me, she loses her composure immediately, growling and snapping and hissing. I've never seen her behave this way. "I don't know what's wrong with her. Fluff! Stop it!"

Flynn takes it in stride, his expression showing amusement even as he keeps his distance from the growling ball of fur.

I snap a leash on her and have to nearly drag her to the door, which is another first. She usually bounds for the door.

Flynn puts his KGB hat back on and follows at an understandable distance as we go downstairs. On the street, Fluff looks up at him, and the hat sends her into another fit of rage.

"I think she's afraid you're wearing one of her relatives on your head."

He laughs and takes hold of my free hand.

I love the easy, casual way he does that, as if we've been holding hands forever. It feels natural to me, like my hand belongs wrapped up in his. It's absolutely freezing, so we stay out only long enough for Fluff to do her business.

Flynn takes the plastic bag from me and cleans up after her.

"That's way above and beyond the call of duty in light of her treatment of you."

"I like to think I'm a gentleman toward all women, even the shrewish ones."

He's got the market cornered on charm, that's for sure. Because I can't stop laughing at the hat, he playfully refuses to go out with me, so we end up ordering Thai and having it delivered. That's more than fine with me since I've had enough of the icy cold. Other than Fluff's continuing hostility toward Flynn, we have a great night together, but the whole time we're on the sofa watching mindless TV, I'm thinking about kissing him and wondering if it will happen again.

How have I gone from wanting no man to touch me again—ever—to wanting this man with a fervor that surprises and astounds me? It's like the last eight years never happened and I'm back to being who I was before my life was shattered. Is it possible that I've actually recovered, finally, and can entertain the possibility of true intimacy with a man?

Since that thought never would've occurred to me before I met Flynn, I decide to table it until I can pick it apart when I'm alone later. Having him curled up next to me requires my full attention.

By ten thirty, I'm trying not to yawn. I'm usually in bed by ten because my alarm goes off at five, and I need every minute of those seven hours of sleep to function the next day. But I don't want this time with him to end.

"What time do you have to get up tomorrow?" he asks.

I wonder if he's a mind reader in addition to his many other attributes. "Five."

"*Ugh*, that's *brutal*. How do you do that?"

"Well, it all begins with an alarm clock."

"Smart-ass. You know what I mean."

"Don't you have early days when you're filming?"

"Yeah, but I always know there's an end in sight."

"So do I. It's called summer vacation, when I sleep until noon as often as I possibly can."

"Now you're talking my language."

"You like to sleep in?"

"I love to sleep in. While you're slogging to work in the morning, think of me sleeping until noon."

"That's just mean." My imagination immediately leaps to what he must look like in the morning, all sleep-rumpled and sexy with stubble on his jaw and his hair standing on end. I nearly sigh from the power of my imaginings.

"I'll let you sleep until noon at least one day in LA."

"Promise?"

"Cross my heart." He looks over at me. "I should go so you can get some sleep. Something tells me those third-graders won't show much mercy to a tired Miss Bryant tomorrow."

"They'll take full advantage."

His fingers trace the outline of my jaw before he leans in to kiss me. The moment his lips touch mine, I forget all about early wake-ups and third-graders. Nothing matters more than the heat that blasts through my body. My powerful reaction to him should frighten me, but rather than push him away, I pull him closer. That seems to trigger something for him, and the kiss becomes more demanding.

We both ignore the low growl from Fluff, who'd been asleep on the floor until Flynn got too close to me for her liking.

He wraps his arm around me and brings me closer to him. Carried away by the desire and the heat, I open my mouth to his tongue and discover I've only experienced the beginning of what he's capable of making me feel.

"Jesus, Natalie," he whispers harshly. His jaw pulses with tension as he leans his forehead against mine. He's breathing heavily. "I should go."

I want to beg him to stay, to kiss me again, to make me feel this way for a little while longer. But his hands fall away from my face, and he withdraws from me, which seems to pain him. I know I must look as shell-shocked as I feel.

"I, um…" Flynn runs his fingers through his hair. "I'm sorry if I got carried away."

"Don't be sorry. I loved it."

He groans as he stands, and that's when I notice he's hard. The prominent outline of his erection inside well-worn denim rivets me.

"Natalie…"

I force my gaze up to meet his. "Don't look at me that way and then tell me I can't have you." He softens his words with a small smile and extends a hand to me.

I take it and let him pull me up and into his embrace.

"Text me the second you know if you can get the time off."

"I will." All I can feel is his heated length against my belly. I want to press against him, but somewhere I find a measure of self-control.

"I'll be holding my breath until I hear from you."

"Don't do that. You'll pass out."

"Then put me out of my misery as soon as you can."

"Thank you again for today, for what you did for Aileen and her children."

"It was my pleasure. Anything to make you smile."

Fluff is at our feet, growling and snapping. Honestly, she's lost her mind since we met Flynn.

He puts on his coat. "Does she need to go out again?"

"Just for a quick one."

"Want me to take her before I go?"

"That's very nice of you, but I won't subject you to her."

"I'm not afraid of her, and she needs to get used to me." He grabs the leash, and when he bends to snap it on her, Fluff launches herself at him, latching on to the same arm she bit the other day.

"Oh my God! Fluff! Stop!" I manage to pull her off Flynn. Thank goodness he's wearing a coat, so no damage is done. "I'm so sorry. I don't know what's wrong with her." I venture a glance at him and discover that he's laughing—hard.

"I know what's wrong with her."

"Care to share?"

"She's jealous. She can tell I like you and you like me, and she's put out by it."

Fluff growls and snaps, which makes me laugh even as I hold her back from attacking him again.

"It's like you've never had a boyfriend before."

Fearful of giving too much away, I roll my bottom lip between my teeth and drop my gaze to focus on Fluff rather than him.

"Natalie?"

I look up to find him watching me closely. "Yes?"

"You've had a boyfriend before, haven't you?"

I'm immediately frozen with indecision. Do I tell him the truth, or do I go with the version of the truth I've created to match my new life? My moment of hesitation is apparently all he needs to draw his own conclusions.

"*Never?*"

"It's complicated." That's the truth.

"How complicated?"

"It's a story for another day."

He leans in so he's nose to nose with Fluff. "Get used to me. I'm not going away."

She replies by showing the ten teeth she has left and growling again.

All I can think about is Fluff taking a piece out of that picture-perfect face of his, so I tighten my hold on her.

Flynn leans around the snarling dog to kiss me again. "I'll talk to you tomorrow."

Thankful he's decided not to immediately pursue the subject of my past dating life—or lack thereof—I close the door behind him and lean my head against it. He's too perceptive for my own good. If I continue seeing him, I won't be able to hide the truth from him for much longer.

I like to think I can walk away at any time, but I'm in his thrall, especially after kissing him. I don't want to walk away. For the first time, I want to push my fears aside and attempt a real relationship with a man. Despite his fame and all that goes with it, I already feel like I can trust him to protect and care for me, especially if my demons try to ruin everything for both of us.

The minute I return from taking Fluff out for a quick trip to her favorite peeing spot, I pull off my coat, scarf and gloves, and rather than heading for bed, I boot up my laptop to log into the automated system at school to request Monday off. Thankfully, I don't have to go through stone-faced Mrs. Heffernan to get the time off. I make the request for a personal day on Monday and submit it before I can talk myself out of this madness that's overtaken my life.

With Flynn's warnings on my mind, I Google my name and scroll through the few mentions that appear, all of them attached to my current school and the college in Nebraska where I got my teaching degree. Since I haven't done an Internet search in a while, I'm relieved to find no connection at all between Natalie and the person I used to be. As far as anyone can tell, Natalie Bryant is a teacher in New York City. That's all she is, and that's all the paparazzi will find if they dig into my life.

Leah comes in as I'm logging off the computer. "What're you still doing up, Ms. I Need My Beauty Sleep or Else?"

"Just finishing up some work." That's when I remember I didn't do any of the correcting I brought home with me. Tomorrow is going to be a very long day. "Where've you been?"

"At the gym and then dinner with some friends from the bar." She drops down onto the sofa. "I gotta tell you something."

"What?"

"I think I'm going to quit teaching."

"No. You can't. You have a contract."

"One of the guys who hangs out at the bar is a lawyer. He's looking at it for me."

"But why, Leah? It's only your first year. You have to give it a chance."

"I hate it. I hate every second I have to spend in that building with those kids. They deserve better than a teacher who hates them."

"You don't hate them."

"I'm starting to. And don't get me going on the parents."

I couldn't argue with that. Leah had gotten some of the worst parents any of us had that year. They ran the gamut from overly involved to hands-off to a fault—until their precious child got in trouble, and then they were parents of the year.

"Nothing will happen until the end of the year. I'll see it through, but I want out. Teaching isn't for me." She glances over at me. "What'd you do tonight?"

I hesitate because if I tell her I saw Flynn, I won't be getting to bed any time soon.

"Did he call?"

"Not exactly." I fill her in on our visit to Aileen and the rest of our evening.

"You're really going to the Golden Globes." At least she doesn't scream, for which I'm grateful.

"If I can get Monday off."

"You will. You've got the time."

"I'm not getting excited until I know for sure."

"That was nice of him. With Aileen."

"He was amazing. He's nice to everyone." I tell her about the cab driver and how he posed for pictures with the driver and the Bugatti. "He warned me if I go to the Globes with him, things will get crazy for me with the paparazzi. They're apt to come after you, too."

"So we'll be famous? How cool is that?"

"I think it's cooler on paper than it is in reality."

"I look forward to finding out." She yawns loudly and stands. "We'd better get to bed so we're ready to face the monsters tomorrow."

I want to tell her not to call them that, but I know she doesn't want to hear it. I'm saddened by her decision to leave teaching, but I understand how it's not for everyone. Maybe if I get a room full of misbehaving kids and their parents next year, I'll hate it, too.

We say our good-nights, and I'm awake long after I should be asleep, thinking about Flynn and the trip to LA and the kissing... The kissing is amazing, and I can't wait to do it again. I wonder if I'll see him tomorrow—or today—I note with a groan as I glance at my beside clock and see that it's long after midnight. Even in the dark, with my eyes closed, his face is all I see. That adorable tip of his head, the shy, sexy grin, the way he lets loose with laughter.

I'm anxious about what will happen if I attend the Globes with him. I won't deny that, but I refuse to live my life in fear of what might happen. I spent years leaving fear behind, and this is no time to start regressing, especially not when I'm enjoying the present so much.

The alarm provides a particularly rude awakening in the morning. If you'd asked me, I would've said I hadn't slept at all, but apparently that isn't true. The first thing I do is reach for my laptop to log in and find out if my request has been approved. Nothing yet.

I check again minutes before my class files into the classroom, but still nothing. I've never requested a day off before, so I have no idea how long to expect it to take. I plan to ask the other teachers at lunch, if I can only get through the morning. Right before lunch, I check again, and the request has been approved. I sit and stare at the screen as a variety of emotions overtake me all at once: relief, excitement, anxiety and desire.

With the kids occupied with an assignment, I reach for my phone to text Flynn.

You can breathe now. I got Monday off.

He writes right back. *Thank goodness. I was starting to get light-headed. Pick you up from school today? 3:30?*

I think about it for exactly one second before I write back. *4 would be better.* As much as I want to see him again, I *have* to get some work done.

4 it is. See you then. Can't wait.

I read those last words over and over again. Flynn Godfrey can't wait to see me. I think about my sisters and how excited they would be to know I'm seeing Flynn, a movie star they both admire, and I'm filled with sadness for all I've lost. Maybe they'll see a photo from the Golden Globes in one of the celebrity magazines they love to devour. I dismiss that thought the minute I have it. I look so different now, they probably wouldn't recognize me as their long-lost sister. Or maybe they never think of me at all anymore and won't care who I'm dating.

The notion of them forgetting about me depresses me profoundly, so I try to stay focused on all the things that are going right in my life now, including a budding romance with a man who can't wait to see me.

I did what I had to do for myself and for my sisters. Maybe someday they'll realize that. In the meantime, I have an afternoon to get through with a room full of third-graders who are hopped up on sugar thanks to the cupcakes Micha's mom brought in after lunch to celebrate his birthday. As much as I dislike what the sugar does to my plans for the afternoon, I'm thankful that the parents participate the way they do.

Micha's mom stays for the afternoon to help out with a science project, and we end the day with her reading them a book. Her cheerful presence helps the day go by faster than it would have normally, especially when I know I'll be seeing Flynn.

After the kids leave, I make quick work of cleaning up my room and correcting the papers I never got around to doing last night as well as today's classwork. The whole time, I'm watching the clock creep closer to four. At ten till, Leah ducks her head into my room.

"Working all night, loser?" she asks with a teasing smile.

"Nope. Just for ten more minutes."

She looks at me suspiciously. "And then what?"

"A little of this, a little of that…"

"You have a date with the movie star!"

"Shush, will you?"

She comes into the room, letting the door slam behind her. "Where's he taking you?"

"I don't know. We'll probably hang out at his place. It's easier for him than going out."

"This whole thing is so fucking cool, Nat."

"Don't say fuck at school."

"Why not? There're no little ears around to hear it."

"Mrs. Heffernan is always listening with her big elephant ears."

Leah snorts with laughter. "She's probably got every room bugged."

"Which is why you shouldn't swear at school."

"So I heard something I thought would interest you."

"What's that?"

"Someone made an anonymous donation to Aileen's fund—a big donation. Like half a million bucks big."

I stare at her, trying to process what she's told me. *"Half a million dollars?"*

"That's what Sue said." Leah is friends with the woman who runs the main office and gets all the best gossip from her. "Who else could it be but your friend Flynn?"

"God... I can't believe he did that. He said he wanted to help them and asked if there's a fund or something. But I never imagined..." Tears fill my eyes when I imagine Aileen's reaction to receiving that kind of money.

"It's good of him," Leah says.

"It's amazing." I'm stunned and overwhelmed and more eager to see him than I was before.

"Pull yourself together. You've got a hot date with a hot man in five minutes."

Still reeling from Flynn's incredible gesture, I force myself to calm down and try to relax. "What're you up to tonight?"

"I picked up a shift at the bar. Still trying to pay off Christmas."

"Which means you'll be a wreck tomorrow."

"It'll be worth it to pay off that beast of a credit card. No tutoring today?"

I shake my head. "Myles's grandfather is in the hospital, so we're not meeting at all this week. But get this—his mom is still paying me because it's not my fault we couldn't get together."

"You have all the luck lately, Nat. We should call you Lady Luck."

If only Leah knew what a huge price I paid for any luck I may be receiving now. For the longest time, I wondered if everyone else had gotten my share of the luck quotient. But lately... Lately things have been good, and I hope they stay that way from now on. No matter what happens, however, nothing could ever be as bad as what I've already been through. Knowing what I'm capable of gives me the courage to face each new day and every challenge that comes my way.

"I need to make myself pretty," I say to Leah.

She rolls her eyes at me. "Puleeze. You were born pretty."

Though I was born a redhead with green eyes and freckles, I bear no resemblance whatsoever to that girl anymore. I wear special contacts that give me brown eyes, and I regularly color my hair, which is much longer than it used to be, to keep it dark. Other than a once-a-month change of contacts, I never see my green eyes anymore. I've gotten used to my new look, but it didn't happen overnight. The new looks were nearly as hard to come by as my new identity, not that Leah would have any way to know that. "Whatever you say."

"Can I stay until he gets here?"

"Sure."

"Am I allowed to talk to him?"

"Yes," I say, laughing, "you can talk to him. I already know him well enough to know he'd want you to be normal around him."

"Not sure I can promise *normal*, but I'll try."

While I run a brush through my hair, she finger combs her much shorter locks and makes funny puffy-lip model faces that have me laughing so hard I worry about tears sending streams of mascara down my face. "Knock it off, will you?"

"Hey, Nat, do you think you'll ever look at him and say to yourself, oh, there's Flynn? Just Flynn. Not Flynn, the movie star?"

I think about that for a second. "I already do think of him that way sometimes. When we're sitting on the sofa chatting about a movie or how we like the same food or something one of his sisters said in a text, he's just Flynn, just a regular guy. Then he gets a call from Marlowe Sloane, and I remember who he is to the rest of the world."

"I don't think I could ever forget that. And Marlowe Sloane… Watch out for her. Rumor has it they're a hot item."

"All rumor, according to him. They're close friends." I hold up a mirror from my purse and apply a light coat of plum lip color. "And besides, what's the point of spending time with him if I can't separate the man from the fame? There's much more to him than his career, you know?"

"Is that right?" She eyes me shrewdly. "Have you kissed him yet?"

I look away, intently focused on my mirror. "Maybe."

She pounces on that immediately. "That's *not* a no!"

"Shut *up*, Leah!"

"Tell me everything, and don't leave anything out."

"Sorry, no time for that. Gotta go. If you're walking out with me, try not to act like a freak."

She links her arm through mine. "Oh, I'm walking out with you, and no promises on the freak thing."

"*Great.*"

CHAPTER 9

Flynn

Sitting outside Natalie's school in the Range Rover, I debate at ridiculous length whether I should wait for her in the car or get out and risk someone recognizing me. That it's fucking freezing keeps me in the car until I see her emerge from the building with Leah.

They're both so young, they could easily be mistaken for students if this were a high school rather than an elementary school. I experience a pang of guilt when Hayden's words resurface to remind me she is way too young and unspoiled for the likes of me. Yet, even knowing that, I can't walk away from her.

She spots the car and heads toward me.

That's when I get out and go around to meet them, bowing gallantly. "Ladies."

"Hi there." Natalie's lips are glistening with some sort of purple gloss that I want to lick off as soon as possible. Yes, that's my first thought, and no, I'm not proud of that.

I kiss her cheek. "How was your day, dear?"

She dazzles me with her smile. "Excellent, you?"

"Long and boring waiting for school to get over. Reminds me of the not so good old days."

"See?" Leah says. "He agrees with me. School sucks."

"Lovely to see you again, Leah."

"Mmm," she says suggestively, "same here."

"Can we give you a lift somewhere?"

She eyes the car longingly and then glances at Natalie. "Home?"

"We can do that," I say before Natalie has a chance to reply. I open the back door for Leah and the front passenger door for Natalie.

When I get into the driver's side, I notice Natalie giving me an odd look. "Do I have something on my face?" I rub the cheek I recently shaved in anticipation of seeing her.

"No," she says, laughing.

"Then what?"

"I'll tell you later."

"When *I'm* not here," Leah says from the backseat.

"Then let's get rid of her ASAP," I say.

"Hey! That's not nice."

Natalie laughs at Leah's pretend outrage. The two of them amuse me. Leah is as mouthy and ballsy as Natalie is reserved. They make for an odd pairing that seems to work well despite their differences.

Natalie's cell phone rings, and she glances at the caller ID. "Aileen," she says, glancing at me. "Hi, Aileen."

I can hear the other woman's high-pitched screams coming through Natalie's phone.

"I heard about that," she says, looking over at me again.

I feign ignorance as to what's happening even though I know all about it. The donation was made anonymously because I don't want anything from it other than to know that Aileen and her kids are taken care of during this difficult time.

"I'll tell him," Natalie says after several minutes of mostly one-sided conversation. "Talk to you soon." She ends the call and stashes the phone in her purse. "Can you believe someone made a *half-million-dollar* donation to the fund we set up for their family?"

"I wonder who could've done something like that," Leah says.

"That's great," I add. "Good for them."

Natalie gives me another of those looks that lets me know I'm not fooling anyone. That's okay. The best thing about having money is being able to help people who truly need it.

When we arrive on their street, there's not a parking spot to be found.

"I can jump out here," Leah says. "You want me to take Fluff out for you?"

"Would you mind?"

"Not at all."

"Thanks. Flynn's not her favorite person."

"Aww, is the old bag of bones jealous?"

"Don't say that about her! She's not a bag of bones."

"But she is jealous," I says smugly.

"Ha," Leah says as she opens her door. "I knew it. See you later. Or tomorrow. Stay out all night. Have a wild time." She closes the door before Natalie can reply.

"She's a freak," Natalie says.

"I kind of like the way she thinks."

She rolls her eyes at me as I pull back into traffic. "You would."

I reach for her hand and love the thrill that travels through me when her skin rubs against mine. I can't even begin to wonder what sex with her would be like if holding her hand is one of the most sensual experiences in what's been a rather sensually indulgent life. With her sitting so close to me, I don't dare *indulge* those thoughts. "You look very kissable with those purple lips."

When the light in front of us turns red, she leans over the center console, her intentions clear.

Being no fool, I meet her halfway and revel in the sweet taste of her lips. "Mmm, hello to you, too. I missed you today."

"I missed you, too."

"So why were you giving me that funny look when I picked you up?"

"I was just enjoying the exceptional view."

"Is it Friday yet?"

"One more day."

"I'll never make it."

She smiles, and neither of us looks away until the driver behind us blows their horn when the light turns green. Damn impatient New Yorkers.

"In California, stoplight kissing is encouraged and supported much more than it is here."

"Is that right?"

"Yep. I'll show you when we're there."

"I can't believe I'm actually going to LA with you."

"Believe it. As soon as I got your text earlier, I had my assistant, Addison, contact some of the stylists we've worked with in the past. She'll have you all fixed up with a million options by the time we get there Friday night." I glance over to find her worrying her bottom lip with her teeth. "What?"

"These stylists you've used in the past... You've done this before? Invited a nobody to an event and then had to outfit her?"

I'm touched and amused by the hint of jealousy I hear in her tone. "First, you are *not* a nobody. Don't say that again. Ever. Second, I've used them for me, silly. Believe it or not, there's a lot more to showing up at all these events than throwing on a tux and combing my hair. I have my favorite labels, but I need to keep up with the latest thing, and I don't have time to be bothered figuring that out on my own."

"Ahh, I see."

I squeeze her hand. "You're the first person I've ever asked to attend something like this with me who wasn't already in the business in some way or another."

"Oh."

"Oh what?"

"Nothing... I'm just... This whole thing is incredibly overwhelming. It's exciting, too, of course, but overwhelming for someone who's never done anything like it before."

"Trust me when I tell you it'll be so much fun. You'll feel like a queen for a day or I'll fire 'em all and make sure they never work again in Tinseltown."

"Stop it. You'd never do that."

"No," I say, laughing, "I wouldn't, but I will make sure you're the most pampered woman in all of Hollywood on Sunday. *That* you can count on."

"I hope you know I don't need all that."

"I know you don't *need* it, which is why it'll be so much fun to make sure you get it."

She takes a deep breath and releases it.

"You okay over there?" It's taking forever to drive uptown in the late-day traffic.

"Yeah. I'm good."

"I got tickets to 'Wicked' for tonight at seven."

She spins around in her seat and stares at me. "Tonight as in *today tonight?*"

"As in two and a half hours from now tonight."

"Oh my God! You're too much, you know that?"

"You said you wanted to see it, didn't you?"

"Yes, I want to see it, but I didn't expect you to go out and get tickets."

"Technically, I didn't go anywhere. I made a phone call, and the tickets are at will-call."

She sagged into her seat. "Are you for real? Am I going to wake up and find out I've dreamed this entire thing?"

"I sure as hell hope not." I glance over at her. "Will you be okay getting home around eleven?"

"And getting to see 'Wicked'? Yeah, I think I can handle that."

"Just to be sure, the 'Wicked' thing is good? Yes?" I can't believe how insecure and uncertain I am around her—two things that I've never been when it comes to women. Well, except for the bitch I married, but who wants to think about her when I've got the lovely Natalie to focus on?

"It's 'Wicked' good, but you know what's even better?"

"What's that?"

"What you did for Aileen and her kids."

I've been expecting her to mention that, and I'm ready for her. "I don't know what you mean."

"Yes, you do, so stop pretending otherwise. It was... It's incredible, Flynn. Truly. I can't even begin to tell you what it'll mean to her, to all of them. And what it means to me... Thank you."

"I still don't know what you're talking about, but you're welcome and so are they."

She encloses my hand in both of hers, and the sweet gesture is a total turn-on. Everything about her turns me on. It's been a long, long time since I've been this attracted to a woman outside my chosen lifestyle. For the first time in more than a decade, I'm entertaining the possibility that what we refer to as a "vanilla" relationship might actually satisfy me.

That doesn't mean I'm prepared to completely give up a lifestyle that has defined me in many ways. It just means that I'm considering making some changes that would've been unthinkable only a few days ago.

Something my father once said to me has been rattling around in my mind since I met Natalie. It was after the disastrous breakup with Valerie when I asked him how he'd known that my mother was the woman he wanted to marry. "Someday," he said, "probably years from now, a woman will come strolling into the room, and all the oxygen will seem to leave with her arrival. Your chest will be tight, your heart will beat a little faster, and you'll *know*. You'll just *know*."

"Is that how it happened for you with Mom?" I asked him.

"Exactly like that. I knew the second I laid eyes on her that there'd never be anyone else for me."

And there never has been. Forty-four years later, they're going strong and more in love than ever. As I get older, I find myself envying them as well as my two oldest sisters, who've found true-love matches with guys I like and respect.

"You're quiet over there," Natalie says. "What're you thinking about?"

I like that she asked. "My parents, actually."

"What about them?"

"Tomorrow is their anniversary. Forty-four years."

"That's awesome."

"I need to send them something, but I'm trying to decide what it should be. What do you get for two people who have everything?"

"I have no idea. Flowers seem too simple. Gift cards would be silly in light of who they are…"

"You see my dilemma."

"Could you take them out for a nice dinner while you're in LA?"

"That I can do." At the next light, I grab my phone and get Addie on the Bluetooth.

"What's up?" We've already spoken about six times today and got the "how are you?" preliminaries out of the way hours ago.

"Can we pull together an anniversary dinner for Max and Estelle and the girls Saturday night if they're available?"

"We can do that. I'll make some calls."

"Include Natalie in the count, and you should come, too."

"Of course I should."

"You're the best, Addie."

"I know. I tell you that every day."

Laughing at the predictable reply, I end the call with the push of a button on my steering wheel. "Done."

"Wow, that was kind of... impressive."

"Addie is fantastic. I'd be lost without her."

"She sounds fantastic, but I mean the whole thing—from idea to implementation in five minutes flat."

"We get things done."

"I see that."

I glance at her tentatively. "Does it all seem... I don't know... pretentious to you?"

"No, not at all. I'm sticking with impressive."

Her reply makes me smile as we finally reach the entrance for my garage after a slow crawl uptown. I punch in the code and drive down the ramp. Without waiting for me, Natalie gets out of the car and meets me at the elevator. I like that she's falling into a comfortable routine in my life.

Upstairs, I take her coat, and she looks down at her clothes. "I wish I'd known to dress up more for the theater." She's wearing sexy black pants, high-heeled boots and a turquoise sweater with a scoop neck that hugs her full breasts, making me want to peek inside for a better look.

"You look gorgeous. Perfect for the theater. People don't dress up like they used to. You'll fit right in." With my hands on her hips, I draw her in closer to me. "In fact, you'll class up the joint."

"Sure I will."

I tip my head and lay my lips on hers in an undemanding caress that I feel all the way through me. Though I don't intend to take it any further than a quick kiss—at least not yet—when her hands slide up my chest and curl around my neck, I'm lost.

Her mouth opens, and her tongue meets mine in a sensual caress that makes me moan from wanting more. I already know, days after I first laid eyes on her, that I'll never get enough of her.

I hadn't intended to devour her in the foyer, but she's totally irresistible, especially when she's pressed against me, kissing me with such innocent eagerness. That innocence has my cock hard and throbbing as I reluctantly withdraw from the kiss, mindful of what she said to me the day we met. If I seduce her into giving me what she said she'd never give, she'll hate me afterward. The thought of that is worse than denying the desire that beats through me like a living, breathing thing.

"Natalie…"

Her eyes are closed, her lips swollen and slick, her cheeks rosy and warm… She's unbearably beautiful.

I nuzzle her neck, and she tips her head, granting me full access to her sweet softness. Her scent defies easy description, but it's bewitching nonetheless. It's simple, clean, fresh… Unlike anything I've encountered before, which leads me to conclude it's the essence of *her*. I roll her earlobe between my teeth, biting down just hard enough to draw a sharp inhale from her.

"Nat…" I don't even know if anyone calls her that. The nickname rolls off my tongue as naturally as I draw air into my lungs.

"Hmm?" Her hands are doing something to my hair that makes my scalp tingle with awareness.

"We should stop this."

She shakes her head. "More."

"Natalie," I say, laughing at her unabashed eagerness, "you're killing me."

"I don't want to kill you. I want to kiss you."

She has no idea what she's doing to me, how she's waving a red flag in front of a bull by looking at me with those sweet brown eyes gone liquid with desire and emotion.

I try to tell myself I can handle this. I can handle holding her and kissing her and maybe touching her, but nothing else. Not now anyway. Clutching her hand, I lead her to the sofa, where I sit and then bring her down onto my lap. The press of her soft bottom against my raging hard-on takes my breath away for a second before I recover and capture her mouth in another kiss that goes from zero to a hundred and twenty in a flashpoint of heat so potent I feel scorched.

I've never, ever reacted to a woman like this before, and it thrills and terrifies me in light of the conditions she laid out the day we met. If I ask for more than she's willing to give, I'll lose her before I ever have her. But with her soft and pliant in my arms, I'm unwilling to end this moment before I have more of her.

I ease her back onto the sofa cushions, pausing to gauge her reaction. For a heartbeat of an instant, I see something resembling fear in her expressive eyes before she seems to recover, reaching for me and bringing me down to resume the kiss.

If I thought the kiss in the foyer was incredible, this is something else altogether, and it truly takes every fiber of self-control I possess to keep from ripping the clothes from both our bodies and having her right here and now. Fighting off those urges is almost as consuming as the kiss itself, which becomes more erotic and more sensual with every stroke of her tongue against mine.

Her sweater is enticingly soft under the hand I lay flat against her back. I work my way under the hem and encounter warm skin that makes me greedy for more. Though it pains me to move, I shift slightly to the side without breaking the kiss and move my hand to the front of her. I'm like a teenage boy in the throes of first passion, trying to gauge whether my advances will be welcome or not. I honestly can't tell, and remembering that flash of fear I saw earlier, I need to be certain.

I ease back from the kiss but keep my lips against hers. "Natalie, I want to touch you."

She arches her back, pressing against my hand.

"I need you to say it's okay. Every step of the way, I need you to tell me."

"Yes, Flynn… Please. Touch me."

"Polite and sexy. What a potent combination." I ease her sweater up and over her head.

She shocks the hell out of me when she tugs at the hem of my sweater and has it off me before I can begin to prepare for the sharp punch of desire that occurs when her skin and mine come together for the first time. Holy fuck. It's electrifying and terrifying at the same time. She scares the hell out of me.

Her fingers continue to comb through my hair as her other hand wanders down my back, leaving a trail of fire in its wake.

I'm literally burning up and beginning to sweat from the effort it's taking to hold back, to go slow, to remember what she said about sex and marriage and rules. But I'm only human, and I want her desperately, so I kiss everything I can reach, beginning with her neck and working my way down to her chest and the upper slopes of plump breasts that are straining at the confines of her plain tan bra, which will go down in history as one of the sexiest things I've ever seen.

On her, the sexiest lingerie in the world wouldn't do a thing to enhance her natural beauty.

"*Flynn.*" She gasps when my chin rubs against the tight point of her nipple. Her entire body arches into me, silently asking for more.

"Tell me."

"I…" She opens her eyes, and again I see fear mingled with obvious desire.

"Talk to me. Tell me what you're thinking." I nuzzle my nose into the valley between her breasts.

"Touch me. Please touch me."

I cover her breast with my hand, squeezing gently and rubbing my thumb over the tight point. "Here?"

She bites her lip and nods.

"Are you sure?"

In answer to my question, she releases the front clasp of her bra, surprising me once again.

Her breasts spring free and fill my hands, testing my control all over again. I want to possess her, but I'm careful, gentle with the gift she has given me and probably no one else. She inferred last night that she's never before had a boyfriend, although how that's possible, I'll never know. Is every other guy in the world blind and stupid? She's a treasure, a priceless gift that came barreling into my life at a time when I'd all but given up on ever finding anyone who could soothe the disquiet in my soul.

Because she is all that and so much more, I move carefully, cautiously as I caress her, working my way slowly to the straining tips that tighten under my hands.

My dick is about to explode from the urge to get in on this, but I try to ignore that urgent need to focus on her. I'm wondering what she'll allow me to do when the tug of her hand on the back of my head guides me toward what I want more than anything.

I run my tongue around her right nipple, and she goes crazy under me, tugging my hair and pressing every part of her against every part of me. Jesus... This is fucking insanity. With any other woman, I'd be deep inside her by now, fucking her senseless. But with Natalie, that's not an option, so I take what she's offered and I feast on her, sucking and tugging and licking her nipple until she cries out from the pleasure—at least I hope it's pleasure she's feeling.

Then I do the same to the other side, working her over until I'm sure she's not thinking of anything other than me and the incredible connection that sizzles between us.

But I can only take so much of her sweet brand of torture. I have to rein myself in and take control of this situation before we move past the point of no return. I drop my head to her chest, which is heaving from the air she's dragging into her lungs.

"Why did you stop?" she asks after a long period of silence in which the only sound is that of both of us breathing hard.

"Because if I don't stop now, I won't be able to." I force myself to raise my head, to look down at her face, which is rosy and flushed with desire. "You told me the day we met what isn't going to happen. If we keep this up..." I drop my head back to her chest. "God, Natalie, I want you so bad. You have no idea."

"I want you, too. I hope you know that. It's just that I... There are reasons. For why I feel the way I do."

"I know, and I'm trying to respect your boundaries, but if we don't stop this now, I'm afraid it'll go further than you want to go." To my profound astonishment and dismay, her eyes fill with tears that quickly spill down her cheeks. She closes her eyes, tightly as if that will contain the flood. "Natalie, sweetheart... Talk to me. Tell me what's wrong."

"Everything," she whispers. "Everything is wrong with me."

I kiss the tears from her face and hold her as close to me as I can. "No, honey. Don't say that. You're amazing, and I'm completely gone over you."

"That's so sweet, and you're so… You're… Incredible. You're incredible, and I should be able to do this, but I can't."

"What can't you do?"

"*This.*" The single word is spoken so emphatically, with such disgust and fury that I'm not sure how to react. "I can't do this because I'm broken. Inside."

"Did someone hurt you, sweetheart?" I feel, for the first time in my life, that I could commit murder at the thought of someone doing harm to her.

She pushes at my shoulder, and I realize she wants to sit up. So I move quickly to release her.

Natalie grabs for her sweater, and I help her into it. When she reaches under it to refasten her bra, I try not to watch, but I can't look away. Then she looks at me, and the pain and agony I see in her normally exuberant gaze shatters me. "I should go. This… You… You're lovely and wonderful, and you've been so kind to me. But I…" She shakes her head, and the stark misery is in such contrast to her normal demeanor that I'm shaken to my core. And I'm afraid. I'm very, very afraid of losing her now that I've found her.

"Natalie, sweetheart, there is nothing you could tell me that would change how I feel about you or that would make me not want to be with you in any way that I can. If things got too heated between us, that's my fault. I shouldn't have pushed you, knowing how you feel—"

Her fingers on my lips stop me and arouse me simultaneously. "You didn't do anything wrong. I loved everything you did. I loved it, and I encouraged it."

"Please don't go. Whatever it is, let's figure it out together. Let's find a way through it. Don't run from me."

"It's not fair. You deserve someone who can give you everything, and that's not me."

I put my arms around her and draw her into my embrace. Only when her hand lands flat against my chest do I remember that my sweater is gone. Her touch is so potent that I want to beg for her hands on me everywhere, but instead I clear my throat and try to find the words she needs to hear.

"I would wait forever for the chance to hold you and make love to you and to worship you the way you should be worshipped."

She's shaking her head before I finish speaking. "You've known me for six days. How can you say such a thing?"

I feel like I'm standing at the edge of a cliff, looking down at what my life would look like after Natalie, but if I take a step back and give her what she needs, I'll never have to experience that wasteland.

"Remember in the car, when you asked me what I was thinking about and I mentioned my parents' anniversary?"

She nods.

"I was thinking about much more than that. I was remembering a conversation I had years ago with my dad about how I would know when I met the woman I'm meant to be with. His exact words were, 'Someday, probably years from now, a woman will come strolling into the room, and all the oxygen will seem to leave with her arrival. Your chest will be tight, your heart will beat a little faster, and you'll *know*. You'll just *know*.'"

With my finger under her chin, I raise her face so I can see her eyes. "From the first second you looked up at me the other day, with your crazy dog attacking me, I knew. I just *knew* it's you. You're the one my dad told me I'd find. That's why I ran after you when I had something else I was supposed to be doing. It's why I wanted to see you again Saturday night. I've wanted to see you every day since and every day from now on. It's *you*, Natalie. So whatever it is that's got you so upset, I want to fix it. I want to make it right."

More tears spill down her face, and I brush them all away. "You're very sweet to say that and to feel that way about me, but no one can ever make what's wrong with me right again."

"How do you know that? Have you ever let anyone try?" I know the answer to that question before I even ask it. The shake of her head confirms it. "Let me help, Natalie. Let me in. I want to understand you. Not just in this way," I gesture to the sofa to encompass what just happened there, "but in every way."

Her expression is tortured, and I can tell by the way she looks at me that she wants to tell me what has her so upset.

"I can't," she says so softly I almost can't hear her. "I'm sorry, but I just can't."

CHAPTER 10

Natalie

I want to. God, I want to. No one has ever said anything to me like what he just said so beautifully. He makes me want to believe that anything is possible, that I can have what other people take so effortlessly from each other, but I know better. On the day I became Natalie Bryant, I made a vow to myself that no one in my new life would ever know about April. She died a traumatic, horrible death eight years ago during the most hellish weekend of her life. When I made the decision to leave her behind and become Natalie, I did so with rules that can't be abandoned, not even for Flynn.

He's the only one I've ever been tempted to tell, and I've known him for six days. I know what I need to do. I need to get up, pull myself together and go home where I belong. The interlude with him has been wonderful, unforgettable in every way. But it's also served as a reminder of my limitations.

First, however, I have to make him understand that this is over. "I want you to know… Every minute I've spent with you has been better than any time I've spent with anyone. You… You're so much more than I ever could've imagined, and you've taught me not to believe everything I read."

He smiles at that, but it's not his usual smile. It's not the one with the deep grooves that line his cheeks when he's truly amused. "If you're saying good-bye to me, don't. We got carried away, Natalie. Won't happen again until you want it to."

"That's just it! I may *never* want it to, and that is so unfair to you."

"Can I say something here without sounding like a total cad?"

"Can I stop you?"

He takes my hand and holds it tightly, as if he's afraid I'll get away before he can express everything he needs to say to me. "I've been with a lot of women. Probably too many. I've kissed them and fucked them and done things with them you'd no doubt find distasteful at best, objectionable at worst. But I have never, ever had a woman react to me the way you do. And I have never reacted to any woman—ever—the way I do to you. So if you tell me all I can do for the next year is kiss you, I'll take it. I'll take that over you walking out that door right now after telling me we're done."

I immediately want details of what he's done with other women that I would find so distasteful or objectionable, but I have no right to ask those questions. Nor do I have the right to ask him to live like a monk so that I can continue along this path I chose for myself.

"I'd marry you tomorrow, Natalie, if you'd have me."

His words shock me and bring more tears to my eyes. "Stop it. You have no desire to be married. You've made that very clear."

"I thought you weren't believing everything you read anymore."

"You told me yourself that one is true."

"It was before you. Before you bowled me over and took all the oxygen with you."

The sad thing is, I want to believe him. I want to buy everything he's selling. I want to wrap my arms around him and never let him go. But I've learned to be wary and distrustful, except I haven't been with him. I've jumped in with both feet and practiced none of the usual caution I usually bring to every new relationship and situation. In my new life, people have to earn my trust. I never give it away like I have with him.

"Do something for me." He gazes earnestly into my eyes. "Give me this weekend. If, after that, you want out, I'll let you go. I'll never forget you, but I'll respect your wishes." After a pause, he adds, "Things got out of control tonight. It won't happen again, unless or until you initiate."

I'm torn in a thousand different directions at once. I want him. God, I want him so badly I burn from the inside for him and all that he's prepared to offer me. In six days, he's made me forget eight painful years spent largely alone while I reinvented myself into the person I am today. I'm risking all that hard-won freedom and emotional well-being with every minute I spend with him, and I'm doing it willingly with my eyes wide open to the potential fallout.

And I don't care. I want him as badly as he seems to want me. I take a deep breath and release it slowly, the way my counselor taught me to do when things get overwhelming. I force myself to meet his gaze, to look directly into intense brown eyes when I say, "Okay."

"Yes?"

Nodding, I cling to his hand like it's the one thing keeping me from hurtling into space, never to be seen or heard from again.

He moves cautiously to put his arms around me. I rest my face against his bare chest, breathing in the scent of soap and deodorant as his chest hair brushes against my cheek. "Whatever it is, whatever you need, I'm here, Natalie. You're not alone anymore."

I want more than anything to believe him, to hold on to his words and his assurances with everything I've got. But I know better than to be that foolish. So I give him the only thing I've got to offer—one weekend. After that, I will leave him, and I'll never look back.

I'm very good at that.

Flynn

After I convince Natalie to stay and give me a chance, we enjoy a subdued dinner before leaving for the show. She loves "Wicked" and brightens visibly as the show unfolds before us. We're in the tenth row in the orchestra section, and since I've seen the show twice before, I watch her as she takes in every detail with her usual enthusiasm and exuberance.

I'm gutted by the memory of her pain, her fear and the tears. Part of me wants to hire someone to find out what happened to her so I'll know what I'm dealing with. But the more reasonable part of me rejects that idea as the stupidest thing I could ever do to her. If and when I find out what or who hurt her, it'll be when she decides to tell me and not before.

She gushes about the show all the way home, how it was funnier than she'd expected and how she'd never thought about how the wicked witch in *The Wizard of Oz* had become so wicked. We talk about the music and the story and the jokes. In other words, we stick to safe topics rather than the ones that are fraught with peril.

There's once again nowhere to park on her block, so I pull up next to two cars and put on the hazards.

"Thank you so much for taking me to 'Wicked.' I loved it so much."

"I'm glad."

She glances at me shyly. "And for being so nice earlier. I'm sorry I had such a meltdown."

"Please don't apologize to me for something you couldn't help. I want you to remember that whatever it is, whatever haunts you, you're not alone with it anymore. You can trust me, Natalie. I swear to you I'd never do anything to cause you another second of pain or fear."

Her small smile is a huge victory for me. "I can certainly see why every woman in American is in love with you, Flynn."

"Fuck that," I say emphatically, perhaps a bit *too* emphatically. "This isn't some line of movie star bullshit I'm feeding you. This is *me*—the real me who is crazy about the real you. All that other crap aside, this is my *life*, Natalie, not my job."

"I didn't mean to imply otherwise."

"And I didn't mean to jump all over you."

"I get it. You're constantly having to separate the real from the imaginary."

"Yes," I say with a sigh of relief that she understands. "And this is as real as it gets for me."

"Thank you for a lovely evening. I'll never forget a minute of it."

"Neither will I." I lean over the center console to kiss her. "Much more to come."

She kisses me back and caresses my face, the gesture so tender and sweet that I can barely breathe from wanting her.

I want to drive her back to my place and take her to bed and never let her leave, but since that's not going to happen tonight or any time soon, I withdraw slowly and painfully. "I'll see you tomorrow, okay?"

"Okay."

I steal one last kiss. "I'll watch you get inside."

"You don't have to."

"Yes, I do."

She leaves me with a smile that doesn't reach her eyes, and that's all it takes to tell me I'm in for the fight of my life where she's concerned. That's okay. I'm willing to wage war to show her what we can have together. Now that I've found her, I'll never let her go.

Neither of us can sleep that night. After exchanging a few texts, I call her and we end up talking for hours about silly things such as the difference between growing up in Nebraska versus Beverly Hills. I notice she never mentions her family in specific terms, always vaguely, as if she's no longer a part of them. I'm desperate for more information, but I'm cautious. I don't push. I can only hope she'll trust me enough someday to tell me her truth. Until then, I summon patience I didn't know I had.

With the film wrapped and time to kill before we leave for LA, my friends are having a wild week at Quantum. They've been calling and texting relentlessly, wanting me to join them, but I've stayed away. Until I know how this weekend with Natalie will play out, I resist the temptation to expend my pent-up sexual energy on someone else.

I'm committed to Natalie for now. If she'll have me, that commitment will go far beyond this weekend. But that remains to be seen.

Hayden is relentless, texting me every half hour about what a pussy-whipped asshole I am for deserting them in their time of celebration. He's even got Kristian, Jasper and Marlowe on my ass, but I ignore them all and stay focused on Natalie.

By Friday afternoon, I'm a wreck. I've never been more nervous about anything than I am about this weekend with her. I've driven Addie crazy, micromanaging the details to make sure everything is perfect for Natalie. I was supposed to fly to LA with Hayden and the others, but I've chartered my own plane. The last thing I want is to share Natalie with anyone, especially friends who've questioned the wisdom of getting involved with her in the first place. I took endless text abuse from them when I let them know I wouldn't be joining them on the flight, but like most of the shit from them this week, I ignore it.

Wait until they hear that I want to do postproduction on the new film in New York rather than LA, as planned. There'll be hell to pay with Hayden, in particular. I'll deal with that on Monday, after the Globes.

I'm waiting outside her school at three o'clock sharp when she emerges with her workbag slung over her shoulder and a suitcase in tow. I figured Leah would be with her, but she's by herself. As she crosses the street to me, I can almost feel the emotions coming from her—hesitancy, excitement, caution, fear, curiosity and maybe, just maybe, a hint of pleasure at seeing me.

Pleasure is too benign a word to describe what I feel at the sight of her. Relief, anxiety, delight, desire and excitement for the adventure I'm about to take her on. I feel all of that at the same time. I feel more for her than I have for any woman, and rather than run from it, I want to wrap myself up in it and in her.

"Hi," she says when she reaches me.

"Hi there." I take her bag and toss it into the backseat with mine and then help her into the car. I'm not sure if I should, but I feel like I haven't seen her in days, so I lean in to kiss her after I buckle her in.

She kisses me back, and I take that as a good sign.

"Missed you."

Smiling, she says, "You texted me constantly."

"No substitute for the real you."

I want to bury my face in her hair, nuzzle her neck and breathe in the scent of her, but I do none of those things. Hopefully, I'll get to do all of them on the plane. I pull myself away from her and close her door. The second I've got the car moving toward our destination in Teterboro, New Jersey, I reach for her hand.

"How was your day?" I ask her.

"Good but busy. We're doing some testing this week, and the kids hate it so they're out of sorts, which means we're out of sorts, too."

"You have three days to decompress."

"Believe me, I know. I'm looking forward to it."

I'm so glad to hear that, I want to sing Hallelujah or some other celebratory song. But like all my other impulses where she's concerned, I resist. It's far too soon to celebrate, especially when she's still deciding whether she's going to give me a chance.

The ride out of the city is slow thanks to Friday afternoon traffic on the Henry Hudson Parkway. I used to think there was nothing quite like LA traffic until I spent time in New York. Most people don't drive in the city, but public transportation can be a challenge for me, so I put up with the traffic. Today I'm annoyed by anything that delays me getting to the airport and onto the plane, so I can be alone with Natalie and focused completely on her rather than the traffic.

"I've been thinking about 'Wicked' all day. Thank you again for that."

"You're very welcome. I love that you enjoyed it so much."

"It was... I need to find a way to expand my vocabulary where you're concerned, but I keep coming back to incredible."

"That's not a bad word."

"No, but I teach my kids that any word that's overused becomes a cliché after a while, and I don't want to become a cliché where you're concerned."

"Not possible." I give her hand a squeeze and wish I could look at her when I say, "Everything about you is fresh and new and interesting to me. And this entire thing between us is the furthest thing from a cliché that I've ever experienced. It's quite possible, in fact, that my entire life up until about a week ago was a *gigantic* cliché and you've saved me from all that ridiculousness."

By now she's laughing, which pleases me greatly. I do love that laugh of hers. It's quite... incredible. Because I already know she hasn't had a lot to laugh about, it's extra special to be the one to give her that, even if it only lasts for a minute or two.

"Where do you come up with that stuff?"

"Despite your insulting laughter, I meant every word of what I said."

Once we get over the George Washington Bridge, the traffic into New Jersey begins to move. Finally.

"Are we leaving from Newark?"

"No, Teterboro. It's a small regional airport."

"Oh. Do the airlines fly out of there?"

"We're not going on the airlines."

"Oh. *Oh!*"

"So here's the thing—commercial flying, like any form of public transportation, can be difficult for me, and while I'm acutely aware that my carbon footprint is way bigger than it should be, I don't really have a choice. I'm not afraid of many things, but crowds and big crushes of people freak me out. You never know who's in that crowd or what their agenda might be."

"I totally understand. It's a safety issue more than anything."

"Yeah, in a way. Besides," I say, trying to lighten the mood, "it's hardly a hardship to fly private. You'll see what I mean in a couple of minutes."

Because I fly out of here often, I have a routine with the charter company. They're waiting for me, and we're able to drive right up to the waiting Gulfstream. If there's any benefit to celebrity, it's moments like this when we're given the ultimate VIP treatment with the car and our bags dealt with quickly and efficiently.

The pilots introduce themselves to me, shake my hand and tell me they're big fans.

"We're expecting a relatively smooth flight today, Mr. Godfrey," the captain says. "There'll be some bumps over the Rocky Mountains, as usual, but nothing major."

"Sounds great, thank you so much."

"See you in LA," the first officer says as they return to the cockpit to prepare for departure.

The flight attendant, Jacob, takes our coats and encourages us to get comfortable in the side-by-side leather seats where they want us for takeoff. Afterward, we can move to the plush leather sofa and get really comfortable.

"This whole thing is crazy," Natalie says when we're alone. "I bet no one would complain about traveling—ever—if everyone could do it this way. No lines, no waiting, no security."

"It does have its perks."

Right after takeoff, Jacob proves my point by emerging from the galley with flutes of champagne and a tray of cheese, crackers, grapes, strawberries and chocolates artfully arranged.

"Are you nervous about this weekend?" Natalie asks as we enjoy the snack and the icy champagne.

I glance at her, not entirely sure what she's asking. Am I nervous about spending the weekend with her? No, I'm thrilled.

"I mean the Globes," she says, apparently tuning in to my internal debate.

"Not really. I mean, it would be nice to win and be recognized for the work, but if I don't, my life will still be great on Monday."

"That's a good way to look at it."

"That's the only way to look at it."

"For what it's worth, I think you should win. *Camouflage* is your best work to date. No question."

"Really? You think so?"

"I do. It was brilliant."

"May I be entirely honest and do you promise never to repeat what I'm about to say?"

Her smile lights up her gorgeous face. "By all means."

"I agree with you. It's the best work I've ever done, and I really, *really* want to win that Globe."

"Ah, now the truth comes out!"

I played a larger-than-life Special Forces officer who sustains devastating injuries in Afghanistan and has to rebuild his life from the ground up. It's loosely based on a true story. "Making that film was the experience of a lifetime. Spending time at Walter Reed with injured service members, witnessing their struggles to regain their lives, to learn to live without some of the essential elements of who they were before… It was life-changing for all of us."

"I loved it. Every second of it. I think I saw it five times."

"Really?" I'm amazed and flattered to know the film I'd poured my heart and soul into for two years had connected with her.

"Really. I could see it a hundred more times and never get enough. It was beautiful. Everyone in it deserves awards, but you… You were just…" She shakes her head. "Transcendent."

It is, without a doubt, the single best compliment I've received in a career filled with unreasonable adulation, and I'm touched to my very core. "Thank you," I say gruffly. "Means a lot to me coming from you."

"You must hear it all the time."

I shrug that off. "It's just words coming from others. The people close to me are the ones who matter. My parents had a lot to say about that film, too, and I won't soon forget any of it."

"They must be so proud," she says with a note of wistfulness I can't help but hear.

"I hope they are. Their voices are always in my head, that's for sure. I consult with my dad on every project before I agree to do it. He's my touchstone."

"I'm very excited to meet them."

"They're looking forward to meeting you, too."

"Oh. So they know about me?"

"Yes," I say with a soft laugh, "they know about you. And they know I must *really* like you if I'm bringing you home to meet them. That hasn't happened very often in the past."

"Oh," she says again, and I can almost feel her trying to process the meaning of what I'm telling her.

"Want to get comfortable?"

"We aren't comfortable now?"

"More comfortable." I nod toward the sofa, and she eyes it with what might be trepidation. "We can stretch out and watch a movie. Anything but *The Sound of Music*."

I watch the tension leave her shoulders when she realizes I'm not suggesting a make-out session. Although if that were to happen... No. That's not going to happen. I want her to trust me and to feel comfortable with me, which is my number one goal for this weekend.

"That sounds good," she says.

We unbuckle from the chairs, kick off our shoes and head for the wide, plush sofa that accommodates us both with ease. Jacob appears out of nowhere with a cashmere throw blanket. He gives me a quick tutorial on the controller for the cabin lights and the entertainment system before gathering the tray and empty glasses. "May I get you anything else for the moment?"

I glance at Natalie, and she shakes her head.

"I think we're set for now, Jacob. Thank you."

"My pleasure. If you need me, just push this button. Otherwise, I'll leave you to relax."

I love that he lets us know he won't be back unless we summon him. He earns himself a big tip with that move.

"This is the life," Natalie declares as she snuggles up to me.

As I dim the lights and flip through the movie menu, I couldn't agree more. Right here, in my arms, is everything I'll ever need.

CHAPTER 11

Natalie

I'm completely blown away by the plane, the luxury and the easy comfort of being with Flynn. I love the way he talks about his parents and how he confessed to wanting to win the Golden Globe on Sunday. He truly deserves it after his magnificent performance in *Camouflage*. I can't imagine what it will be like to be there with him, waiting to hear if he'll win or not.

Everything new I learn about him chips away at my plan to leave him. He's not making it easy to keep this casual, that's for sure. Take, for instance, the way he holds me in his arms, comfortably but respectfully. His hand strokes my hair in a soothing, undemanding caress.

I feel his affection for me in every look and every touch. He's made me remember what it was like to be loved by my parents and siblings before everything changed and they were lost to me. I've been so alone in the world since then that Flynn's affection is like a balm on the raw wound I carry with me everywhere I go.

Changing my name and appearance and rewriting my history are all surface things. Inside, where April still lives and breathes, the truth of who I really am is also with me always. Every minute I spend with him makes me want to take a chance I thought I'd never take. Every minute I spend with him is a risk to the future I fought so hard for.

With his fingers running through my hair and his hand warm against my back, I don't care about any of that.

"Flynn?"

"Hmm?"

"I was thinking…"

"About?"

"What happened last night at your place." I feel his entire body go tense.

"What about it?"

"I'm so embarrassed about the way I reacted." We haven't spoken about it again, but it's been on my mind.

"I don't want you to be embarrassed." He arranges us so we're looking directly at each other. His hand is warm and comforting on my cheek. "Do you have any idea how much I value honesty of any kind? Or how rare it is to witness a genuinely honest reaction from a woman that has nothing at all to do with who I am in the business or what I can do to advance her career?"

"I hadn't thought of it that way." I look away from his intense gaze for a moment before summoning the courage to continue. "After what happened last night, all I could think about was how I should end this before it goes any further."

He closes his eyes, and his cheek begins to twitch. After a long pause, he opens his eyes. "And now?"

"Now I'm wondering if you'll ever kiss me again after what happened."

"Natalie," he says on a deep exhale, "you have no idea how badly I want to kiss you and hold you and touch you. But more than anything, I want you to trust me. I want you to tell me what I need to know so I won't do the wrong thing and make whatever is troubling you worse than it already is."

His words are like a key in the lock that guards my secrets. He is so genuine and kind. "I want to trust you."

"You can. I promise you, with everything I have and everything I am, you can trust me to guard and protect you. I've known you for a week, and I'd already give you everything, if you'd let me."

I lay my hand on his face and kiss him. I can tell that I've surprised and pleased him by initiating the kiss.

He kisses me back, but there's no urgency, no flashpoint of desire like there was last night. This kiss is about safety and comfort and taking steps forward together.

I break the kiss and close my eyes, needing some distance from him for what I'm about to say. "You've probably already figured out that I was raped. It happened when I was fifteen." The words, once I decide to release them, tumble forth in a rush. "It was a particularly vicious and brutal assault that left me damaged in every possible way. There's a lot more to the story than that, but the rest is stuff I don't talk about. Ever. It's in the past where it belongs." I take another minute to collect my emotions before I open my eyes to find tears in his.

"I... I'm so sorry that happened to you, baby." He takes a deep breath that rattles in his chest, and I can tell he's fighting hard to maintain his composure, which only makes me fall that much faster and harder for him. "I'll never ask you to share things that are too painful for you." With the soft flutter of his fingers over my cheek, he slays me with tenderness. "Thank you for telling me. I can't begin to fathom how hard that was for you."

"I wanted you to know... What happened last night, it wasn't your fault."

"It wasn't yours either," he says fiercely.

I love him so much for saying that. "It took years of therapy for me to acknowledge it wasn't my fault. I didn't do anything wrong. This was done *to* me."

He gathers me in even closer to him, his arms tight around me, and all I feel is loved and protected when only a week ago I would've freaked out if a man had tried to hold me so possessively. There's no place for fear when I'm in his arms. "We're going to figure this out together. One day at a time, one step at a time. Whatever you need, whenever you need it. I'm in this so deep, Nat."

"So am I. A week ago... The thought of something like this would've been impossible to imagine. And now... Now everything seems possible."

"Please don't leave me. Don't walk away. Give me a chance. Give yourself a chance. If anyone deserves to be happy and loved, it's you."

He's a dream come true. He's my dream come true. He's the dream I never dared to have all sewn up into one irresistibly wonderful package.

"Will you kiss me again?" I ask him. "Please?"

"Only because you asked so nicely."

We're both smiling when our lips come together. I can feel his caution, his hesitancy. He's worried about pushing me too far, about losing control of himself and the situation. I already know him well enough to gauge these things just from the way he kisses me. There's none of the heat that nearly consumed us last night, and I miss it. In spite of my fears, I want it back but I know it'll never come from him after what I've shared with him.

Summoning the courage to take what I want so badly, I run my tongue over his bottom lip and experience the profound pleasure of feeling his entire body react.

"What're you doing to me?" he asks on a gasp.

"Kissing you."

Laughter rumbles through his chest and makes his lips vibrate against mine. "Sure you are, you little vixen."

I use my tongue again to tease and entice him.

"*Natalie.*"

"Yes?"

"I'm so afraid I'll do the wrong thing here. Help me."

To hear this strong, confident, capable man asking *me* to help *him* give me what I need is awe-inspiring. "Just kiss me the way you did last night. You can't do it wrong. I'm prepared now for what it'll be like."

"Tell me to stop, at any point. Just say stop, and it's game off."

"Okay."

He looks at me for a long, intense moment, his eyes burning with desire and affection and so many other things I can't begin to process. And then he takes possession of my mouth. There is no other word for it than *possession*. Complete and utter possession. As his tongue strokes against mine, the fire ignites the way it did before, and I'm carried away in a sea of heat and desire.

He fists a handful of my hair to keep me anchored in place, but he doesn't touch me anywhere else yet. This is all about lips and tongues and teeth and raw, desperate need. His leg sneaks between mine as his hand moves down my back to pull me in closer to him, so close my sex is pressed tight against his muscular leg.

I squirm to get even closer, to gain relief from the ache between my legs. Every part of me wants every part of him, which is a startling discovery for someone who has avoided any contact with men for the last eight years. But all he does is kiss me and kiss me and kiss me until my lips are tingling and my lungs are about to burst.

When I can no longer deny the need for air, I break the kiss and suck in greedy deep breaths as he turns his attention to my neck. The plane hits a bump that knocks us out of the sensual haze we've slipped into. He raises his head to meet my gaze and smiles at me. I love that smile. It's so sexy and potent. I could look at it all day and never get tired of seeing it.

"How're you doing?" His gaze is so tender, so totally focused on me.

"Great. You?"

"Never been better."

I snort out a rather unladylike laugh. "Sure you haven't."

"Nat."

"Hmm?"

"Look at me."

I do as he asks, and what I see there… God. All of that for me.

"I've never been better than I am in this moment with you."

Though it's against my better judgment and my inner cynic is crying out to be heard, I believe him. Whether that will prove to be a mistake remains to be seen. "Do you think we could…"

"What, sweetheart? What do you want to do?"

"I'm feeling kind of warm in this sweater." I wore a black sweater with a skirt to school that day, hoping I'd look sophisticated enough to take this trip of a lifetime after school.

His gaze shifts to my chest. I can almost tell he's trying to gauge whether I have anything on under it. I don't, except for a bra, of course. "Do you want me to do something about the cabin temperature?"

I shake my head.

"Natalie… I want to do the right thing here. If we start taking clothes off, it's going to get even warmer in here."

I can hear the torture and inner turmoil he's struggling with in his tone. It's much more rigid than normal, as are the muscles that are pressed against me. He's waiting for some sign from me about what's going to happen. Reaching for the hem of my sweater, I pull it up and over my head. I'm left in only the black bra I wore under it.

"God, you're beautiful, and that was about the sexiest thing I've ever seen."

Once again my first thought is that can't possibly be true, but I keep it to myself this time. I want to believe him so badly. I want to believe *in* him. I dip my hand under his sweater and encounter the warm skin underneath. "Take yours off, too."

After a slight hesitation, he complies.

I love the way his chest hair feels against my skin. My eyes close as I take a moment to enjoy the simple pleasure that comes from being close to him this way. It fills a void inside me I didn't know existed until him.

"Could I ask you something?" he says after a long period of silence.

"Of course you can." Whether I'll answer is another matter.

"Has there been anyone since that happened?"

I shake my head. "No."

"I feel like the luckiest bastard in the world that you've chosen to be with me this way. But I'm also so scared of doing something to upset you. I can't bear to see you cry again. That killed me."

"I'm sorry about that—"

"No," he says, kissing me softly, "don't apologize, baby. You didn't do anything wrong. You're beautiful and perfect in every way. I feel like you've given me a priceless gift by letting me in, and I want to be so careful with you. But then you kiss me, and I forget all about being careful."

"What do you think about when I kiss you?"

Smiling, he shakes his head. "Can't tell you. If I do, you'll find the emergency parachute and jump right out of this plane."

I know I'm playing with fire, dangling red in front of a bull, but I can't resist the need to know more. "Tell me anyway. I promise, no parachutes."

"You're not ready to hear those thoughts."

"Can you give me a hint? A little sneak peek?"

Groaning, he buries his face in my hair, and his lips find my neck. "I think about what it would be like to be completely naked with you, to have your long smooth legs wrapped around me and your gorgeous breasts pressed tight against my chest while I make love to you. I think about what it would be like to be inside you, so deep there's no way to tell where I leave off and you begin. I think about what it would be like to be able to do that every day and every night, to know you're mine and I'm yours and there'll never be anyone else for either of us."

For a moment, I'm too stunned by the raw desire in his voice to formulate a reply. But then I realize he's waiting for me to say something. "All that from a kiss?"

Nodding, he touches his lips to mine in a tentative caress. "And that's just the sneak peek. There's so much more where that came from."

"I want that. I want all of it. I want to be the woman you described. I want to be her with you."

"You can have anything you want from me. Anything at all. You only have to ask."

"That's the hard part for me."

"Tell me what you want, sweetheart. Tell me so I can give it to you."

"What we did the other night…"

He cups my breast and runs his thumb back and forth over the nipple. "This?"

I nod because he's stolen my words with the subtle gesture that sets off a firestorm inside my body.

"You liked that?"

"Yes," I say, covering his hand with my own when the sensations become too intense. After a deep breath, I remove my hand, hoping he'll continue.

"More?"

"Yes." I'm finding I don't possess more than that one word to tell him what I want. I've never had to say the words before.

Flynn runs his finger along the top slopes of my breasts. "Bra on or off?"

I look up to find him watching me in that intense way that has all my walls crumbling down around me. "Off."

He reaches behind me to release the hooks, and my breasts spill free of the tight confines of the cups. Leaving a trail of goose bumps in his path, Flynn pushes the strap down my arm.

My only goal is to get through this without having another meltdown. I want to be like any other woman being touched by a man she's come to care about. I don't want to be a victim. Not anymore. But then he cups my breast, dragging his thumb back and forth over the sensitive tip, and my mind is wiped clean of every thought that doesn't involve the sublime sensations that spiral through me. I arch into him, wanting to be closer.

His lips close over my nipple, drawing it into the heat of his mouth as his tongue swirls around it. The sensory overload is intense, but I stay focused on the present rather than spiraling into the past the way I did the last time we got this far. I want more. I want everything, but I'm so afraid I won't be able to follow through when the moment is upon us.

"Why did you just get all tense?" he asks.

"I... I don't want it to happen again."

"Do you feel like it's going to?"

I draw in a sharp deep breath. "No, but I'm still afraid."

"If it happens a hundred times, we'll keep trying until it doesn't."

Here, in my arms, looking at me with affection and tenderness and desire, is the man I never expected to find. He's patient and kind and understanding. Despite my intense desire to get through this without them, my eyes fill with tears anyway.

"Hey! What's this? What happened?"

"It's... It's you. What you said. It was perfect."

"So these are good tears?"

"The best kind." I close my eyes, keeping them tightly shut until the tears are contained. And then I open them to find him watching over me. "Could we..."

"What, sweetheart? Just say it."

"Could we keep going?" I told him I wouldn't have sex with him unless we're married, and I meant that. That's been my rule for eight long years, a rule I've hidden behind because I never expected to get close enough to any man to actually consider marrying one. But now... Now, everything is different, and he's the reason.

"Help me out here. How far are we talking?"

"A little further?"

"I can do that." He arranges me so I'm lying flat on my back and settles between my legs, leaning over me to give my other breast some attention.

I grasp a handful of his hair, needing to hold on to something as he sets off another frantic wave of desire. Then his hand is on my leg, moving from my knee to my inner thigh, opening me. I hold my breath, waiting to see what he'll do next.

"Breathe, sweetheart. Try to relax. I promise I'll never hurt you. Not in a million years."

I do what I'm told, drawing in greedy breaths as his hand creeps closer to my core. I don't know whether I want to pull him closer or push him away. While his hand tortures me with the slow slide, his lips pull and tug on my nipple, splitting my focus squarely in half. I suspect that's his intention, to scramble my brain so completely there's no possibility of going to the bad place. There's only pleasure and desire.

"Doing okay?" he asks gruffly as his tongue swirls around my nipple.

"Mmm."

"Words, Nat. Give me the words."

"Yes! I'm okay. *Flynn...*"

"What, honey?"

"Touch me. Please touch me." I've never been so desperate for anything in my life as I am for his touch.

His hand is warm and large as he does exactly what I want, pressing his fingers against the place that throbs for him, with only the thin silk of my panties between us. He knows exactly where I need him most, and I cry out from the pleasure that scorches me.

Lifting my hips, I silently ask for more, but he distracts me with another deep pull on my nipple. The combination has me climbing toward some sort of summit, something dark and mysterious and altogether out of reach until right now. He doesn't do anything more than press rhythmically against me as he continues to torment my nipple. The pleasure builds and grows until I feel like I'm going to explode from within. "Flynn..."

"It's okay, baby," he whispers. "Let it happen." He doesn't stop until I'm crying out from the overwhelming pleasure that detonates from between my legs and travels through my body like a lightning strike. "God, that was amazing. You're so beautiful. I can't wait to be inside you when that happens."

I cling to him, breathing hard as he brings me down with gentle strokes of his fingers. His words permeate the fog that has invaded my brain, and for the first time since I was attacked, the thought of allowing a man inside me doesn't make me cringe with horror or disgust. It makes me burn with longing, especially as I feel him hard and throbbing against my leg.

"Talk to me, sweetheart. Tell me what you're thinking." His voice is rough against my ear, making me shiver.

"I think you've wiped my brain clear of all thoughts that don't involve you."

"Excellent," he says, chuckling. "Then my work here is finished."

I push my pelvis against the hard thrust of his erection. "Not everyone got to finish." Running my hand down the muscular contours of his chest, I summon the courage to take what I want. "Could I... Would it be okay..."

"*Natalie*," he says through gritted teeth, "Christ, do whatever you want to me. Touch me anywhere. Any time you want."

"*Any* time?" I ask, smiling up at him.

He responds with a savage kiss, seeming to pour every ounce of pent-up desire into one blistering kiss. I'm so distracted that, for a second, I nearly forget what caused him to kiss me this way. Then the insistent press of his erection against my leg reminds me of what I wanted to do. Without breaking the kiss, I slide my hand down over the front of his well-worn jeans where I find him long, hard and thick.

Groaning, he comes up for air wearing an agonized expression I've never seen before. He covers my hand with his and shows me how to touch him, his eyes rolling back in his head when I follow his lead. I've never willingly touched a man there before, and it's a revelation to watch such a strong man become powerless because of me.

Then he pulls my hand away. "I can't."

"What's wrong?"

"Nothing. Nothing at all."

"Why did you stop me?"

"I can't take any more."

Suddenly, I'm swamped with regret and dismay. How long can a vital, virile man like him deny his desires? How long before he loses interest in the traumatized woman who can't give him what he needs?

"Whatever you're thinking right now, knock it off."

His terse tone takes me by surprise, and I try to pull away from him.

He holds me closer. "I'm sorry. I shouldn't have said it that way. I can tell you're putting thoughts in my head that simply aren't there. I'm not thinking about anything other than how much I love being with you. I swear."

"But you want more."

"Of course I do, Natalie. You're sweet and gorgeous and sexy and smart. I'm only human. I want you. I'll never deny that. But I'm on your schedule here."

"How long will you wait for me to get over my issues?"

"I don't expect you'll ever completely get over what happened to you. Who would?" As he speaks, he runs a finger over my cheek. "There's no timetable. We've known each other a week, and I've loved every second I've gotten to spend with you. The physical stuff is only part of it. I like talking to you as much as I like kissing you. I can't wait to introduce you to my family and to spend this weekend with you. I can't wait for everything with you. It doesn't matter if it takes a week, a month, a year... I'm not going anywhere for as long as you want to be with me."

I have so many emotions swirling around inside me—and so many questions. "Could I ask you something?"

"Anything."

"You told me not to believe everything I read, and I'm trying to do that."

"But?"

"You've had a lot of girlfriends, women..."

"I like women. I'd never deny that either."

"You like to have sex with women."

"Yes."

"A lot of sex."

"Sometimes."

"But not with me?"

He leans his forehead against mine, his chest hair tickling my breasts. "I hope someday you and I will have a *lot* of sex. I hope someday you and I will start and end each day wrapped in each other's arms. I hope maybe someday, you'll be able to do whatever you want with me any time you want to do it and know that you'll *always* be welcome and safe in my arms, in my bed, in my life. And because I *know* when all that happens it'll be extraordinary, to say the least, I'm willing to wait. For as long as it takes, I'll wait." He kisses me. "I'll wait for you."

"Flynn… How can you say that? You have no idea what a mess I am."

"You're not a mess. You're beautiful, and I adore you. Something terrible happened to you, but that doesn't define you."

"It has. For the last eight years, it's defined me."

"That doesn't mean it has to forever. There's so much more to you than that one incident, and I'm going to help you see that. If it takes the rest of my life, you're going to see what I see when I look at you."

I reach up to caress his clean-shaven face. "Does it scare you to feel that way about someone?"

"It scares the hell out of me, but not for the reasons you think." He pauses before he continues. "It scares me that you don't feel the same way, that you'll try to leave me rather than trusting that I'm sincere when I tell you I truly care about you and I can see my life unfolding with you by my side. I can *see* it."

"I do feel the same way, and it scares me, too. How is that possible when we just met six days ago? If you had told me last Friday, I'd be on a private plane, half-naked with a guy—any guy—I would've said you were crazy. But now… Now it doesn't seem so crazy."

"No, it doesn't. Sometimes these things just happen, Natalie. Does it make sense? Not really, but does it matter if it makes sense when it feels so good?"

"Has this happened to you before?"

"Never. Not like this."

My heart beats faster in light of his confession.

"What else do you want to know?" he asks with a hint of amusement lighting his eyes.

"When was the last time a woman made you wait to have sex with her?"

"Other than tonight?"

I poke him in the belly, making him grunt with laughter. "Seriously."

"It's been a while, but a little dose of humility might be good for me."

"No one makes you wait for anything."

"No, they don't, but can't you see how refreshing it is for me to have to work for what I want with you? To have to put in the time and the effort and the care to make sure that when we get there, we're both in the right place at the right time?" He gathers me in close to him. "Stop thinking so much. Holding you this way is better than sex with other women who meant nothing to me. Try to relax and go with it. When the time is right to move forward, we'll know."

His words and the sincerity behind them bring me the kind of peace that's been largely elusive in my life since I left home. Running from the past is exhausting, especially when you can never run fast enough or far enough to truly escape the demons. But here in his arms, with the low hum of the plane's engines lulling me, I'm able to close my eyes with the comfort of knowing he's there, and he's not going anywhere. Not now, anyway.

CHAPTER 12

Flynn

If a man could die from unspent desire, I'd be on my deathbed. Watching her come apart in my arms was the single most erotic thing I've ever experienced, particularly because I suspect I just gave her the first orgasm of her life. What an honor and a thrill it is to hold her and to feel her beginning to trust me.

I caress her soft skin in small circles as she drops off into a light sleep.

I truly meant every word I said to her, but she's right about one thing—I'm not accustomed to denying my stronger-than-average sex drive. With my need for her still pulsing through my body, my cock hard and throbbing, I have to get myself together.

Moving slowly so I don't disturb her, I get up from the sofa and cover her with the blanket. Her lips move as she settles into her nap, and she's completely adorable.

In the small bathroom, I splash cold water on my face, trying to summon the control I need for her. Thinking about what she told me earlier, that she'd been attacked and raped as a fifteen-year-old, makes me crazy with rage and thirsty for revenge on her behalf. I want to find the guy and cause him twice the pain he caused her. I want to know if he ever paid for what he did. Is he rotting in jail where he belongs or living his life like nothing ever happened?

The latter possibility makes me seethe. I have so many questions but can't ask them without venturing into territory she's marked off-limits. I could hire someone and have the answers I crave within days, but I won't do that either. I'd never violate her privacy that way.

The thought of her turning on me is worse than not knowing. But it pains me not to know the full story. How can I protect her if I don't know my enemy? This is all new territory for me—these intense feelings for a woman and the knowledge that I'd kill to protect her.

I've always been a live-and-let-live kind of guy. I've created a monster career without leaving a trail of enemies behind me. My father taught me early on that ours is a small community with a long memory. "Be a gentleman in all your dealings," he advised, "and never forget the director you disdain today could be the producer you're wooing tomorrow."

It was good advice and words I live by. Sure, I've had my detractors and people who looked on with envy as my career took off while theirs stalled. I've had fellow actors and others in the business snidely imply that I am where I am because of who my parents are. I've always shrugged off that shit. Did my parents give me a leg up when I first ventured into the business? Without a doubt. But I've done the rest, and I know how hard I've worked for everything that has come my way.

But I already know I'll never work harder for anything than I will for the future I want with the gorgeous young woman currently sleeping on the sofa. I grip the edge of the countertop as I summon the innate control I need to manage this situation. I stare into the mirror at my reflection, surprised to realize the man looking back at me seems unfamiliar in many ways.

He wears a hint of fear in his eyes, and an unusual amount of tension tightens his jaw. It's not lost on me that I'm the last guy in the universe Natalie should be with. When you're into the kind of sex I want and need, there's no place for a woman traumatized by sex in the past. It's a testament to how strongly I already feel for her that I'm willing to put aside my own needs to tend to hers. But will I be able to do that forever? I can't answer that question, which is why I fear I'm setting up both of us for disaster.

My ringing cell phone tears me out of my uneasy contemplation. Surprised to have reception at altitude, I withdraw the phone from my back pocket and take the call from Hayden. "What's up?"

"Where are you?"

"In the air. You?"

"Just landed. We're hanging at the club tonight. Will we see you?"

"Not tonight. I've got some stuff to do when I land."

"Not tonight, not last night, not all last week. What's the deal, Flynn? Was it something we said?"

Well, sort of… I thought it, but I'd never say it. For all his pain-in-the-ass qualities, Hayden is my oldest and closest friend. "Don't be stupid. Nothing to do with you. But listen, while I have you, I've been thinking I'd like to do postproduction in New York rather than LA." A long pause follows my statement. "Hayden?"

"I'm here. I'm just wondering where the hell you are."

"What's that supposed to mean?"

"You hate the cold, Flynn, almost as much as I do. You hightail it back to LA the second you wrap a film—every single time. And now you're telling me you want to spend the next few months freezing our asses off in New York when we could be surfing in LA? And you wonder what's wrong with *me*?"

I pinch the top of my nose, which I hope will keep my head from blowing off my neck. "You know damned well why I want to be in New York right now."

"And you know damned well why I don't."

"Fine, then I'll commute. Forget I said anything."

"Come on, man. Let's at least talk about it."

"What's there to talk about? I want to be in New York. You don't. Neither of us is about to budge, so I'll figure something out."

"You're really that into this girl?"

"She's not a girl. She's a woman—an amazingly strong, resilient, smart woman."

"Who also happens to be hot as fuck."

"Shut the fuck up, Hayden. Don't talk about her that way."

"We *always* talk about women that way."

I'm ashamed to admit he's right. "Not this one."

"Dude, I don't even know what to say to you these days. Everything I do is wrong, and you're all edgy and shit. What's up with that?"

He's right. I can't deny it. I changed after I met Natalie and recognized she could be someone special. It's not Hayden's fault that our usual rules of engagement are no longer in effect, and I failed to tell him that. "I just need a little time to deal with a few things that are going on right now. It's nothing to do with you. We're cool."

"Are you sure? Because I haven't been getting the 'we're cool' vibe from you at all in the last week. I've been getting the 'Flynn's pissed at me and won't tell me why' vibe. And part of me doesn't give a shit, because if you're pissed, you'll get over it. You always do. But this feels different somehow."

"It is different. She's different. I need you to respect that and give me a little space."

"How much space and how long do you need?"

"I don't know. I'll let you know. But I won't be around much next week."

"I thought you were sticking around LA until the SAGs," he says of the Screen Actors Guild Awards that are two weeks after the Globes.

"I'm going back to New York in between."

"You're crazy, man, but whatever. Do what you gotta do. Just remember we've got a film to finish and not a lot of time to do it."

"I'm well aware of the timing."

"Could I ask you one other thing?"

"Sure."

"Have you prepared her for what'll happen after she appears in public with you? Arranged security and all that?"

"Addie's on it, but thanks for asking."

"No problem. Well, I guess I'll see you Sunday."

"See you then."

The click on the other end indicates that Hayden is gone.

I'm playing with fire in every aspect of my life, risking my reputation for having my priorities straight when it comes to my career and the people I work with, but Natalie is worth the risk.

Hayden's question about security puts me right back on edge. Because of what she's endured in the past, I have to warn her again about the media blitz that will follow our coming-out party. I have to be sure it won't cause a setback for her after she's worked so hard to build a new life for herself. In light of what she shared with me earlier, I shouldn't take her with me on Sunday. I have to give her the chance to beg off and spare her the insanity.

Selfish bastard that I am, I hate the thought of her deciding not to come with me. But she's already been violated once before, and that word aptly describes what will happen to her once the press catches wind of the fact that I have a new woman in my life, and that I'm serious about her.

I take a deep breath, steeling myself to deal with the disappointment that will follow her decision. But this isn't about what's best for me. I have to think of what is best for *her*. I will do the right thing by her no matter what it costs me— emotionally and physically.

With the steady drumbeat of desire thrumming through my veins reminding me of what I can't have, it's hard to say what price will exact the greater toll on me—the physical or the emotional.

Natalie

Flynn wakes me with kisses that begin at my shoulder and end at my fingertips, leaving a tingle of sensation that reawakens the desire. "We land in about an hour, Sleeping Beauty."

"How long have I been asleep?"

"About three hours."

"Oh my God. I'm so sorry. You must've been bored."

"Not so bad. I watched a movie when I wasn't watching you sleep."

I'm immediately embarrassed at the thought of him watching me sleep.

He runs a finger over my frown. "You were adorable. As always."

I shift under the blanket, and the rasp of soft wool against my breasts reminds me that I'm half-naked. My nipples tighten under the blanket, and I swear he knows that my body is reacting to his nearness.

As always, he shows restraint, but I can tell it doesn't come naturally to him. He's a man who reaches out and takes what he wants, and he clearly wants me. That he can't have me, at least not the way he'd like to have me, hasn't driven him away.

"I would give anything to know what goes on in that pretty head of yours when you look at me that way."

"What way am I looking at you?"

"Like you have a million questions you're dying to ask me, but can't bring yourself to do it." He bends over me to rub his nose against mine. "I wish you'd ask rather than worry about things that are probably no big deal."

"This whole thing is a big deal to me. A huge big deal. You have no idea how big."

"I think I have a small idea—and it's a huge big deal to me, too. Just in case you thought otherwise."

"I feel like Cinderella at the ball, and any second the clock is going to strike midnight, and the handsome prince will disappear in a wisp of smoke, never to be seen or heard from again."

"As you well know, the prince showed up the next day with her slipper, and they all lived happily ever after."

"That's how it works in fairy tales. Not real life."

"Not to give myself more credit than I deserve, but if I'm playing the role of the prince in this fairy tale of yours, I can assure you I'm not going anywhere. No wisp of smoke, no team of mules or ten men could drag me away from you. So whatever you're thinking, just say it. Put it out there and have one less thing on your mind."

He makes it so easy to lay myself bare before him in more ways than one. Words come to mind that I can't imagine saying to anyone, let alone him, but because he makes it easy, I find myself saying them. "I see the way you look at me."

"How do I look at you?"

"Like you're starving, and I'm the only food for miles around."

A broad smile unfolds across his sinfully handsome face. "You do make me rather ravenous. Have we moved on from Cinderella to the Big Bad Wolf?"

I laugh at the playful growl that accompanies his question. "I want you to know... I'm aware that you have... needs... and if you wanted to go elsewhere for that—"

"Natalie! Jesus. What do you take me for? A rutting beast with no self-control?" He stands and pushes his hands through his hair, his entire body rigid with impatience and irritation.

"I didn't mean it that way." I hate that I've upset him.

"You wouldn't care if I went off and fucked someone else because you're not ready to put out? Is that what you're saying?"

His crude language is shocking to me, but not as much as the flash of jealousy that roars through me at the thought of him having sex with another woman. Clearly, I didn't think this suggestion all the way through.

His face relaxes into a smile that's full of male satisfaction. "Thought so."

"Did you say that to make me jealous?"

He returns to the sofa, bracketing me with his arms on either side of my body. "No, silly girl, I said that to show you how ridiculous you're being. I want *you*. Only you. When I said I'd wait, I didn't mean until a more convenient vagina comes along, tempting me to stray."

"That's gross!" I sputter with laughter even though I find him outrageous. "I can't believe you just said that. Although I'm sure you've met many a convenient vagina in your time."

"Vaginas are rather readily available for big movie stars like me."

I love that he laughs so easily at himself and his lifestyle. I love that he cares enough to make me jealous. "You were right."

"About?"

"I was jealous at the thought of you with someone else."

"Good. You should be. I'm all yours." He pauses and takes a deep breath. "And because you're all mine and I want to protect you, we need to talk again about Sunday. While you were asleep, Hayden called, and when we talked about the Globes, he asked if I've arranged security and properly prepared you for what'll happen afterward."

"You arranged security? For me?"

"Hell yes, I did. The media will be relentless when they put two and two together with you and me. Since I can't be with you every minute of every day, I'm not going to risk you being hurt or overrun by them."

I swallow hard at the thought of being pursued.

"And," he says haltingly, "because of what you told me earlier and the possibility of that making headlines, I'm wondering if we should change our plans for Sunday."

"There's no chance of that making headlines. It's buried so deep, they'll never find it."

"If there's something there to be found, babe, they'll find it."

"No, they won't."

"You're sure?"

"Positive. But I'll understand if you don't want to go to the trouble and expense of security. I can watch it on TV and cheer you on that way."

"I couldn't care less about the cost of security—or the trouble. I want you with me, but I'd never do anything to cause you further pain. You've already had enough."

"I won't lie to you. The thought of being pursued by reporters is unnerving to me, but I'd really like to go with you. If that's all right."

"It's more than all right. We'll have a fantastic time."

I smile up at him, and he bends to kiss me. He roots around under the blanket until he finds my bra and sweater. "How about some dinner?"

"That sounds good."

Without making a fuss of it, he helps me into my clothes. I don't miss the flash of desire that overtakes him at the sight of my bare breasts. Knowing he wants me so badly is a powerful thrill.

Once I'm decent, he rings for Jacob, and we enjoy a delicious meal of tender filet mignon and cheesy scalloped potatoes.

"These potatoes are my new favorite food ever," I tell him.

"They are pretty damned good." He refills our wineglasses.

Between the rich red wine, the delicious food, the sexy man keeping me company and the restorative nap, I'm feeling more relaxed than I have in years—a thought I share freely with him when my inclination is to keep most thoughts to myself.

"I'm so glad to hear that. I want you to relax and enjoy everything this weekend. You so deserve to be pampered."

"I don't know if I *deserve* it, but I won't say no to it."

"We're going to have a lot of fun. I promise you that."

The approach into LAX is bumpy due to wind, and I cling to Flynn's hand. When the wheels finally touch down on the runway, I can finally breathe normally again.

"You okay?"

"Much better now that we're back on the ground."

"Me, too."

"You don't like to fly?"

"It's not my favorite thing to do, but a necessary evil in my life."

We say good-bye and thanks to Jacob before we deplane on the tarmac, where a car is waiting for us. In the short minutes we're outside, I appreciate the warmth after the deep freeze in New York. Flynn helps me into another low-slung black sports car while someone else sees to our luggage.

We're driving away from the airport minutes after we arrive. "This is all very impressive."

"What is?"

"The efficiency with which you travel."

"Another necessarily evil. The last time I flew commercial, the airline 'invited' me not to fly with them again because my presence on the plane caused a one-hour delay in departure, *and* I got mobbed in the airport, which isn't as much fun as it sounds."

"They actually came right out and asked you not to fly with them again?"

"Not in so many words, but the message was received loud and clear. I'm apparently too disruptive."

"Wow."

"See what I mean when I tell you it's not all champagne and tuxedos?"

"I'm beginning to see there's a definite downside to fame."

"Not that I'd ever complain about my truly amazing life."

"You always have to add that disclaimer, don't you?"

"Last thing in the world I'd ever want anyone to think is that I'm ungrateful for what has been a truly astonishing career and life. The only downside has been the loss of anonymity and the ability to move around freely. Every outing has to be carefully choreographed, and that gets tiresome. But again—not complaining, just stating the facts of my reality."

"Which is another thing the entertainment websites and news shows don't cover when it comes to celebrities."

"Exactly. That's because if they cover it, they'd have to acknowledge their role in creating the insatiable desire for personal information about celebrities. They'd also have to take responsibility for the fact that they often endanger us—and themselves—in the pursuit of the big story. It's a catch-22 for them."

"It's all very interesting to me, to see it from your point of view."

"We go into this business knowing that's part of it, but until you've lived it, you can't imagine how invasive it can be." He glances over at me. "Which is why I'm so concerned about exposing you to it."

"And I appreciate your concern. I really do. But if my choices are to put up with some attention from the media or never see you again, I'll take my lumps with the press."

He reaches for my hand and gives it a squeeze. "I'll keep you safe, sweetheart. I promise."

"I know you will. So what kind of car is this?" I ask, looking to take the conversation in a less intense direction.

"This beauty is an Aston Martin Vanquish."

"You do love your cars."

"It's one of my two addictions—neither of them illegal."

As we exit the freeway, I ask, "Where're we going?"

"My place in the hills tonight and tomorrow night. We're staying in town on Sunday." He looks over at me again. "Is that okay?"

"Sure. It sounds good." Though he's told me repeatedly that he has no expectations, what happened on the plane has changed my expectations. I want to be close to him. I want to let him in. I want things I've never wanted before. Am I prepared to give him everything? No, not yet. But I want more than nothing.

"Now what're you thinking?"

"I don't know how to say it."

"I told you before—just put it out there. Whatever it is, we'll figure it out."

"Remember when you asked me to come on this trip and you promised separate bedrooms?"

"I haven't forgotten. My place has four extra bedrooms. You can have your pick."

"What if I pick your room?"

"That's fine, too. I can sleep anywhere."

When I realize he's missed my meaning, I begin to laugh. His baffled glance only makes me laugh harder.

"What the hell is so funny?"

"You are. We are. I'm trying to tell you I want to sleep with you, and I'm bungling it badly."

"Oh. You do?"

"Yeah. Is that okay?"

"Baby, that is the best news I've ever gotten."

"I'm not saying I want to, you know, do everything. But I want to be with you."

"I want to be with you, too, and I can't wait to sleep with you in my arms."

I shiver in anticipation of spending a full night with him—something I never thought I'd want from any man until this one came along and showed me what's still possible despite everything I've been through. I also acknowledge that I'm falling in love with him, one sweet moment at a time. He seems to understand me innately, in a way that no one ever has. And that he's willing to let me set the pace is a precious and priceless gift to me.

Flynn's house is way up in the Hollywood Hills in a location I could never find again if I had to. He punches in a code that opens the big iron gates that guard the property and drives into a circular driveway, coming to a stop outside the front door.

A young woman with long blonde hair comes rushing out the front door to greet us. "You're here! Welcome home." She gives Flynn a huge hug before turning to give me the same greeting. "*So* nice to meet you, Natalie."

"Um, you too."

"Natalie, this is Addison, my assistant."

I'm shocked by how young and beautiful she is.

"My friends call me Addie."

"Nice to meet you, Addie. Flynn says he'd be lost without you."

"Flynn had better say that."

"I speak only the truth," Flynn says, like the wise man he is.

Addie hooks her arm through mine. "We're going to have so much fun this weekend. I've got stylists standing in line for a chance to dress you for Sunday. And two weeks from now, too. Is she coming to the SAGs, Flynn?"

He follows us into the house, hauling the luggage. "We haven't gotten that far yet."

I look over at him. "SAGs?"

"Screen Actors Guild Awards. They're at the end of the month. 'Tis the season."

"Oh, well, I doubt I can do two weekends in one month, with work and everything."

"That's what I figured, but I did plan to ask."

"Sorry if I beat you to the punch," Addie says with playful chagrin. "Anyway, I just wanted to be here to say hello when you got home. I hit the grocery store, so you're all stocked up. I'll be here tomorrow around ten so Natalie can choose her dress. Sound good?"

"Sounds great." Flynn kisses her on the forehead. "Thanks for everything and for getting the car to the airport for me."

She waves off his thanks. "Johnny did that." For my benefit, she adds, "He won't let me drive the Aston."

"I'm only protecting the car."

"A girl has one or three fender benders in a year, and suddenly no one will let her drive their two-hundred-fifty-thousand-dollar car. It's so not fair."

I laugh because how can I not? She's hilarious.

"It's more than fair. Now get out of here before I kick you out."

"Yeah, yeah, I'm going. I got better things to do on a Friday night than deal with you."

Listening to them, I get much more of a brother-sister vibe than I do a lover vibe, and I'm relieved.

Addie takes off, leaving me alone in the gorgeous one-story house with Flynn.

"How about a quick tour?"

"I'd love it."

He leaves our bags in the foyer and takes my hand to lead me into a warm, cozy kitchen that I immediately fall in love with. "This is fabulous!" It's all dark wood and cool marble that I run my hand over reverently. A center island is surrounded by barstools, and I can picture gatherings happening right there.

"The kitchen is new, but I should start with the pedigree. This house once belonged to Marlena Davis. She sold it to Frank Thompson, and his estate sold it to me."

"That's some pedigree. Three of the biggest movie stars in history have owned it."

"Check out the view." He leads me over to floor-to-ceiling windows that look out over an in-ground pool with Los Angeles spread out in all her glory far beneath us. "It's even better than your view in New York."

"I know. I love it. In the daytime, we can see all the way to the Pacific from here. Come see the rest."

He shows me his cluttered office, the room that doubles as an at-home movie theater and a game room, and the four extra bedrooms, all of them neat and nicely decorated and each with an en suite bathroom. "This is my room," he says, flipping on the lights in a spacious room with the same view of the Hollywood Hills as the living room.

"That's the biggest bed I've ever seen."

"It's a California king."

"Figures you all do everything bigger and better out here."

"So much I could say to that."

"But you won't."

"But I won't." He kisses my nose and then my lips. "The bed is so big, you won't even know I'm there."

"What's the point of that?"

His mouth opens and then closes as he apparently thinks better of whatever he was about to say. "How about a swim?"

"Now?"

"Why not?"

"Sure, we can do that."

"Hang tight, and I'll get the bags."

I take advantage of the opportunity to take a closer look at his room, including the family photos displayed prominently on his dresser and bedside table. He's obviously close to his bevy of nieces and nephews, who hang all over him in the photos. I pick up one of him with three blond little boys squirming on his lap, and the happy smile on his face touches me deep inside. This is a man who loves fiercely.

"Those are my sister Annie's kids—Connor, Mason and Garrett. Little monkeys."

I return the photo to his bedside table. "They're adorable."

"Yes, they are." Flynn opens a door to a huge walk-in closet. "I'll stick your bag in here, okay?"

"Perfect."

"Is it too much to hope for a really skimpy bikini in there?" he asks with a salacious grin.

"Maybe. Maybe not." I'm now really glad I bought what I consider a very sexy bikini when he told me to bring a bathing suit on the trip, and I didn't have the heart to tell him I didn't own one. I bought it online, hoping it would fit, and paid more than the suit cost to have it delivered in time for the trip.

"Mmm, don't keep me in suspense for too long." He leaves me with a kiss. "I'll be outside when you're ready. The door is off the living room."

"I'll be right there."

I take a minute to unpack my cosmetic bag and put it in the huge bathroom that adjoins his room. After I brush my hair and teeth, I reach for the bathing suit. My hands tremble ever so slightly as I change into the red bikini. By Leah's standards, it would be considered massively conservative. By my standards, it's racy. Perhaps too racy, but it's the only suit I have, so I'll wear it. Thinking of Leah reminds me I need to check on Fluff, so I shoot off a quick text to my roommate, who graciously agreed to watch her this weekend.

Leah writes right back. *All is well here. She's decided she wants to sleep with me since you're not available.*

Aww, she loves you.

No, she loves YOU, but you've abandoned her for Hollywood. How is it out there? I bet it's awesome.

It's really nice. We're at his place in LA, about to go in the pool.

I hate your guts. Have I told you that lately?

Ha! Did I mention the private jet that brought us here?

No, I really do hate you.

Love you too. Smooches to you and Fluff. Take good care of my baby.

Will do. Send pictures and have FUN!

XOXO

CHAPTER 13

Natalie

I pull on the cover-up I bought to match the suit, thankful now that I spent the extra money on the cover-up. The thought of parading through his house wearing only a bikini freaks me out. And then his words from the plane come back to remind me of what's possible with him.

"I hope someday you and I will have a lot *of sex. I hope someday you and I will start and end each day wrapped in each other's arms. I hope maybe someday, you'll be able to do whatever you want with me any time you want to do it and know that you'll always be welcome and safe in my arms, in my bed, in my life. And because I know when all that happens it'll be extraordinary, to say the least, I'm willing to wait. For as long as it takes, I'll wait. I'll wait for you."*

My insides quiver the same way they did when he first said those words to me. Though my inclination is always to be skeptical, with him I'm not. I believe him when he says he'll wait for me, no matter how long it takes me to get there. He'll wait. Knowing that takes the pressure off and allows me to relax enough to enjoy this adventure he's taking me on.

I walk through the house to the living room and notice he's left the door open for me. The lights are now on inside the pool, casting a glow over the deck where Flynn waits for me, dressed only in a pair of board shorts. His back is to me, but I can tell he's checking his phone while he waits.

"Hey."

He spins around, and once again, his mouth opens and then snaps shut. After a short pause in which he only stares at me, he says, "You're so beautiful, Nat. You literally steal the breath from my lungs."

Equally taken in by him, I cross the pool deck. "You're quite beautiful yourself." His chest and abdomen are ripped with well-defined muscles that make me want to run my fingers—and my tongue—over them.

"I ain't got nothing on you."

"I know a few million women who would disagree."

He slips his arms around me and brings me in close. "The only one who matters is right here."

I go up on tiptoes to kiss him.

"What did I do to deserve that?"

"You're very sweet."

He scowls at the term. "No, I'm really not."

"Yes, you really are."

"Natalie…" He seems tormented as he appears to weigh whether he wants to say more.

"What is it?"

"Nothing, sweetheart." He kisses my forehead. "Let's swim."

Despite what he says, I can see something is troubling him. I decide to wait for another chance to ask him about it.

We swim, we snuggle underwater, and we laugh—a lot—when we're not kissing, which is most of the time. As promised, he's a perfect gentleman. His hands never wander from my hips or back. By the time we get out of the pool more than an hour later, my skin is pruned and my body is craving more of what he gave me on the plane.

My first orgasm. It's beyond embarrassing to admit, even to myself and especially to him, that at nearly twenty-four, I'd never experienced that particular bliss until he took me there. I'm so accustomed to keeping everything to myself that sharing something like that will take courage I don't have quite yet.

I'm beginning to believe, however, that I'll get there. Eventually. I'm beginning to believe the day will come when I share most of my thoughts with him.

With the sun long gone, the evening air is chilly. Flynn wraps a big towel around me and leads me straight to the massive shower in the master bathroom. There are knobs and valves and a wide variety of showerheads as well as room for a family of six. "I'm going to need a shower tutorial here."

"I gotcha covered." He turns on the water and sets it to fall from the rainforest showerhead above.

"I left shampoo and stuff on the counter. Would you mind grabbing it for me?"

"No problem." He returns with the shampoo and the conditioner bottle he's opened to smell. "Mmm, so that's the source of the most incredible scent."

I take the bottles from him, but he shows no signs of leaving.

"Want some help with the shampoo?"

"Is that a metaphor?"

His laughter echoes through the bathroom. "No, that's my genuine attempt to get my hands on your gorgeous hair."

"In that case, come on in."

Still wearing the board shorts, he steps into the stall and takes the shampoo from me. He takes his time massaging my scalp and running his fingers through the length of my hair. By the time he's finished with the conditioner, I'm leaning against him because my legs no longer feel sturdy under me.

The cloud of steam around us adds to the erotic atmosphere. His every touch and caress sets me on fire for things I thought I'd never want from any man. But in his arms, I've discovered that underneath the trauma and the scars on my soul is a normal young woman with all the same desires other women have.

I turn to him, slide my hands from his chest to his shoulders and draw his head down for a kiss. "Flynn?"

"Hmmm?" His eyes are closed and his jaw is tight.

"Every time you touch me, you take me apart, piece by piece. And then you kiss me and put me back together."

"God, Natalie... You do the same thing to me. You said it so perfectly." He cups my face and kisses me again. "I'm falling so hard and so fast for you."

"I'm falling just as fast."

"Are you scared?"

"Terrified."

"Don't be. You're safe with me. I promise." He holds me close as the warm water rains down upon us. His erection presses insistently into my belly, reminding me of what he wants from me. What would've terrified me a week ago now intrigues me. I want to touch him there. I want to touch him everywhere.

With a tender kiss to my forehead, he releases me to finish my shower. When I step out a few minutes later, I find a stack of dry towels and a robe. He's thoughtful and sweet and sexy as hell. Though I don't want to be nervous about sleeping with him, I am nonetheless. Mostly I'm worried that I'm not being fair to him by sleeping with him but not allowing it to go any further.

The robe is so big, it could wrap around me twice. I tie the belt tightly and hang the towels to dry. I venture into his bedroom, where he is lying on the bed, propped up on his side on a mountain of pillows, wearing only a pair of loose-fitting pajama pants and black glasses as his fingers fly over his phone. The glasses are hot. Seriously hot. He catches me staring at him and smiles.

"Glasses?"

"Took my contacts out."

"Ahh. I like them."

"Yeah?"

Nodding, I go to the closet, where I fetch my hairdryer and something to sleep in. By the time I get dressed, dry my hair and return to the bedroom, he has traded his phone for an e-reader. He sees me coming and turns down the covers on the other side of the bed, inviting me to join him.

I slide between soft, cool sheets. I feel awkward and uncertain about where I should put my hands and what will happen now that we're in a big, comfortable bed together.

He puts down the e-reader, takes off his glasses and moves closer to me, covering my fussing hands with one of his. "Don't be nervous, Nat. It's just me and you, and I'm so happy you're here."

Turning to face him, I give his hand a squeeze. "How do you always know just what to say to me?"

"I don't know anything. I'm always afraid of saying or doing something that will scare you away from me." He holds out his arm, inviting me to come closer to him.

I scoot across the silky sheet and sigh with pleasure when his arms encircle me. "The last thing I'm thinking about now is running away from you." He's becoming essential to me one minute at a time, and the thoughts I had days ago about getting out of this seem foolish now.

"You must be so tired," he says, his lips brushing against my hair. "It's after one in the East."

"I had a three-hour nap."

"That's true." He releases me to turn off the light but comes right back to where he was with his arms around me.

"Are you tired?" I ask him.

"Not really. I tend to be a bit of a night owl."

"We don't have to go to bed yet if you don't want to."

"Natalie," he says, laughing softly, "do you think wild horses could drag me out of this bed right now?"

"Is that your charming way of saying you like having me in your bed?"

"I *love* having you in my bed and in my shower and in my pool. But mostly in my life."

I raise my hand to his arm and set out to learn the contours of his muscles.

"Tell me about your family," he says.

The request catches me off guard and unprepared. How to answer without giving too much away...

"Is it okay to ask about them?"

"Yeah, sure. I have two younger sisters, Candace and Olivia." I don't mention that I haven't seen them in eight years, that I miss them every day, that Candace would've graduated from high school last year, and I wasn't there to celebrate with her. They were still little girls when I left, when I sacrificed myself to save them.

"And your parents?"

"My dad works in state government." Or he had the last time I'd bothered to check three years ago. "My mom works for an insurance company."

"Are you close with them?"

"Not really. We had... We had some issues when I was growing up, and I don't see much of them." I can't tell him that my parents let me down when I needed them most, and left me twisting in the wind alone and broken. I don't want him to know I come from people like them.

"I'm sorry. I don't mean to poke at something painful."

"You're not. It's a fair question."

He raises his hand to my face before he kisses me. "You're not alone anymore, Natalie. I hope you know that."

"I do, and it helps. Thank you."

"Don't thank me, sweet girl. Being with you makes me so happy. Happier than I've ever been."

"I still can't believe you feel that way about me."

"Believe it. It gets stronger every day." He kisses me again, more intently this time, and I open my lips to his tongue. His kisses strip me bare and leave me reeling from the powerful punch of desire I experience every time.

Flynn breaks the kiss suddenly. "Sorry," he mutters. "I didn't mean to get so carried away again."

"I like when you get carried away."

"*Natalie...*" He groans. "You're killing me. You know that, don't you?"

"I wish I could be like other women and give you what you want, but—"

His finger over my lips stops me. "Please don't ever say that. You're perfect just the way you are, and I don't want you to be like anyone else. Close your eyes and relax. I've got you, and everything is okay."

He will never know how much it means to me to hear him say that, how long I've yearned for someone to tell me everything is okay. Despite the steady thrum of desire zipping through my veins, I find myself drifting into sleep.

CHAPTER 14

Flynn

I'm wound so tightly I fear I will break in half if I so much as move. Holding Natalie in my arms as she sleeps is both heaven and hell at the same time. I want her so badly, but not just physically. I want to possess her heart and soul. I want to share her life and her passion. I want it all with her, which is why I forced myself to end a kiss that was spiraling out of control.

I know how much courage it took for her to tell me she wanted to sleep with me. I don't want to take advantage of her close proximity by pushing her for things she's told me she's not ready to do.

I'm restless, and the desire-driven tension that grips my body has me buzzing like I've ingested a week's worth of caffeine. With Natalie warm and soft in my arms, my thoughts are free to roam. The last time I attempted a relationship similar to what's happening with Natalie was with my ex-wife, Valerie. We'd been married two years before I let her see the full extent of my sexual desires. I was unable to deny that part of myself any longer. When I told her what I wanted—what I really wanted—she was horrified and said I was depraved. Shortly afterward, she arranged for me to catch her having sex with another man, which was her way of telling me we were done.

Our marriage was a disaster in more ways than one, which is why I publicly stated I'd never marry again. Despite the intense feelings I already have for Natalie, I still believe I'm better off not being married. What would sweet, lovely, wounded

Natalie think if I told her I want to tie her up, clamp her nipples, spank her sweet ass, and then watch her take a thick plug there. I want to fuck her senseless and watch her suck my dick while I flog her.

Yeah, I can only imagine how that conversation would go. Frustrated and turned on thanks to the direction my thoughts have taken, I drag a hand through my hair. Hayden is right about me. When I try to deny who and what I am, it usually goes bad for me and the women who have the misfortune to get involved with me. The majority of them never knew why I wasn't satisfied by what we did together, just that it was over between us.

Even knowing why it's a bad idea to let this continue, I already can't imagine a day without Natalie in it. I try to picture telling her, after everything we've already shared, that I've changed my mind, that I've decided we aren't compatible after all. Those words would hurt her, perhaps so deeply she'd never take a chance with a man again. The thought of that hurts me.

I'm a fucking heartless bastard because I know I'll never let her go, despite all the reasons why I should.

I fight off the sleep that would claim me because I don't want to miss a second of the sweet pleasure of holding her while she sleeps. When I can't fight it any longer, I drift into uneasy rest, filled with dreams of me chasing after something I can't have. Every time I get close, it slips away again. I can't see or touch what I'm after, but I can feel it so intensely, I wonder how I can breathe through the painful surge of desire.

Then I'm at the club in New York. It's dark except for the single light that illuminates the table where Natalie stands, still wearing the robe I provided for her and afraid of what I'm going to do to her. I like that she's afraid. Though she has come here willingly, her underlying fear fires my desire.

Here in my dreams, she's not a rape survivor. She isn't broken inside. She isn't fragile or hesitant. I'm confident she can handle what I have planned for her.

"Take off the robe," I tell her, my tone leaving no room for negotiation. She's my sub, and I'm in charge.

She looks around the big room full of people, many of whom are looking on in eager anticipation of our scene, which has been many months in the making. We've spent hours playing at home, building up to tonight, the night we go public at Quantum. It's the fulfillment of every dream I've ever had to bring her here, to my place, with my friends watching and supporting us.

Her hands tremble as she tugs on the knot, the robe falling open to reveal the creamy skin that has been the source of all my fantasies since I first laid eyes on her. My gaze falls to her pussy and the thin strip of light hair that covers her. I prefer her bare, so my first order of business will be to shave her. I've told her I want to do it, but I haven't told her it'll happen here tonight.

"The robe," I say again, watching her closely as she shrugs it off her shoulders and holds it to her for a long moment before letting it drop to her feet.

She is exquisite. Her breasts are large and full, her nipples like dark red berries and standing at attention. At her waist, her fingers link and unlink in an unconscious show of nerves.

"On the table, sweetheart."

She gives me an uncertain look before she hesitantly does what I've asked her to do.

"Tell me your safe word." We've negotiated this in advance, along with her hard and soft limits. I know how far I can push her, what will break her and what won't. I'm not interested in breaking her, though. I'm far more interested in worshiping her in the best way I know how.

"Fluff," she says softly.

"And when should you use it?"

"If something is too much for me or if it hurts."

"And what will happen if you say that word?"

"Everything stops."

"Good." I give her a soft, reassuring kiss and help her to lie back on the table, noting the deep tremor that has overtaken her thighs.

Seeing that makes me hot and harder than I've ever been in my life. Bringing Natalie into my world and showing her my inner self is the culmination of every fantasy I've ever had about what true love would be like. There's no hiding, no evasion, no denial. I'd have her and everything else I want, too. Before Natalie, it seemed I'd never have it all, and now I have everything.

I've prepared in advance for our scene, so I'm ready for her. I ease her legs apart and place her feet in stirrups that I pull from under the table. I tug her bottom to the edge of the table. The bowl of warm water, shaving cream and razor are waiting for me. As I lather her up, she raises her head for a look.

"Wha... What're you doing?"

"Making you ready." I drag the razor over her most sensitive skin, and she moans. The sound travels like an electrical current straight to my already hard cock. I take my time to shave her clean with slow, even strokes of the razor.

As I work, I notice the quivering in her thighs has become more intense, forcing me to place my free hand over her lower belly to keep her from moving. The last thing I want is to cut her or cause her real pain. That's not the goal here.

By the time I finish, her eyes are closed and her lips parted in supplication that makes my cock throb in anticipation. I wipe away the remaining shaving cream with a warm cloth and reach for a tube of lubricant. With my index and middle fingers coated with lube, I press against her back entrance, preparing her to take a plug.

She fights back, resisting the intrusion. "No," she gasps. "Not there."

"Yes, there. Be still." I push against the muscles that are determined to keep me out, drawing a whimper of protest from her but no safe word. This is the first time I've touched her there, and I can tell she's shocked and aroused. It's a battle, but she eventually cedes and lets me in. Her moans and groans feed the beast inside me, making me ravenous for her and satisfying me in ways that nothing else ever could. I keep my fingers buried deep inside her ass as I bend to lick her pussy, stroking my tongue over her clit until she's squirming from the need for release.

"Don't come," I say harshly. "I own your orgasm, and I say when."

"Flynn..."

"That's not my name here."

"Sir... Please... Let me come."

"Not until I say you can."

All around us, everything has come to a halt in the club, and we are the main attraction. I want her to see that, so I order her to open her eyes and look around. When she realizes everyone is watching me fuck her ass with my fingers while I deny her orgasm, her entire body flushes with heat. "Does my baby like to be watched?"

"No."

"Are you lying to me?"

She squirms, trying to dislodge my fingers. I press them deeper and her back arches in response. "*No.*"

I drag my free hand between her legs, where she is fairly dripping. "I've discovered evidence that says otherwise."

Natalie shudders from the need to come, a need I won't let her give in to until I'm good and ready.

"Do you know what happens to bad girls who lie to their Doms?"

"No," she says on a whimper.

"They get their sweet asses spanked until they're so red and rosy that they can't sit for a week without remembering how they got so sore." My words bring a new rush of moisture from her pussy. "Mmm, the thought of that turns you on, too, doesn't it?"

"No!"

I slap her ass—hard—drawing a sharp cry from her and another gush from between her legs. God, she's perfect. She responds to me like no one else ever has. I pull my fingers back, almost to the point of removing them. Natalie holds her breath while she waits to see what I'll do. I don't leave her hanging for long. I drive them back into her and suck on her clit at the same time, sending her into a screaming orgasm that has her ass clamping down hard on my fingers.

I can't wait to feel that hard clamp around my cock.

"I don't recall giving you permission to come," I say as she floats back to reality after the scorching release. "You know what that means, don't you?"

She licks lips gone dry. "No. What?"

"It means you must be punished for your bad behavior." I pull my fingers free of her ass so quickly, she gasps. After I wipe my hand clean with a towel, I reach for one of the jeweled clamps that sits on my tray. Bending over her, I lick and suck her left nipple until it is standing up tall and proud and then affix the clamp before she has time to process what I plan to do.

She screams from the pinch of the clamp.

I give her other breast the same treatment and then wipe away her tears. "Do you need your safe word, sweetheart?"

She bites her lip and shakes her head. She's so brave and willing, the woman of my dreams. The one I thought I'd never be lucky enough to find. I love her more than life itself.

"Turn over." When she complies with my demand, moving carefully so as not to test the clamps, I arrange her so her feet are on the floor and her upper body is bent over the table. My hand finds her ass cheek and squeezes, testing her pliability.

Her head falls to the cushion of her arms as her legs continue to tremble.

I deliver a sharp spank to her lower left cheek, right where her leg meets her bottom.

Other than a sharp intake of breath and the quiver of her bottom cheeks, she doesn't react. I do it again on the other side, waiting all the while for the safe word that doesn't come. I spank her until both cheeks are rosy red and then rub them until the heat from her ass spreads to the rest of her body.

Separating her cheeks, I home in on her anus, which still glistens from the lube I applied earlier. I reach for the plug I've chosen for her and press it against her entrance. It's big, but it has nothing on me, and I want to prepare her to take me. Eventually.

"God, Flynn... I can't."

"What do you call me here?"

"*Sir*... Please, sir... I can't take that."

"Yes, you can."

"*No*."

"Do I hear your safe word, Natalie?"

When she remains stubbornly silent, I smile with satisfaction and continue to work the plug into her, all the while rubbing the heated skin on her ass and making her squirm.

"This is the biggest part," I tell her. "Push out and let it in."

"I *can't*."

I deliver another sharp slap to her left cheek, and she immediately yields to the plug, crying out as it settles into place.

"That's my brave girl." I kiss from her shoulders down her back to her ass, which glows from the attention I've given it. I hold her cheeks apart and lick her pussy and back to where the plug stretches her skin obscenely. She is so wet and so ready. Since this is my dream and we're in a fully committed relationship, I don't bother with a condom before I push my cock into her pussy, slowly and carefully, since space is at a premium due to the plug.

She grunts and groans and moans, her tight channel rippling around my cock in what feels like a constant orgasm.

"Talk to me, baby. How does it feel?"

"So tight."

"Mmm, so *good*." I push on the plug to remind her she's being filled from both ends, and her pussy clamps down on my cock so relentlessly I nearly come on the spot. Grasping her hips as I fuck her hard and deep, I lose myself in her in a way I never have with anyone else. I'm transported, right out of this room and straight to paradise. My balls tighten and my spine tingles. As I get closer, I pick up the pace, pounding into her relentlessly. Because I want her with me when I come, I reach around to find the hard nub of her clit. I pinch it between my fingers, giving her no quarter.

I can tell she's on the brink of an epic release, so I use my other hand to remove the clamps, making her scream as the blood flows back into her tortured nipples at the same second she comes. The squeeze on my cock is so intense that I see stars as I empty myself into her.

I wake with a start to realize I've come in reality as well as in my dream. My cock is throbbing, my pants are wet, and I'm sweating profusely. Beside me, Natalie sleeps on, undisturbed. I'm rattled and mortified and shocked. I haven't had a wet dream since I was a teenager, and even then it was a rare occurrence.

The dream comes back to me in erotic snippets… Natalie standing nude in the midst of Quantum. The pale skin on her ass reddened from my hand. My fingers gliding into her ass in preparation for the plug.

My cock hardens all over again at the memories that come back to me one after the other to torture me, as if I didn't just have the single most explosive orgasm of my life. Moving slowly so I won't disturb her, I get out of bed and go into the bathroom, where I remove my soiled pants.

"Jesus," I whisper to myself and the almighty. What the hell just happened? I splash cold water on my face until my breathing calms and my heart stops racing. I'm ashamed and appalled to have had such a dream about Natalie, but underneath it all, I'm insanely aroused at the idea of sharing an experience like that with her.

And then I'm just as quickly despondent at the knowledge it'll never happen. It will be all she can do to handle regular sex, let alone my kind. I tell myself I can live with that as long as I get to be with her, but deep, lacerating doubts plague me nonetheless.

I take a long shower as images from the dream continue to taunt and arouse me. I'm like a live wire by the time I step out of the shower and pull on a clean pair of pajama pants. If I were here alone, I'd wear nothing. But out of respect for Natalie, I wear the pants. I venture into the living room, pour myself a couple fingers of Bowmore and take it with me to the windows that look down over the bright lights of Hollywood.

I'm tormented by what I should do where she's concerned. The dream has helped to solidify how impossibly out of reach this relationship really is. I have to let her go while I still can. After this weekend, I'll do what I should've done right from those first minutes in the park.

I'll let her go, even if it kills me. It's what's best for her.

CHAPTER 15

Natalie

I wake up alone, which is profoundly disappointing after taking the momentous step of sleeping with him in the first place. The robe he lent me last night is laid across the foot of the bed. I put it on and tie the belt at my waist. In the bathroom, I use the facilities and brush my teeth and hair before wandering into the hallway to look for Flynn.

He isn't in the office, but I take a moment in the light of day to check out the framed photos that cover the walls. There are pictures of him with some of the biggest names in the business. In them, he's always wearing that wide, appealing grin I've become so fond of.

Like his desk in New York, this one is also piled high with scripts and other piles of paper and folders. Just as I'm wondering why he doesn't have someone clean up the office, Addie appears in the doorway.

"He won't let me touch a thing in here," Addie says as she hands me a mug of steaming coffee. "I took a guess on the cream and sugar."

"It's perfect, thank you."

"No problem. So about this office… Total disaster, right?"

"It is kind of a mess."

"He says he has a system and I'm not to touch a single speck of dust in here." She shrugs. "If there's a system, I've yet to discover it."

"Where is he?"

"He went for a run. He'll be back in an hour or so."

I'm surprised he left without telling me and that Addie is here earlier than expected, but I certainly don't share those thoughts with his assistant. "How did you two meet?"

Leaning against the doorframe and holding her own mug, she says, "He didn't tell you? Huh, well, my mom died when I was twelve, leaving me with a dad who had no idea what to do with me. He's a cameraman and has done a lot of work for Quantum, Flynn's production company. Flynn's friend Marlowe Sloane took an interest in me, took me shopping for prom gowns and was like my fairy godmother."

She takes a deep breath and continues. "When I graduated from UCLA and couldn't find a job to save my life, she suggested Flynn hire me to run his. I've been with him five years now, and it's the coolest job ever. I never know what's going to happen on a given day. Like when he called me to tell me he's bringing a date to the Globes who needed a stylist to get her decked out. So I put the word out that Flynn is bringing a date who needs a stylist, and I've had every stylist in Hollywood—and every designer in the universe—kissing my ass all week. See what I mean? I love my job!"

She's so adorable and delightful that I can't help but laugh at her enthusiasm. She's several years older than I am, but I feel like the adult here for whatever reason. There's a lightness about her that's infectious. I find myself lightening up and getting excited about the stylists.

"*Sooooo*, you want to see some dresses?"

"Now?"

"Right now."

"Yes!"

"Right this way."

I follow her to Flynn's living room, which has been converted into a dress boutique while I was sleeping. I bring my hands to my mouth to muffle the gasp of delight at the sight of gowns in every color imaginable hanging on racks that have been artfully arranged throughout the room.

I'm so overwhelmed, I have no idea where to begin.

"Don't stress out. Tenley is on her way. She's the best stylist in Hollywood, and Flynn told me to get only the best for you."

Hearing that makes me smile, even though I'm slightly annoyed that he left me alone with people I don't know on our first morning in LA. I try not to let it ruin my delight in the dresses, but it nags at me anyway.

The doorbell rings, and Addie goes to answer it while I tie the robe tighter around my waist. If I'd known this was happening first thing, I would've gotten up earlier and gotten dressed.

Addie returns with a tall woman with long dark hair and sharp dark eyes that immediately zero in on me. She's wearing super-skinny jeans with sky-high heels and a blue blazer over a formfitting tank. She carries a huge leather purse that might be Louis Vuitton. I'm immediately intimidated.

"Oh, he wasn't kidding. You're stunning." Tenley approaches me with an almost deranged look in her eyes that has me taking a step back.

"Don't be scared," Addie says, laughing. "She doesn't actually bite."

"You're flawless. I hope you're prepared to be the next It Girl, because the minute the paps get a look at you, they're going to be ravenous."

"Don't scare her off, Tenley," Addie admonishes. "Flynn wants her to enjoy this."

"Oh, we are going to enjoy this. We're going to enjoy it so much."

Despite my initial impression of her, Tenley is savvy and astute. She studies each gown with a critical eye and narrows the choices down to two that she feels best suit me. One is an incredible plum color that clings to my body, leaving nothing to the imagination. It's sexy and demure at the same time. I love it.

Addie gives me a thumbs-up when I emerge from the bedroom in the plum gown. "That is awesome."

"I agree," Tenley says, tugging at the bodice and checking the fit through my hips. "But I want to see the black one, too." She grabs the one she wants. "You're going to need help getting into this one."

I didn't have sleepovers. I didn't get a chance to play team sports. I spent one full year in high school. Other than the one time I wish I could forget but never will, I don't have any experience with showing my body to strangers, and I hesitate now.

Tenley immediately senses my hesitation and softens. "This is my job, honey. I'll be discreet. I promise."

Because Flynn has a right to his privacy, I take her into one of the guest rooms rather than his room. She makes quick work of getting me into the dress. This one shows a lot more of my breasts and my left leg, thanks to a split that extends nearly to my waist.

I tug on the bodice that refuses to budge any higher. "I don't know about this."

"Come out and see it in the mirrors. You might feel differently."

I doubt I will, but I follow her anyway.

Addie gasps. "Oh, wow, Natalie… The other one is pretty, but that one's a knockout. That's the one."

I stand before the double mirrors that came with the dresses, and immediately see what they see. This one is special. I barely look like me in it. I look like someone brave and fearless, someone who is perhaps on the verge of a whole new life she never could've imagined for herself.

"Will you be comfortable in it, Natalie?" Tenley asks. "If not, the plum is perfect on you, too."

"The plum is the safe choice." I can't stop looking at myself in the mirror. I can't believe that's me. I look like the women in the magazines after the award shows. "This one's a bit riskier."

"It is," Tenley agrees, "but it's still classy and sexy."

"Who is it?" Addie asks.

"Gucci Couture."

"Gucci," I whisper. "For real?"

"As real as it gets and one of a kind. And apparently made just for you."

"What happens at midnight?" I ask them.

In the mirror, I see them exchange perplexed glances.

"Do you mean tomorrow night?" Addie asks.

"I'm thinking about Cinderella and what happened when the clock struck midnight."

"In Hollywood," Tenley says, "that's when things are just getting interesting." She unzips the dress. "You're going to blow them away."

"You're going to blow *him* away," Addie adds.

I like the idea of that. "Okay, ladies. Gucci it is."

"Fantastic," Tenley says, her satisfaction apparent. "Now, about the shoes."

CHAPTER 16

Natalie

Tenley and Addie are long gone by the time Flynn finally returns. He's sweating profusely and breathing hard when he comes into the house. Sweaty has never looked so sexy to me.

"Oh, hey, you're up." He goes straight to the fridge for a bottle of water that he downs in three big gulps.

"I'm up, and I've been styled, too."

"Tenley was already here?"

"Yep. All done."

"What'd you pick?"

"I'll let you see for yourself tomorrow. They took it to do a few alterations, and she'll meet us in town tomorrow for finishing touches."

"You're happy with it?"

The question makes me laugh. "Yes, Flynn, I'm happy with the Gucci Couture dress I get to wear to the Golden Globes tomorrow night. And I'm *thrilled* with the Valentino sandals I'll be wearing with the one-of-a-kind dress."

"Good. As long as you're happy, I'm happy."

He says the words the way he always does, but something is different.

"Are you okay?"

"Yeah. Why?"

"You seem... I don't know... distracted or something."

"Sorry about that. I had a couple of work things crop up early, and they're on my mind. I'll shake it off in the shower and then make you some breakfast. Sound good?"

"Or I could make you some breakfast while you're in the shower."

"Only if I get to do the dishes."

"Deal."

"I'll be quick."

I want to know what happened, what has him so distracted, but I figure he'll share it with me if he wants to. I don't want to be, but I'm disappointed that something has changed since our wonderful afternoon and evening together yesterday.

As I withdraw a carton of eggs from the fridge and begin making an omelet with cheese, tomatoes and peppers that I slice into thin strips, I wonder if I did something wrong. But what could I have done in my sleep?

Oh God… Did I *say* something? Did I talk about the attack? I falter mid-slice, and a searing pain in my finger requires my full attention. Blood pours from the cut on my index fingertip. I run it under cold water, but the blood keeps coming. I can barely bother to focus on the cut with the possibility looming over me that I said something I didn't mean to in my sleep.

Flynn returns to the kitchen, where I'm applying pressure to the cut with a paper towel wrapped around my finger. "What happened?" He's wearing gym shorts and a gray T-shirt.

"Knife met finger. I wasn't paying attention." I can't even look at him as the fear pulses through me like a heartbeat, leaving me panicked and light-headed. As much as I don't want to know, I have to ask. "Did I do something or say something in my sleep?"

He looks up from examining the cut. His expression is nothing short of stricken. "What?"

"Something happened. You're different. I want to know if it was me. Did I say something or—"

"No, God no, Natalie."

"Then what's wrong? You came in from your run, and everything feels different. Have you changed your mind about wanting me here? Because if you have—"

"No." He puts his arms around me and holds me. I'm immediately enveloped in the fresh clean scent he brought with him from the shower. "I haven't changed my mind. I had a dream that upset me. I was up most of the night. I'm sorry I wasn't here when you woke up. I expected you'd sleep in, so I went for a run. I saw Addie coming in as I was leaving, so I knew she'd be here when Tenley came."

"Do you... Do you want to talk about your dream?"

"I... No, not really."

"You know how you tell me I can trust you?" He nods. "You can trust me, too. I hope you know that."

"I do, sweetheart. I trust you. If I didn't trust you, you wouldn't be here."

"You trust me with your home, and I'm honored by that. But that's just real estate. If you don't trust me with what's in here," I say as I rest my hand over his heart, "the rest doesn't mean very much."

He stares at me in that intense, all-consuming way of his. "You know how there're some things you said you won't talk about—ever?"

"Yes."

"I have a few things that fall into that category, too."

"Fair enough."

"Maybe someday we can have a 'share our secrets' conversation."

"Maybe."

"Until then, I'm kind of starving."

"Me, too."

He tends to my cut finger with antibacterial ointment and a bandage before we enjoy the omelets and toast as well as the fresh fruit he tells me he eats every day at breakfast. We discover we like our coffee exactly the same way—with cream and a quarter teaspoon of sugar. Real sugar. None of the fake stuff for us. After breakfast, I get dressed in shorts and a tank top.

Flynn hands me a tube of sunscreen. "You're going to need this. And this." He puts a ball cap on my head.

"How come?"

"We're taking a convertible and going sightseeing."

Yet another car awaits us in front of the house. This one, he tells me, is a Porsche Boxster. It's a beautiful bright red.

"Is it new?"

"Nope. It's a '96. First-generation Boxster. A bit of a collector's item."

"So this car thing goes back a while, huh?"

He opens the passenger door for me. "Um, yeah."

"Your sisters might be right about that twelve-step program."

"Again I remind you there are worse addictions I could have. There's heroin and cocaine and meth and booze and pills and women and—"

"All right. I get it."

He starts the car and hits the gas, launching us into motion. "I don't like to think of it as an addiction so much as a *collection.*"

"And how many cars make up this *collection?*"

"You want like a number?"

"Yes," I say, laughing at his obvious discomfort, "a number would be good."

"I don't know. Like sixty, maybe?"

"*You own sixty cars?*"

"It's a *collection.* Often, when you collect things, you have a lot of them."

"You have sixty cars."

"That's an estimate."

"So it could be more?"

"Or less."

I start to laugh, and I can't stop. He's so cute and funny and embarrassed.

"I give a lot of money to charities of all kinds, especially the starving-children kind, so don't tell me there're a lot of starving kids out there who could benefit from the money I spend on cars. I take care of them first."

I wipe laughter tears from my eyes. "It seems you may have mounted that ready defense in the past."

"All the time with my sisters, who think my collection is 'obscene.' They also like to remind me that he who dies with the most toys is still dead."

"I think I'm going to like them."

"They do help to keep things real for their little brother," he says with a chuckle. "I don't get away with much around them. And, seriously, starving kids are a thing for me."

"I already knew that about you."

"That's one thing they write about me that you can actually believe. I hate that there are kids going hungry in this land of plenty. It astounds me that a country with our resources can still have hunger problems. So I do what I can to shed some light on that issue."

"I have kids who come to school hungry in the morning. I keep breakfast bars and juice boxes in my desk drawer. They all know they're welcome to them and they don't have to ask first. It breaks my heart every time one of them visits that drawer. Even at that young age, they're embarrassed."

He grips the steering wheel so tightly, his knuckles turn white. "God, I hate that. It makes me fucking furious that hunger exists as a problem in this country."

"Me, too."

"If celebrity is good for anything, it's for stuff like this. I never miss a chance to raise money or draw attention to the fact that while we're sitting fat, dumb and happy in our big rich lives, kids are starving from coast to coast." He glances over at me. "I'm actually starting a foundation to put my money where my mouth is on this issue."

I'm immediately intrigued. "Really?"

Nodding, he says, "It bugs the shit out of me that so much of what I donate to other organizations goes to overhead. I hate going to fancy, costly benefits to raise money for hunger issues. Screw that. Hungry people don't need the glitterati having another black-tie event on their behalf. They need *food*. Right now. I want to work on ways to make that happen more efficiently. Develop networks across the country, tap into my own network for funding. That kind of thing."

"I love that idea."

"It's starting to look like it might happen. I've had a couple of recent meetings with people in LA and New York about what it would take to get it started. We're planning to begin in the biggest population centers and work our way out from there. We've got another meeting coming up soon."

"So many people would benefit from that kind of project."

"That's the goal. So am I forgiven for my car collection?"

"You didn't just make up the foundation idea hoping I'd forget about the cars, did you?"

His guffaw makes me smile. "Not hardly. I can provide witnesses that the foundation was in the works long before today."

"It's really admirable, Flynn. All kidding aside, I absolutely love the idea."

"I'm glad you do. I feel good about it."

"You should. When I first moved to New York, I gave money to every homeless person I encountered on the street until Leah told me I had to stop or go broke myself. It kills me every time I have to walk by someone who's living on the street, especially in the winter."

"I used to do the same thing when I was able to walk around in the cities."

I smile at him as we discover another trait we have in common. "So where are you taking me?"

"I figured since you've never been to LA before, we'd do a little windshield tour starting with Beverly Hills and Rodeo Drive. Then we'll hit the coast and check out Santa Monica and Malibu. Sound good?"

"Sounds great. Those are places I've heard about all my life but have never seen."

"The only thing is," he says tentatively, "we can't really get out of the car. I don't go out in public very often anymore without security. That's why we snuck into 'Wicked' after the lights went down and left before they came back up. After what happened in London last year—"

"What happened?"

He sighs deeply. "I was working a rope line at the UK premier of *Camouflage* when a guy pulled a knife on me. He managed to slice me in the ribs before security swooped in and took him down. It all happened so fast. Scared the shit out of me, though."

"How did I not hear about this?"

"We kept it hush-hush. The guy is mentally ill, and I didn't see any reason to make his life more of a living hell than it already is. Luckily, he just broke the skin, so they were able to bandage me up, get me a new shirt and send me on my way to the premier. But my hands shook all night."

"Jesus. You could've been killed."

"It really scared me, and I'm not easily scared. Ever since then, big crowds freak me out, and I don't go very many places without security except for in a car. It's the one time I get to be totally free, you know?"

"And I'm teasing you about your car obsession. It all makes sense now."

"It's okay to tease me. My obsession is totally over the top, and I know it."

We drive through Beverly Hills, where he shows me the stately home where he grew up. It's two stories, white sandstone with black shutters and a black iron gate.

"My folks have lunch plans today, or we'd stop by to see them. We'll see them tonight."

"I'm not exactly dressed to meet Max Godfrey and Estelle Flynn."

He laughs at that. "They don't stand on pretense, so you don't need to worry about what you're wearing when you meet them."

"Right. Whatever you say. You're their son. Of course it matters what I wear to meet them."

"I'm telling you, they aren't hung up on superficial crap. You don't have a thing to worry about where they're concerned. They'll love you."

"I like them already from the way you've described them."

"I like them, too. I enjoy every minute I get to spend with them and my sisters, even if the girls drive me nuts."

"They keep you humble."

"That they do."

We zip past his famous high school before taking a slow ride down Rodeo Drive, where all the top designers have storefront boutiques. The street is all about high style, from the buildings to the cars to the women on the sidewalk, and I'm mesmerized.

"Sorry we can't get out and walk around."

He sounds genuinely regretful, and I feel for him. "It's okay. I'm happy just to see it all."

We head out to the Pacific Coast Highway and check out Santa Monica and the famous Ferris wheel on the pier, before driving north to Malibu. I gaze longingly at the beach, which I can see is crowded on this particularly warm day. The Pacific stretches out before me, huge and blue and sparkling in the sunshine.

"What do you think of your first look at the Pacific?"

"It's beautiful."

"I grew up on these beaches, surfing and partying and generally loving life."

"Can you believe I've never stepped foot on a beach?"

"*Seriously?*"

"Believe it or not, there aren't a lot of beaches in Nebraska."

"Well, we have to fix that. Immediately." Reaching for his cell, he makes a call. "Are you decent?" he asks. "I'm going to stop by, and I'm bringing a friend who's never been to the beach before." After a pause, he says, "I know, right? I told her we have to fix that immediately. See you in a few, Mo."

I'm practically bouncing in my seat with excitement at the thought of going to the beach. A short time later, we pull into a driveway, and Flynn punches in a code to open the gates.

"Whose house is this?"

"Marlowe Sloane," he says casually, as if he's not speaking of one of the biggest female movie stars in the world.

"*The* Marlowe Sloane?"

"The one and only. She's one of my best friends." He shuts off the car in front of a dark wood bungalow that's much smaller than what I'd expect for a star of Marlowe's caliber. But then again, what do I know about movie stars and where they live? "Come on. Let's go check out Marlowe's slice of paradise."

With a quick knock, Flynn walks right into Marlowe's house. I follow, feeling hesitant and concerned that we might be bothering her. He, apparently, has no such worries.

"Mo! Where are ya?"

"Back here! Come on in."

The single-story house is much bigger than it seemed from the driveway and the view of the beach and ocean is nothing short of breathtaking. We find Marlowe on the back deck, stretched out on a lounge chair enjoying a cup of coffee. She's wearing aviator sunglasses and a barely there black bikini. Her gorgeous red hair is contained in a messy bun on top of her head.

She jumps up to greet Flynn with an enthusiastic hug. "This is a nice surprise."

"Mo, this is Natalie. Natalie, Marlowe, but we call her Mo."

She raises her sunglasses to the top of her head, exposing warm green eyes. The toothy smile that helped to make her a star is on full display as she hugs me, too. "So great to meet you. We've all been buzzing about Flynn's new girlfriend, and I was looking forward to meeting you this weekend."

"Thank you." I'm so starstruck, I can barely get the words out or process the fact that Marlowe Sloane considers me Flynn Godfrey's girlfriend. "I'm a huge fan."

"Aww, that's so nice to hear. Come in, have a seat, make yourselves at home."

"Your place is incredible," I say, immediately feeling foolish for stating the obvious. Like she doesn't already know that.

"Isn't it? It's my favorite spot on the planet. Any day I get to spend on this deck is my idea of heaven."

"You sure we're not disturbing you?" Flynn asks as he proceeds to make himself right at home as directed. He produces bottles of water from an outdoor fridge and hands one to me. We sit together on the lounge next to Marlowe's. I wish I could text Leah and tell her I'm at Marlowe Sloane's house in Malibu. She'd totally flip out. Maybe I can take some pictures for her before we leave.

"You're not disturbing me at all. I'm glad you came by." With the sunglasses back in place over her eyes, she returns to her lounge. "How are you feeling about tomorrow night?"

"Surprisingly nervous," Flynn confesses. For my benefit, he adds, "I've been nominated five other times, but I've never won."

"He's the front-runner this time, and rightfully so," Marlowe says. "If he doesn't win—"

Flynn holds up his hand to stop her. "Don't jinx me."

"Knock on wood to your heart's content, but I'm predicting a sweep for you this year—Globe, SAG, Oscar."

"For fuck's sake, Marlowe," he grumbles.

She unleashes a lusty laugh that makes me smile. It's that contagious. She makes a big show of knocking on the teakwood arm of her lounge chair. "Better?"

"Much."

I'm surprised and delighted to discover Flynn's superstitious side. I wouldn't have suspected it of him. He always seems so confident and in control.

"So, Natalie, tell me everything about you," Marlowe says. "I understand you're a teacher?"

"Yes, third grade in New York City."

"Good God, woman. How do you stand being with little kids all day?"

I laugh at her bluntness. "I got really lucky with a great group this year. I love them. I'm having a great time. I hear I can't count on that every year, so I'm enjoying it while it lasts."

"We should all be thankful for teachers like Natalie," Flynn says, directing a warm smile my way. "They're making sure the next generation doesn't grow up to be ignorant idiots."

"That's certainly one way to put it," I say, making them both laugh.

"Is it really true that you've never been to the beach?" Marlowe asks.

"Yep. As I said to Flynn, there aren't many beaches in Nebraska where I grew up."

"Well, let's get you down to the beach!" She jumps up again and goes to a cabinet where she pulls out towels for each of us. "Do you want to borrow a suit so you can swim? I have tons of them, and you're welcome to them."

"That's so nice of you, but I'll be happy to put my feet in the water."

"Good enough. Let's go."

She opens a gate on the deck that leads to stairs that go right down to the beach.

I'm giddy with excitement that I try to hide from them, lest they think I'm a silly nitwit. But when Flynn smiles at me, I realize I'm not hiding my giddiness from him. He sees right through me.

For the first time all day, he takes hold of my hand as we walk onto the warm sand and kick off our shoes.

"You can leave them there," Marlowe tells me. "No one will touch them."

I'm immediately in love with the feel of the sand between my toes, the scent of fresh air and other smells I've never experienced before. Overhead, seagulls dot the cloudless sky.

"You got a perfect day to see LA," Marlowe says. "January weather can be anything from sixty to eighty. You got the better end of it."

"It's beautiful and such a nice relief from the freezing cold in New York."

"I was there last week and froze my ass off. I don't know how people can stand a full winter there."

"You're going to think I'm a total weirdo, but I love the winter in New York."

"You're right—you are a weirdo."

I laugh as I fall a little bit in love with this incredibly successful woman who is so down-to-earth I feel like I've known her far longer than half an hour. She's put me immediately at ease, and I appreciate that more than she'll ever know.

We walk to the water's edge, where I splash gleefully in the frigid water. It's so cold, my feet quickly go numb. But I couldn't care less about that as I gaze out at the massiveness of the Pacific. Light, rolling waves deliver the surf gently to the beach, another sight that leaves me mesmerized.

Flynn comes up behind me, resting his hands on my shoulders. "What do you think?"

"I'm in love—with the beach and with Marlowe." I look back at him. "Thank you for this."

"My pleasure."

"This has been an incredible week, Flynn. Thank you for all of it."

"It's been just as incredible for me. I should be thanking you." He wraps his arms around me from behind, and I lean back against him, enjoying the sun and the water and the rare feeling of serenity that has been so elusive in my life.

CHAPTER 17

Flynn

Who am I kidding thinking I can end this thing with Natalie after the weekend? Every second I spend with her has me wanting a lifetime of her sweetness and infectious joy. Watching her dance in the ocean for the first time packed an emotional wallop for me, knowing I had done that for her. I had given her a wonderful new experience.

Now, holding her in my arms as we look out on the endless blue ocean, the thought of not being with her anymore makes me feel sick and sweaty. The fear reminds me of the aftermath of the knife attack in London last year, as if something has changed that can never be undone.

I'm tormented by the raging internal debate about what's best for her versus what I want more with every breath I take. I want her—desperately and fiercely. Talking to her about my hunger foundation and hearing her thoughts fed my soul, which has been hungry for a woman who feels the same compassion I do for people in need. I've had too many vapid, gold-digging, career-climbing women pass through my life not to recognize a true gem when I find one.

And Natalie is the most flawless of gems.

She tuned right into my disquiet this morning, calling me out on the fact that something is different. She pays attention to me—the real me—in a way that no one else before her ever has, even the woman I married.

When Natalie has had her fill of the freezing cold Pacific, we walk up to join Marlowe on the towels she's spread on the sand. The warm sunshine beats down on us, but the cool breeze coming off the water makes for a comfortable temperature.

I enjoy watching the two women talk to each other like old friends rather than new acquaintances. I love that Marlowe is so warm and unaffected by her massive fame. We appreciate that in each other, and though we were together a long time ago for a brief time, we quickly discovered we're much better friends than lovers.

I wonder if Natalie would be annoyed to learn that Marlowe and I were once more than friends. No one really knows that. It happened early in our careers, long before we were stalked by reporters. We went to great lengths to keep our relationship private, but a few people found out about it anyway. The paparazzi speculate endlessly about what really goes on between us.

"What're you thinking about over there, Flynn?" Marlowe asks me.

"I'm just enjoying the beach, but we should head back soon. We're taking my parents to dinner for their anniversary tonight." It occurs to me that I should've invited Marlowe, who loves my folks and doesn't have much in the way of family of her own. "You want to come?"

"I don't want to crash a family party."

"You *are* family, Mo. Please come if you'd like to. I should've thought of it before now."

"Sure, I'd love to help my adopted parents celebrate another year of wedded bliss. Thanks for the invite."

"I'll ask Addie to add to the reservation." I pull out my phone and dash off a quick text. Addie writes right back. *Will do!* "All set."

"I'm so jealous of his Addie, I could eat my heart out," Marlowe says to Natalie. "Did he tell you I basically gave her to him?"

"No, but she did," Natalie replies.

"You need to get an Addie of your own," I tell her. We've been having this argument for years.

"I know, I know. One of these days."

We shake out the towels and walk back to the house. Natalie asks to use the bathroom, and Marlowe tells her where it is.

"Be right back," Natalie says as she leaves the room.

The moment we're alone, I look to my longtime friend for a reading on what she thinks of Natalie.

"Stunning and delightful," Mo says quietly.

A knot in my chest seems to unfurl at her approval, that she sees what I do in Natalie.

"She's young but surprisingly mature," Marlowe adds.

"She's been through a lot. I'm not so sure I'm good for her."

"Yet you're in love."

I shrug. "I think I have been since the second I first saw her a week ago today."

Mo squeezes my arm. "Nothing has to be decided right now. It's only been a week."

"I know." I agree with her despite my misgivings. The more time I spend with Natalie, the deeper my feelings for her become—and I suspect she would say the same about me. Though we've known each other only a week, a lot has happened in that time. I'm old enough and experienced enough to know this is different. "I already feel more for her than I ever did for Val."

Marlowe's mouth falls open, but before she can respond, Natalie returns.

I'm well aware that I've dropped a bomb on my friend, but all my attention is on Natalie. "Ready?"

"Whenever you are."

I kiss Mo's cheek. "Thanks for having us."

"My pleasure. And it was great to meet you, Natalie."

"The thrill was all mine," she says with that adorable smile I've grown to love.

Marlowe laughs and hugs her. "See you guys at dinner."

When we're back in the car and on the way to my house, Natalie says, "So did you two talk about me while I was in the bathroom?"

"Only a little. She really likes you."

"She's so cool. I was trying so hard not to act like a total dork around her."

"I never would've known you were dorking out inside. You were very composed."

"It was all an act."

"You might be in the wrong business with those skills." I can think of a million places I'd like to take her for a late lunch, but the potential hassle has me going home instead. We make sandwiches that we take out to the pool and pass a relaxing afternoon enjoying the sun and each other.

My middle-of-the-night decision to end things with her seems ridiculous now. I'd much rather live without the things I dreamed about than without her. She's become as essential to me as the air I breathe. "Make room. I'm coming over."

Natalie

I scoot over to allow Flynn to join me on my lounge. Whatever was troubling him earlier seems to have passed. That he wants to be close to me fills me with relief and the jolt of excitement I've come to expect when he's near. He's very smooth as he arranges things so I'm lying in his arms, our legs intertwined and his lips a heartbeat away from mine.

"Hi," he says with the sexy smile that makes me weak.

"How's it going?"

"Never been better. This has been the nicest day I've had in longer than I can remember."

"Me, too. Nicest day ever."

"I'm dying to kiss you."

"I'm dying to kiss *you*."

"Really?"

I roll my bottom lip between my teeth and nod.

He cups my cheek as he brings his lips down on mine. The kiss begins slowly with just the gentle glide of lips, but the fire that simmers between us erupts as it always does. His hands are everywhere as his tongue takes possession of my mouth. He shifts ever so slightly, moving me so I'm on top of him.

The position is new to me, but he knows just what to do. With his hands on my bottom, he pulls me in tight against the hard length of his erection.

I try to get closer, and he groans, a deep rumble that vibrates against my lips.

Then his hands are on my breasts, stroking and rolling my nipples. My bikini top disappears while I'm lost in the kiss.

Flynn breaks the kiss and draws my nipple into his mouth, tugging and sucking until I'm nearly delirious from the desire that has me pressing against him, trying to get closer. All I care about is being as close to him as I can get.

"Flynn…" My hands are buried in his hair, holding him to my chest as he continues to suck on my nipple.

"What, honey?"

"I want…"

"Tell me. Anything. I'll give you anything you want."

"More. I want more."

"I want to touch you." His hand moves from my bottom to the front, pressing between my legs. "Here."

"Yes. *Yes.*"

He tugs on the bow that holds my bikini bottoms together, and the fabric drops away, leaving me bared to him. "You're a goddess, Natalie. A fucking goddess." His fingers slide into the dampness between my legs, and he knows exactly where I need him to touch me. I feel like I'm going to break into a million pieces.

"Natalie… I want to put my fingers inside you. Can I do that?"

"*Yes.*" I love that he asked first, that he's careful with me. It shows me how much he cares.

His fingers slide inside me, and I want to scream from the pleasure that seizes me. Then he curls them and pushes on a spot I didn't know existed. I detonate, nearly pulling the hair from his head as I come hard. I float down from the incredible high to realize he's trembling and his fingers are still buried deep inside me.

"Flynn…" I lick lips that have gone dry. Flattening my hands against his chest, I feel his heart pounding. His eyes are closed, and his jaw is doing that pulsating thing it does when he's trying to control himself. "You're making me forget all about my vows to never do any of this until I'm married."

"You're making me think about Vegas."

"Vegas?" I have no idea what he means. "What about it?"

"Wedding chapels. They have a lot of them there."

How is it possible to laugh when I'm lying naked in the arms of a man—willingly—for the first time in my life, with his fingers still inside me?

"Natalie…" His eyes are still closed. "I want you so badly. I know it's happened so fast and I need to be careful with you."

"You have been." I kiss him, and his eyes open to meet my gaze.

"I'm afraid I'm going ask for more than you want to give and scare you in some way. You push every button I have."

"I'm being terribly unfair to you."

He withdraws his fingers, making me gasp from the pleasure of his touch, and then shocks me when he brings them to his mouth to lick them clean. I've never witnessed anything so sensual or earthy. "No, you're not. You're teaching me that waiting for what I want builds character. You're showing me that anything worth having is worth waiting for. And you're showing me that it's possible to care for someone else more than I do for myself."

His words touch me profoundly. "Flynn… I care just as much for you. I hope you know how badly I want what you want."

An odd look crosses his face, but it's gone as quickly as it came. "We should get cleaned up for dinner." He helps me back into my suit, his fingers skimming over my skin repeatedly until I'm covered with goose bumps.

We walk inside together, and he starts the shower for me, but he doesn't join me this time. While I wash and condition my hair, I think about what happened just now and how it felt to be held and touched by him. There were no demons, no fears or worries. There had only been pleasure unlike anything I could've imagined before him.

I'm officially wavering. My plan to avoid men and sex has been shattered by one incredibly handsome, sexy, kind, sweet man, but I can't get past the fact that I've known him only a week. How could years of resolute determination be undone so quickly?

I need Leah, but she's working a day shift at the bar. When I get out of the shower, I go directly to my phone to text her. *Can you talk?*

Yeah, it's dead here. Call me.

"Hey," I say when she answers.

"How's LA? Tell me everything."

"I'll tell you everything as soon as you tell me how my baby Fluff is doing."

"She's been a raging bitch all day because her mama went away and left her."

"Don't say that about her!"

"She's in her usual cranky mood, but we're hanging in there. Now tell me about LA!"

"It's awesome. I met Marlowe Sloane today."

I have to hold the phone away from my ear when she screams. "*Shut the fuck up!* What was she like?"

"Imagine the coolest person you've ever met."

"Oh my God, I'm so jealous, I'm seething. First Flynn and now *Marlowe.* This is too crazy. Are you having so much fun?"

"We are. It's been... Leah, I'm so confused."

"How come?"

"I want to have sex with him."

"*Halle-freaking-lujah!* It's about fucking time!"

"It's been a *week*, Leah."

"He's *Flynn Godfrey*, Natalie."

"That's got nothing to do with this. I don't care what he does for a living. I care about *him*."

"If you care about him, Nat, there's nothing wrong with sleeping with him."

I don't bother to mention that I've already slept with him, because I know that's not what she means.

"Nat?"

"I'm here."

"Look, I don't know your whole story, but I've managed to put two and two together to get that you went through some sort of trauma. I'm sorry for whatever happened to you. But if you care about this guy, really care for him and he cares for you, there's nothing at all wrong with *being* with him. You know that, right?"

"I do. I know." For some reason, tears are rolling down my face. Frustrated by them, I brush them away.

"Are you okay?"

"Yeah, I think I am."

"I'm here if you need a friend."

"Thank you. You said exactly what I needed to hear."

"That poor guy won't know what hit him when he gets pent-up Natalie in his bed."

"On that note…"

Her laughter rings through the phone and makes me smile.

"We're going to dinner with his family."

"Jesus H. Christ! *You're going to meet Max and Estelle?*"

"Yep," I say, laughing at her reaction. "It's their anniversary."

"I think I just passed out over here. Have a fantastic time and don't do anything I wouldn't do, which gives you permission to do anything and everything."

I'm still laughing as we say our good-byes. She promises to give Fluff lots of kisses from me. I dry my hair and take the time to apply eyeliner, shadow and mascara before finishing up with lip gloss. I put on the same black dress I wore a week ago tonight for my first date with Flynn. As I take a final look in the mirror, I think about how I asked him to take me home after we left Leah's bar.

I'm thankful he talked me out of that, because I would've hated to miss out on what's happened since.

A soft knock on the door has me taking a deep breath to prepare for the evening ahead. "Come in."

He steps into the room wearing a gorgeous gray suit with a black button-down shirt and no tie. He's so beautiful.

"Natalie… You look lovely."

"Funny, I was just thinking the same thing about you."

He holds out his hand to me. "Shall we go?"

I take his hand. "Flynn."

"What, honey?"

"Later, after we get back, I think I might want to try."

His body goes rigid with tension. "By *try*, you mean…"

"I want to have sex. With you. Tonight."

Flynn releases a deep breath. "And you expect me to be able to function tonight after you've told me that?" He puts his arms around me and brings me in close to him, so close I can feel how aroused he is.

"I don't know if I can."

"Sweetheart." He drops his head to my shoulder. "Please don't do this because you feel you have to. You don't. I meant it when I said I'm in no rush. In fact, I think we should wait. More than anything, I want you to be sure."

"I am sure."

"Can I call in sick to my own dinner party?"

"Absolutely not. Let's go."

CHAPTER 18

Natalie

I take him by the hand and pull him behind me as I leave the bedroom.

Outside, I discover tonight's vehicle is a silver Mercedes sedan.

"Is there a car for every occasion?" I ask after we're on our way.

"Just about."

"Where do they come from?"

"I have a garage nearby and another in town. Plus the cars in New York."

I run my hand over the black leather on the passenger door. "I like this one."

"Consider it yours whenever you're in LA."

"I don't have a driver's license."

"*What?*" He nearly drives off the road.

"Flynn! Watch where you're going!"

"You really don't know how to drive?"

"I'm sure I could if I had to, but I don't have a license. I never have." I don't tell him that I left home before I got a license, that I was too busy trying to feed myself and get through school to be bothered with something like driving.

"Do you want a license?"

"I suppose I'll get around to it at some point, but right now I don't need it. I can walk everywhere or take the subway."

"I'm going to need to teach you to drive. You know that, don't you?"

"You need to, huh?"

"I do."

"I might let you, but only if I can drive the Bugatti."

"Oh, um, well…"

I bust up laughing at his stammering reply. "Relax. I'm just kidding. I'd probably wet my pants from fear of wrecking that gorgeous car."

"Oh thank God. I was trying to figure out how to tell you no freaking way."

"Anything you want, Natalie," I say in a mocking tone. "Anything except my precious Bugatti."

"You're a brat," he says on a rumble of laughter.

"At least you're not thinking about what I said earlier."

He blows out a deep breath. "How did I end up so outmatched by you, Natalie Bryant?"

Pleased to have gained the upper hand, for a minute or two anyway, I try to prepare myself to meet his family.

Tuned in to me as always, he reaches for my hand. "Don't be nervous. They're going to love you."

I'm not sure what I was expecting when Flynn asked Addie to set up a dinner for his family, but it definitely wasn't Frankie's Steakhouse.

"Welcome back, Mr. Godfrey," the valet says. "Nice to see you again."

Flynn shakes his hand. "You, too, Anton." I watch him slip the young man a bill. "Take good care of my baby."

"Always do. How's the Bugatti?"

"It's loving life in New York."

"Aww, man. That's too far away. Have a nice dinner."

"Thanks again." Flynn rests a hand on my lower back and ushers me into the restaurant.

There's nothing particularly posh about it, but the atmosphere is warm and welcoming. An older man with wispy white hair and a cane hobbles over to greet us. "Flynn, so nice to see you, son."

Flynn hugs him. "You, too, Frankie. Thanks for putting this together for us tonight."

"Always our pleasure to have the family here."

"This is my friend, Natalie. Nat, this is Frankie, a Hollywood legend."

He bows gallantly over my hand. "I don't know about the legend part, but I do cook a mean steak."

"That you do," Flynn says. "Is everyone else here?"

"They're all in the back room waiting for you."

"Join us for dinner?"

"Wouldn't miss it for the world. I'll be right in."

Keeping his hand on my back, Flynn doesn't appear to notice all the people who notice him as we make our way through the dining room. "My parents had their first date here. It's been their place ever since. Every important event in the Godfrey family is celebrated at Frankie's."

That they are faithful to their traditions and their friends endears his parents to me before I even meet them.

"Frankie is one of my dad's best friends. They've had a running poker game with a bunch of other guys for fifty years. His wife died a year or so ago, and he hasn't been doing very well. Dad's been worried about him."

"It'll lift Frankie's spirits to be with friends."

"Hope so." He opens a door to a room full of people, who turn to greet him en masse. A bevy of kids surrounds him, forcing him to let go of my hand. "Whoa! Easy, savages. You're going to scare off my friend."

"Unca Flynn, pick me up," a towheaded blond boy demands.

Unca Flynn does what he's told, seating the boy on his shoulders. "Natalie, this is Mason. He's four."

The little boy holds up four fingers, and I fall in love with his adorable little face. The sight of Flynn holding him on his shoulders does crazy things to my insides. He'll make a wonderful father someday. Yikes! Where did that thought come from?

Before I can process the odd direction my brain has taken, we're surrounded by gorgeous women, all of whom are tall, fair and athletic looking. None of them looks like their brother.

"Natalie, these savages are my sisters—Aimee, Ellie and Annie. Ladies, this is Natalie. Try not to be yourselves and scare her off."

"Shut up, Flynn, and get out of our way," Annie says.

Each of them hugs me and welcomes me, and one of them—it might be Ellie—asks what a nice girl like me is doing with an asshole like Flynn.

"Nice, El," Flynn says with a laugh. "Thanks a lot."

They all talk at once, overwhelming me with questions and excitement and a sense of belonging I hadn't expected to feel with them.

"Ladies," a stern female voice says from behind them. "Back off and let me say hello to Natalie."

They step aside, and there is Estelle Flynn, and my brain goes completely blank as she approaches me.

"Mom, this is Natalie. Nat, my mom, Estelle."

She embraces me in a cloud of delicious-smelling perfume. "It's lovely to meet you, Natalie. We're so glad you could join us tonight."

I know I should say something, anything, but I'm completely starstruck.

Flynn's hand on my back steadies me, and I find my voice. "It's so nice to meet you, Ms. Flynn. Thank you for having me."

"It's our pleasure, and, please, call me Stella."

I'm going to faint. Surely I can't remain standing in the presence of such an amazingly accomplished woman. She's stunningly gorgeous with pale blonde hair that's beautifully styled into a coif that highlights her pretty face. I try not to stare at her, but it's hard not to. She's magnetic and warm and smiling widely as she hugs her only son.

"So nice to see you, my love."

"You, too, Mom. Happy anniversary."

"Thank you for that and for throwing this together."

"Addie gets all the credit."

"Yes, I do," Addie says from where she's standing with Marlowe.

"Let me see my boy." His booming voice precedes Max Godfrey as he approaches Flynn and greets him with a bone-crushing hug that Flynn enthusiastically returns. Max is about the same height as Flynn and has a mane of salt-and-pepper hair and Flynn's gorgeous brown eyes. He's every bit as good-looking as his son, who closely resembles him. Looking at him is like seeing Flynn in thirty years.

"Hi, Dad."

Max releases Flynn and places both hands on his face. "You're looking sort of ugly, boy. What're they feeding you in New York?"

Since there's not one single thing about Flynn that's ugly, I can't help but laugh at his father's comment.

"Dad, this is Natalie. Nat, my dad, Max, who never minces words."

I'm treated to the same sort of hug he gave his son, but not quite as bone crushing. I quickly discover it's one thing to see pictures of Max Godfrey in magazines. It's another thing altogether to experience him. I've never met anyone more instantly magnetic in my life, except for maybe his son.

"Natalie," he says, his hands on my shoulders, "welcome to our family."

"Dad—"

"Hush, son. Let me talk to your girl." He slides his arm around me and deftly wrests me away from Flynn.

Despite my usual wariness around strangers, there's no way to be anything other than charmed by Max Godfrey, who takes me to the bar. "What can I get you, honey?"

"White wine would be great."

He orders Scotch, and with our drinks in hand, he says, "Tell me all about yourself."

"Not much to tell other than I'm from Nebraska originally and teach third grade in New York now."

"And how did you meet Flynn?"

I tell him the story of our encounter in the park last weekend, and he howls with laughter at the part where Fluff bit his son.

"It really wasn't funny."

"Oh yes, it is." He wipes his eyes. "You've probably seen the way people fawn over him, so the thought of a twenty-pound dog getting the better of him is definitely funny."

"Well, as Fluff's mother, I wasn't amused by her bad behavior. Luckily, Flynn wasn't hurt too badly."

"Dad, quit hogging my date," Flynn says as he joins us.

"We're just getting to know each other. Leave us alone."

Flynn puts his arm around me. "No chance of that."

"He ruins all my fun."

I'm absolutely in love with Max Godfrey, and I can see where his son gets his considerable charm and good humor.

I meet Flynn's brothers-in-law—Trent, who is married to Aimee, and Hugh, who is married to Annie. I learn that Ellie, who is single, works as an executive for Quantum, Flynn's production company. Annie is an attorney. And Aimee owns a dance studio. I'm introduced to Flynn's nephew Ian, who is eleven and does bear a striking resemblance to his famous uncle, as well as his nieces India and Ivy, ages seven and nine, all of whom are Aimee's children. Unlike their cousins, they have dark hair and eyes.

We're seated for dinner, and Hugh ends up on my left and Flynn is on my right, locked in conversation with his parents. Across from me are Addie and Marlowe, and I'm thankful to have familiar faces nearby.

"Don't let the Godfreys overwhelm you," Hugh says in a conspiratorial whisper. "They're harmless underneath it all."

"Good to know, thanks."

Without missing a beat in his conversation, Flynn finds my hand under the table and gives it a squeeze. The gesture fills me with warmth and a sense of security I haven't experienced since I left home. It's beginning to feel like I belong to him and he belongs to me, and I like that feeling. I like it a lot.

A sense of serenity overtakes me as I sit back and watch this amazing family interact with each other. There's lots of laughter and teasing and talk about Flynn's foundation. Each of his sisters apparently plans to play a role, as do his parents, which seems to please him greatly.

As we're served a delicious Caesar salad that is made tableside, talk turns to the Globes.

"You're going to win," Ellie says bluntly, earning a scowl from her brother. "What? I'm just stating the facts. No one else came close to what you did in *Camo*, and everyone knows it."

"I agree," Max says.

"As do I," Frankie adds as he joins the party.

"Me, three," Marlowe says, smiling as she raises her glass in tribute to Flynn.

He covers his ears and pretends he can't hear them. I adore this superstitious side of him.

Dinner consists of prime rib, huge baked potatoes and asparagus that melts in my mouth. It's the most delicious meal I've ever had, a thought I share with Frankie, who beams with pleasure.

"Thank you, honey." To Flynn, he adds, "You need to keep this one. She's top shelf."

"I couldn't agree more," he says with a warm smile for me that makes my insides quiver with awareness.

"He never brings anyone to family things," Hugh says for my ears only. "Ever."

As I smile at him, I decide Hugh is my new best friend.

After Frankie's attentive staff clears the dinner dishes, Flynn releases my hand and stands, glass in hand.

His sisters groan in unison.

"Here we go," Annie says.

Ignoring them, Flynn focuses on his parents. "I just want to say happy anniversary to Max and Stella. You guys have made marriage look easy for forty-four years, and we should all be so lucky to have what you have. We love you both very much."

"He's good," Annie says begrudgingly as she raises a glass to her parents, who are positively beaming after their son's toast. "We gotta give him that."

"He's a *pro*-fessional," Aimee says to laughter from her sisters.

Flynn just rolls his eyes at their teasing as he retakes his seat and reaches for my hand immediately.

"That was lovely," I tell him.

"Thank you."

"Thank *you*, son," Stella says. "I agree with Natalie. That was lovely."

"Did he tell you he's Mom's favorite?" Ellie asks. "Little baby Flynn could do no wrong in Mom's eyes."

"That's because he was well-behaved and sweet from the second he was born," Stella replies with a saucy smile. "All of you could take a lesson from him."

While his sisters make gagging noises that have the kids giggling, Flynn smiles at their antics. "Yes, you should follow my lead."

Cloth napkins come flying across the table, all of them aimed at his head.

"Girls!" Stella gazes at me apologetically. "We have a guest tonight, and we're showing her our very worst."

"This is nowhere near as bad as we can get," Aimee says, making everyone laugh.

"That is so true," Max says. He's obviously enjoying every second with his boisterous family. "Just ask Frankie. He's seen us at our best and our worst."

Frankie holds up his hands. "I see no evil, I speak no evil."

"A wise man," Flynn says, his arm around his niece India, who has worked her way onto his lap.

We're served delicious chocolate cake and offered coffee and after-dinner drinks.

Flynn orders coffee drinks for both of us. "You'll love this," he assures me.

And he's right, I love the smooth heat of the Bailey's, something I've never had before with coffee.

The party begins to break up when Annie says it's time to get her kids home to bed. The littlest one, Garrett, is asleep on Hugh's shoulder. The adorable blond boy has his thumb planted firmly in his mouth as his father rubs his back.

Looking at them, I'm hit with an undeniable sense of yearning. What would it be like to watch the man I love hold my sleeping child? I've never had much of a hankering for children of my own. I've been too busy trying to piece together a life and make a living to think that far ahead.

But now...

Flynn's arm encircles me, and I turn to him. "Ready to go?" he asks.

"Whenever you are." My heart beats erratically at the thought of what will happen when we get back to his house.

We say our good-byes, and his parents tell me they'll see me tomorrow at the Globes. I'm happy to know I'll see them again soon.

"Thank you for including me tonight. Your family is wonderful."

"They do have their moments," Stella says as she hugs me. "We're absolutely thrilled to meet you, Natalie. I hope we'll be seeing a lot of you."

"Mom..."

"What? I only speak the truth." She kisses her son on the cheek. "And don't 'Mom' me."

"Let's get out of here before they make you change your mind about me."

"Thank you for a wonderful evening," I say as he leads me from the room.

"Our pleasure, honey," Max says.

Once again, Flynn turns heads as we walk through the dining room on our way to the exit. His car is waiting outside the door, and he helps me in. I watch him press another bill into Anton's hand. Everything is handled so smoothly and efficiently that I can't help but be impressed.

"I hope you had fun," Flynn says when we're on the way home. He took hold of my hand the second we pulled away from the restaurant.

"It was great. Your family is amazing, but of course you know that."

"Yeah, I do, even if they drive me bonkers sometimes."

"I liked Hugh. He seems really nice."

"He's a great guy. So is Trent. The three of us play a lot of basketball when I'm in LA. I tell my sisters they finally became useful to me when they got me a couple of badly needed brothers and some nieces and nephews."

"They must love that."

"You know it's all in good fun, right? There's nothing—and I do mean *nothing*—I wouldn't do for any of them, and vice versa. The three of them would kill for me, and a few times, they nearly have."

"I totally got that. You can give each other a hard time because underneath it all is a foundation of love and respect that comes right from your parents."

"Yes," he says gruffly, glancing at me with an odd expression.

"What? Did I say the wrong thing?"

"No, sweetheart, you said exactly the right thing. The last woman I dated... She met Annie and Aimee once and thought they were shrews because of the way they talk to me. She didn't get it, and you do. You get it."

I certainly understand better than most the way family dynamics can make you or break you. He has the former. I got the latter, but being around the Godfreys tonight has restored my faith in the institution of family, even if I got the short end of the stick.

The ride home is quiet, but a low hum of tension exists between us now that we're alone again. By the time we get home and into the house, I'm a mess of nerves and fear. What if I can't do it? What if I freak out or have a panic attack or—

"Hey, Nat," he says softly. "Come over here and talk to me for a minute." He leads me to the sofa and takes a seat next to me, turning to face me.

"Is something wrong?"

"No, sweetheart, everything is perfect. Tonight was so special for me, to be able to introduce you to the people I love the most and to watch you fit right in with them like you belong with us. My parents loved you, just like I knew they would." He slides his fingers through my hair, making me lean in to get closer to him. "I've been thinking about what you said earlier all night long. It's a wonder I could string together two coherent words."

"I didn't mean to distract you."

"Yes," he says with a low chuckle, "I think you did mean to distract me, and you've distracted me thoroughly. But here's the thing… I think we ought to wait a while before we make love. A week ago, you were very resolute in your feelings on the matter, and I would hate to be responsible for you doing something you're not ready to do only because you think it's what I want."

"I want it, too. It's not just you."

"I know, sweetheart, but still… I think we should wait. I could feel your nerves take over the second we were in the car on the way home."

"I'm nervous. I won't deny that, but that doesn't mean I don't want to."

"There's a lot of really fun stuff we can do without doing everything. I want you to be sure, and I promised I'd respect your boundaries. I'm so afraid of doing something to frighten you, Natalie. You have no idea how afraid I am. The more time I spend with you, the more essential you become to me." He gathers me into his arms. "I'm not going anywhere. We've got all the time in the world to let things happen when we're both ready."

"I want to be normal," I whisper. "I want to be like any other woman who's found a man she cares about."

"You are perfect exactly the way you are. Everything you've been through has made you strong and resilient and incredibly mature for your age. I admire all those things about you so much. And when the time is right for us, we'll know it. There won't be any fear or nerves or worries about the past. It'll be just you and me and everything we feel for each other."

"I feel like this has to be a dream. I never expected to find someone like you, who understands me so profoundly."

"I feel exactly the same way. After having been with a lot of women who were far more interested in what I could do for them than they were in me, it's a breath of fresh air to find someone like you and to feel understood by you."

"If we're going to wait, does this mean you don't want to sleep with me?"

"I would love to sleep with you, if you'll have me."

"Yes, Flynn, I will have you." I smile at him, surprisingly relieved by the reprieve. While I was determined to try, I'm okay with waiting, too.

He kisses me, and I can sense the control he's exerting over himself as he keeps the kiss sweet and undemanding. "Let's go to bed and watch a movie."

"Okay."

We go through the motions of getting ready for bed and come together in the center of his big bed. He's wearing pajama bottoms that look new, leading me to wonder what he normally wears to bed. I'm wearing a tank with lightweight pajama pants. I've taken the time to brush my hair until it's smooth and silky.

He runs his fingers through it appreciatively.

My entire body is alive with awareness of him. "I thought we were going to watch a movie."

"We are."

"Umm, well…"

"I'd much rather look at you than at a movie."

I put my arms around him and sink into a kiss that starts off slow and sultry and accelerates into hot and bothered in a matter of seconds. By the time we come up for air, our legs are intertwined, his hand is full of my breast, and his erection is throbbing against my belly.

He withdraws from me, seeming disgusted with himself.

"Flynn?"

"I'm sorry. I gave you that whole speech about waiting, and then I practically attack you."

"Um, I believe we attacked each other."

"Still…"

"I know you're older than I am and far more experienced and all that, but everything that happens between us is because we *both* want it. Not just you. I want it, too. I want *you*."

"I want you, too, Nat. So badly. I've never wanted anyone more than I want you. But I don't just want you in bed. I want all of you. I want to make this work with you. With us."

"I want that, too. All of it."

"Maybe I shouldn't sleep with you if I can't keep my hands off you."

"You mentioned there were other ways to have fun without doing everything."

"I did say that, didn't I?"

"Uh-huh." I run my finger over the well-defined muscles in his abdomen and watch in fascination as they quiver under my touch. I love that I can make that happen. "What did you mean?"

He blows out a long deep breath, his torment apparent. "I have to be honest with you."

"I wouldn't want you any other way."

"I'm afraid to touch you the way I want to. I'm afraid I'll get carried away and forget what we agreed to." He buries his face in the curve of my neck. "You make me so crazy, Natalie."

I wrap my arms around him, and discover his entire body is trembling. "Could I touch you?"

"You can do whatever you want to me, whenever you want."

I begin by running my hands over his back, hoping to calm and soothe him. But judging by the way his fingers dig into the muscles of my back, I'm failing spectacularly.

Bending over him, I kiss his chest. His hands burrow into my hair, his grip causing a bite of pain that has me shuddering with desire. Even in this position, at my mercy, I can feel him fighting to maintain control of himself. I work my way down to his stomach, running my tongue over the sharp outlines of his abdominal muscles.

"*Natalie…*"

"Yes?"

"Come up here."

"I'm enjoying it down here."

"*Fuck.*"

I smile as I continue to kiss and lick him. I have no idea what I'm doing, but because he seems to be reacting positively, I keep it up until I'm hovering above the waistband of his pajama pants, where the outline of his erection has my full attention. As I try to summon the courage to take the next step, he grasps my hand and places it on top of his hard length.

"Show me how to touch you," I say.

Groaning, he moves his hand and mine up and down, faster and more aggressively than I would've done on my own. Then he pushes his pants aside, freeing himself from the fabric.

God, he's huge, and I'm immediately intimidated and curious and overwhelmed by the idea of taking him inside me.

"Christ," he mutters as our hands move together.

His skin there is surprisingly soft, and my curiosity grows as he hardens and lengthens before my eyes. I'm curious about things that have terrified me for years. I want to know him in every possible way, and the thought of that would've made me sick only a week ago.

Before I can overthink it to death, I bend over him, push his hand away and take him into my mouth.

"*Motherfucker,*" he whispers harshly. "Natalie, you can't... Ahhh, Jesus."

Once again, I haven't the first idea what I'm doing, but the tight grip he has on my hair tells me I'm doing something right.

"Use your tongue," he says.

I run my tongue around the head. "Like that?"

"Yes. God, *yes. Nat...*"

"Tell me what to do. Show me how."

His chest is heaving as he looks down at me. "Open your mouth wider. Take as much as you can." He curls my hand around the base. "Stroke me at the same time."

Despite my best efforts, I can take only about half of him, which has me wondering how I'll ever accommodate him when we actually have sex.

Out of nowhere, a flashback surfaces. Of being forced to perform this act. Of being choked and suffocated and…. I pull back from Flynn, covering my mouth to suppress a sob. My chest aches as I try to erase the memories of the past from my present, which has nothing at all to do with that horror.

Flynn sits up and puts his arms around me. "Breathe, honey. Come on." He gives me a little shake that rouses me from the swamp of painful memories. "Breathe."

I draw in a deep, shuddering breath. "I'm sorry."

"Don't ever feel you have to apologize to me for anything." He gathers me up and arranges me on his lap, my head on his shoulder.

I deeply resent the tears that roll down my cheeks. I hate that the past still rears its ugly head to remind me I'm broken inside, even when I think I've healed. I'm despondent to discover otherwise eight long years later.

Flynn rocks me gently, his lips soft against my forehead. "Natalie, please don't cry. Everything is just fine."

"No, it isn't! Don't you see? If I can't do that, how will I ever do anything else?"

"Nat… This is the first time you've tried. Maybe it didn't work this time. Maybe it'll be okay the next time or the time after."

"What if it's never okay? What if I can't ever be with you that way?"

He takes hold of my chin, imploring me to look at him. "I love you. I'm crazy in love with you. We will get there together. One day at a time, until the ghosts from the past have been exorcised and there's only you and me."

It has been a very long time since anyone said those words to me. At first, I can only cry harder as his words fill the empty places inside me.

"I love you, Natalie. I've loved you since the first second you looked up at me from the ground in the park. I've loved you since Fluff bit me and since I chased you from the park. And if it takes the rest of our lives, we'll get there. I have no doubt about that."

"You can't know that." I wipe away more tears. "You don't even know what happened to me."

"No, I don't. If you want to tell me, I'll listen and I'll hurt and I'll rage, and absolutely nothing will change for me except I'll probably love you more than I already do."

"I don't want to tell you. I don't want to ever talk about that again."

"Okay." He kisses my forehead and my nose and then my lips. "The reason I have no doubt we'll get there is because we've already gotten close. What we were doing this time was different, and it triggered a memory for you."

"I wanted to do that. I wanted to give you something special."

"You give me something special just by being here with me. You give me something special every minute I get to spend with you."

"I want to be what you need."

"You are, sweetheart. You're absolutely perfect for me." He lies back, bringing me with him. His hand slides over my hair. "You're so strong and resilient. I have total faith in you. Everything is going to be okay."

His words lull and calm me. They give me hope.

"Close your eyes and get some sleep. We've got a big day tomorrow."

"Flynn?"

"Yeah?"

"I love you, too."

His arms tighten around me. "There you go, giving me something special again."

CHAPTER 19

Flynn

I hold her as she sleeps, but rest proves elusive for me. I'm overwhelmed with a thousand different emotions that churn through me relentlessly. I'm relieved to have been able to share my feelings with her, and I'm enraged by what she was forced to endure. If the man who hurt her is still alive, I want to find him and kill him with my bare hands.

In that moment, I acknowledge there's nothing I wouldn't do for her, including commit murder if it would give her the peace she deserves so greatly. I'm also forced to acknowledge that even though I've said the words before, I've never been truly in love. Not like this, anyway. This is different from anything I've ever experienced. It's deeper and richer.

I think about some of the lines I've delivered in movies while playing a man in love and how silly they seemed to me at the time. Now I look back at them with new perspective, because there's nothing silly about my feelings for Natalie. And I realize I have a naughty little twenty-pound dog to thank for bringing her into my life. That she could've walked right by the park that day and I never would've known that everything I ever wanted was passing me by...

She loves me, too. I'm relieved and tormented by what I'm keeping from her. But what does it matter? If I'm willing to live without some things in order to have others, well, so be it. Life is about compromise and finding middle ground. I can do this for her, or so I tell myself.

In truth, I honestly don't know if I can live permanently outside the lifestyle I chose for myself more than a decade ago. But I'm willing to try if it means having a chance with Natalie. After what happened tonight, it's apparent to me that there's no way I can share that lifestyle with her.

And if the choice is to live without the lifestyle or live without her, well, there's no choice at all. She is essential to me in a way that nothing and no one else has ever been. I will do whatever it takes to make this work with her, even if it means giving up something that has meant a lot to me.

It won't be like it was with Val. I was new to the lifestyle then and still testing my own limits. I pushed her too far. I know that now. She exacted her revenge by sleeping with the director of the film we were shooting at the time. I exacted mine by sleeping with her friend. The entire incident was ugly and unfortunate. With hindsight, I can acknowledge my share of the blame for the disaster our marriage became at the end.

It will be different with Natalie because I already love her more than I ever loved Val, who was ambitious to a fault, willing to stop at nothing to get what she wanted, which was superstardom. She certainly succeeded at that, but at what cost? At least I didn't sell my soul for my career the way she did for hers.

I don't like to think about her or the difficult, humiliating end to our marriage. The divorce got so ugly that I publicly renounced the institution of marriage altogether, a move my mother later told me hurt her deeply. Those were some of the darkest days of my life, and Hayden is right to remind me of how bad it got.

I have no desire to ever go through anything like that again, which is why I would give up the lifestyle before I'd try to force it on Natalie, who wouldn't be able to handle it. With her in my arms in the dark of night, a decision is made, and I'm able to relax enough to sleep.

I'm tortured in my sleep again with erotic dreams that put me in the dungeon with Natalie, where she's a willing partner in every scenario I dream up. She loves it as much as I do. She loves to be dominated and forced to withhold her pleasure until I give her permission to take it.

I have her bent over the spanking bench, her hands are tied and her bottom raised, tempting me to do anything I want to her—and there are so many things I want to do. She is mine, completely and totally. She trusts me implicitly. I love her madly. I crave her sweet body and want to stretch the boundaries of my own creative imagination to take us places I've never been with any other partner.

I bring my hand down on her soft white skin and the slapping sound resonates through the cavernous room. Natalie gasps and then moans when I rub the red handprint. Pain becomes pleasure with the stroke of a hand. I do it again and again and again, until her bottom is cherry red and her breathing raspy and uneven. Her pussy glistens and moisture coats her inner thighs, which tells me she's enjoying this every bit as much as I am.

After coating my fingers with lubricant, I stroke her back entrance, drawing a prolonged groan from her. "What's your safe word?"

"Fluff," she says breathlessly.

"Fluff what?"

"Sir. Fluff, Sir."

I swallow a lump of emotion that comes with hearing her call me that, from knowing I own her body and soul. It's the greatest gift anyone has ever given me. "That's my girl." I drive my fingers into her bottom and remove them just as quickly, replacing them with the largest plug I own. When she resists the intrusion, I spank her again, which distracts her long enough to press the widest part of the plug past her resisting muscles.

She cries out from the pleasurable pinch of pain, and I stroke her clit to take her mind off the pressure of the huge plug in her ass.

I give her a minute to breathe and adjust, but not too long to slip out of the scene. Taking her by the hips, I drive my cock into her pussy and have to give myself a moment when her muscles contract and my balls draw up tightly. I close my eyes, summoning the control I pride myself in, wanting to see this through to a finish neither of us will ever forget.

It's a tight fit thanks to the large plug in her ass. It's the last step before I take her there with my cock. The pleasure is sublime. It's hot and thrilling and deeply satisfying because I love her more than my own life. I give it to her hard and fast, forcing her to take all of me, and then I give the plug a brisk tug, and she screams.

Her pussy contracts around my cock as she comes hard, so hard I see stars from the power of her release. Knowing I've taken her there is all I need to let go, to find my own pleasure, although that's too tame of a word for how it feels to be in this moment with the woman I love.

I wake to realize it's happened again. I've dreamed my way to orgasm. I'm sweating and trembling from the sheer power of the connection I've found with her in my dreams. Moving carefully, I disentangle myself without waking her.

For a long time, I sit on the edge of the bed, running my fingers through my hair repeatedly, trying to find some sense in what's happening. I'm crippled by the fear that this will be my new reality—nightly wet dreams about what I can't have while the woman of my dreams sleeps in my arms.

Natalie

The next day unfolds like something out of a fairy tale that begins with waking up in Flynn's arms and continues when Addie arrives with hair and makeup people who treat me like a princess for the next couple of hours. They seem to have a vision, so I let them do their thing and try to relax.

Flynn is on edge about tonight, so I encourage him to go for a long run. He comes back to find my hair in huge rollers that have him laughing as he reaches for his phone.

"Flynn! No pictures!"

"Why not? You're too cute."

"No pictures."

"Spoilsport."

We take lunch out to the pool deck while Addie and the others eat inside.

"No woman should ever let the man in her life see the prep for an event like this," I say between bites of the delicious chicken salad Addie had delivered.

He goes completely still and gives me that intense look that always evokes a strong reaction within me. "Am I the man in your life, Natalie?"

"I believe you have been since you chased me down last Saturday and insisted I go out with you."

His smug grin is full of male satisfaction. "I did do that, didn't I?"

"You've made a complete nuisance of yourself, and I've enjoyed every minute of it."

"Me, too." He leans over to kiss me, and one of the curlers smacks against his face, making him laugh. "That's very sexy, sweetheart."

"I'm told the end result will be worth it."

"Mmm," he says against my lips. "I can't wait."

Flynn

I have never been so dazzled by anyone as I am by Natalie in sexy, slinky black Gucci Couture with her hair flowing down her back in big, sexy curls—and I can only see the back of her. A twinge of fear knots in my gut when I realize the paparazzi are going to eat her up.

I've instructed my publicist, Liza, to give only her first name and no other information about her to anyone who asks—and they'll be asking. I'll do whatever I can to protect her privacy, but that doesn't keep me from feeling like a selfish bastard for wanting her with me so badly on what could be the biggest night of my career.

When I step into the master bedroom, Addie and Tenley are still fussing over her. "How's it going in here, ladies?"

Natalie turns, and I'm left breathless by the sight of her. She's positively radiant and so fucking beautiful.

Tenley gives Natalie a careful hug and whispers a few words that leave Natalie smiling.

"Thanks, Tenley," I say as she goes past me on her way out.

"My pleasure. Entirely my pleasure."

"You look fantastic," Addie says to Natalie. "A vision in black. You'll be on all the best-dressed lists."

"Only thanks to you and Tenley and the others."

"Have the best time ever."

"Thanks again, Addie. For everything."

I bestow a warm smile on my assistant as she comes toward me.

"She's a keeper," Addie whispers as she walks past me and out the door.

Of course I already know that. I've known it from the beginning. As I approach her, I can see that her eyes are fairly sparkling from the excitement. "There simply are no words to properly tell you how incredibly beautiful you look."

"So do you." Her hands lay flat upon the lapels of my tuxedo coat.

"I'm afraid to touch you. You're a goddess come to life before my very eyes."

"Would you do me a favor?"

"Anything."

"Take a picture for Leah? I promised her I would."

"I'd be happy to, but first you need the finishing touches."

"What finishing touches?" She turns to consult the mirror. "Tenley said I was all set to go."

I remove a blue velvet box from my suit coat pocket and reach around her with it in my hand. "She didn't know about these finishing touches."

"*Flynn!* What is that?"

"Open it and find out."

"I can't. My hands are shaking."

"Then allow me."

She turns to me, watching as I open the box to reveal the elaborate diamond necklace and matching chandelier earrings, compliments of my brother-in-law Hugh, an exclusive Beverly Hills jeweler. "You... Those... Those aren't real, are they?"

"Sweetheart..." I laugh at her sweet innocence. "Of course they're real."

Natalie takes a step back. "I can't wear them. What if I lose them?"

"You won't lose them. Now stand still and let me put the necklace on you."

"Flynn, seriously... I don't need this."

Could she be more adorable and sweet? "I know you don't, but I need to give it to you."

I secure the necklace and place a kiss on the back of her shoulder, which is bare. "You do the earrings." I hand them to her and watch her fingers tremble as she puts them on. "Now let me see."

Her hands drop, and I admire my handiwork. "Absolutely perfect. I'll be the envy of every guy there tonight."

"This has already been the most exciting day of my life. Thank you."

"Thank *you*. I'm thrilled to have you here with me."

"How're you holding up?"

"Okay. I guess. I hate that I really want to win this time. That makes me feel so shallow when there are far bigger problems in the world than whether Flynn Godfrey will finally win a major acting award. I have them for producing, but not acting."

"How about we put aside all those other problems in the world and give Flynn Godfrey one night to be a self-absorbed movie star who deserves to win big?"

"Well, when you put it that way... Are you all packed up?" I told her earlier that we wouldn't be returning to the house tonight.

"Yep. My bag is in your room."

"I'll grab it."

"Flynn?"

"Yeah?"

"The necklace and earrings are lovely. Thank you so much."

"My pleasure, sweetheart. Be right back."

CHAPTER 20

Natalie

All the way into town in the back of a limousine that Flynn assures me he doesn't own, I'm constantly checking to make sure the priceless necklace is still there. I can't believe he did that.

"It's fine. It's not going anywhere, and if it does, it's insured, so don't worry."

"If it's so valuable it needs to be insured, I will worry."

He takes hold of both my hands to stop me from continuing my regular checks of the necklace. "When we get there, the reporters are going to stop me for interviews and general B.S. When they ask me who you are, I'm going to just say you're my friend Natalie, okay?"

"Sure, that's fine."

"You are so much more than that to me, but they don't need to know that. Not yet, anyway. They'll ask who you're wearing, and it's okay to reply, but you can ignore the rest of the questions that'll fly our way."

"Okay."

"I'll be right there with you the whole time, so don't let it freak you out."

"I won't." I tug my hands free of his hold and wrap them around his arm, resting my head carefully on his shoulder. "Don't worry about me. I'm planning to enjoy every second of it."

"Did you send the picture to Leah?"

"Uh-huh. She wants to see one with you in it, too."

"Take a selfie."

"Good idea." I withdraw my phone from the clutch Tenley chose to go with my dress and set up the selfie. "Ready?"

"Whenever you are."

We laugh our way through a series of selfies until we finally get one that doesn't look awful. I shoot it off to Leah.

She writes right back. *You look amazing and I'll be watching on TV. Good luck to Flynn!*

"Leah wishes you good luck tonight."

"That's nice of her. How about sending it to your family?" he asks. "Wouldn't they like to see what you're up to?"

I say the first thing that comes to mind. "They don't have smartphones." In truth, I don't know what kind of phones they have these days, but I do know for certain they wouldn't care where I am or who I'm with. Not after I ruined all their lives.

Praying he'll drop it, I stare out the window as the scenery rushes by. I love the palm trees and the bright blue sky. Addie and Tenley were talking about how it "monsooned" last year on Golden Globes day and what a challenge the rain presented to getting everyone into the theater without looking like drowned rats.

"Did I say the wrong thing by mentioning your family?" he asks quietly.

"No... I... We... I don't talk to them."

"Ever?"

This is the last thing I want to talk about now or ever, but I suppose it's inevitable. "No."

"How long has it been?"

"Eight years."

"That would've made you fifteen, Natalie."

"I know how long it's been." I turn to him and can see he's agitated by this information. "Can we please not talk about this?"

"Natalie—"

"Please, Flynn. I really don't want to talk about it. It's part of the stuff I never talk about." I can see him struggling with the need to pursue it further. "Please?"

"Okay, but I hope you know there's nothing you could tell me that would change how I feel about you."

"I do know, and I appreciate that more than I can ever express, but I've put all that behind me a long time ago. That's where I want it to stay."

An uncomfortable silence descends upon us as we join the line of limos heading for The Beverly Hilton. I hate that my unfortunate past has come back to haunt this most important evening for him.

I reach for his hand. "Hey."

He smiles at me, but it's not that big megawatt Hollywood smile I've grown to love so much.

"Good luck tonight. No matter what happens, I think you were the best of the best. By far."

He leans across the seat to kiss me. "Thank you for that and for being here with me."

"Thanks for bringing me. I'll never forget any of it."

"Hopefully, this is just the first of many such nights for us."

"That would be nice." I can't yet conceive of how this life he has in mind for us would work, but I don't need to figure that out now, not when there's a red carpet to walk on the arm of the man I've fallen in love with.

A roar from the crowd gathered outside the hotel greets Flynn when he emerges from the limo. He reaches for me and helps me out before he waves to acknowledge the fans.

"We love you, Flynn!"

He smiles and waves some more before we proceed toward the hotel, stopping to chat with TV reporters.

One of them, a willowy blonde, greets him with a kiss on his cheek. "We're here with Golden Globe nominee Flynn Godfrey. How are you feeling tonight, Flynn?"

"I feel great. It's always nice to be nominated by the Hollywood Foreign Press."

While he talks to her, I stand by his side, taking it all in as stars I recognize from TV and movies walk by. I try not to stare like the awkward newbie I am, but it isn't easy.

"We're hearing that this is going to be your year. Anything to say to that?"

"I've had a great year. No matter what happens tonight or in the next couple of weeks, I have no complaints."

"Who's with you tonight?"

"My parents are here somewhere, and this is my friend Natalie."

"Nice to meet you, Natalie."

"You, too."

"Who are you wearing tonight, Natalie?"

"Gucci Couture."

"Well, good luck to you tonight, Flynn. We'll be pulling for you."

"Thanks, Debra. Nice to see you."

Reporters covering the red carpet stop us four more times, each of them asking similar questions. The last one tries to get Flynn to spill the details about us, but he deflects with his usual brand of charm and humor. As we walk away from him, I can tell Flynn is annoyed.

"Sorry about that," he says.

"It's fine. You handled it perfectly."

"They think they have some sort of right to the details of my private life just because my job is public."

"Oh my God," I whisper. "There's Johnny Depp!"

His low rumble of laughter wipes the tension from his face. "Do I need to be jealous?"

"Not at all, but that's *Johnny Depp*." I sure do wish I could share this night with my sisters, who would never believe the people I'm seeing in person. It's the who's who of Hollywood, all in one place. And I'm right in the middle of it wearing Gucci Couture and dripping in diamonds on the arm of Flynn Godfrey, who loves me. Someone please pinch me so I'll know this is really happening.

Flynn waves Johnny over, and they do the man-hug routine. "This is my girlfriend, Natalie. She's a big fan."

To my profound surprise, Johnny Depp *hugs me, too*. I'm going to faint. Seriously. I'm not sure which is more exciting—meeting Johnny Depp or hearing Flynn introduce me as his girlfriend.

"That's long enough," Flynn growls when Johnny shows no sign of ending the hug.

"He's a buzz killer, eh, love?" Johnny asks.

"Um, in this one particular case, yes, he is."

The two men laugh and shake hands before Johnny kisses my cheek. "You're a lucky man, Godfrey. Good luck tonight."

"Thanks, Johnny. See you inside."

"That was the second-coolest thing that's ever happened to me," I tell Flynn when we continue on our way into the hotel.

"Dare I ask what took first place?"

"Meeting you, of course."

"That's a very good answer, sweetheart."

"You called me your girlfriend just now."

"Did I?"

"You know you did."

"I must really love you to be telling people you're my girlfriend." He puts his arm around me and kisses my temple.

I feel like I'm floating through a dream as we walk into a massive ballroom filled to overflowing with Hollywood's glitterati. Everywhere I look, I see someone I recognize, and in many cases, people I've admired most of my life. It's surreal in every sense of the word.

Flynn is greeted warmly by everyone, and it's obvious he's well liked by his peers, most of whom wish him well tonight. He introduces me to everyone as Natalie, just Natalie. When Meryl Streep compliments my dress, I'm so tongue-tied I can barely squeak out a thank-you.

We're seated up front with the other nominees. As producers on the nominated film *Camouflage*, Marlowe Sloane and Hayden Roth are at our table. I haven't forgotten the way Hayden talked to me the day we met, but he seems slightly less scary in a tuxedo with his mane of dark brown hair combed into submission. He's every bit as handsome as Flynn, but I don't feel a shred of attraction to him. First impressions are lasting, and he's going to have to work really hard to convince me he's worth my time.

Marlowe hugs me like we're old friends and raves over my dress. She's in white, which is offset by the light tan from yesterday. Her long red hair has been gathered into an elaborate updo, and she's glowing from excitement.

"This is going to be a big night for Quantum, boys," she says. "I can feel it in my bones."

Flynn scowls at her. "Shut up, Mo. You're going to jinx us."

She rolls her eyes at him. "It's too late to change the outcome now, so calm yourself."

Flynn glares at her as he knocks on the tabletop.

I love that he's superstitious and doesn't take anything for granted. That underlying humbleness is one of his most attractive qualities.

The show begins with great fanfare as Tina Fey and Amy Poehler take the stage to welcome everyone. I wonder if Leah has seen us on TV yet, and my belly flutters at the thought of how many millions of people are watching at home. The ladies are hysterical as they roast the nominees.

"And check out Flynn Godfrey," Tina says disdainfully. "They finally did something about his chronic ugliness. I mean, really, how can someone so ugly be such a huge star?"

My heart stops at the mean-spirited commentary until I realize Flynn is cracking up laughing next to me.

"And that smile," Amy adds. "So gross, right?"

"Ugh," Tina says. "How anyone can kiss that face. It's truly a face only his mother could love."

Estelle Flynn's laughing face appears on the screen, and the entire theater joins in as she blows a kiss.

Flynn shakes his head at the two women, who are congratulating each other on their successful bit.

I'm not quite sure what comes over me when I lean over to kiss his "ugly" face. I realize the whole theater saw it on the big screen when their applause nearly deafens me. Flynn gifts me with a huge smile that tells me I did exactly the right thing.

The evening takes off from there with award after award, touching acceptance speeches and musical entertainment. I'm dazzled by the gowns, the gems, the gorgeous women and the handsome men.

I can feel Flynn's body tightening with tension as we get closer to his category—best actor in a motion picture, drama. He leaves me only for a few minutes to present the best screenplay award with Marlowe. They are greeted with enthusiastic applause as they take the stage.

Watching them together, I'm struck by what a gorgeous couple they would make. The same chemistry they've demonstrated time and again on the big screen is readily apparent as they banter their way through the award presentation.

He returns during the next commercial break, stopping along the way to shake hands with friends. The stage managers call for quiet as we return from the commercial to the segment that will include Flynn's category.

I reach for his hand and cradle it between both of mine.

He gives me a squeeze and a smile that tells me he appreciates my support. I want him to win so badly, my stomach is filled with nervous butterflies.

Finally, it's time, and Dustin Hoffman takes the stage to announce the nominees for best actor in a motion picture, drama. When I hear Flynn's name called, it takes a second to sink in that he actually won. Oh my God, he *won!* And then he's leaning over to kiss me before heading for the stage.

I'm on my feet clapping and crying and hugging Marlowe, who is also crying.

"About fucking time," she says for my ears only.

The applause goes on long enough that Flynn finally calls an end to it by beginning to speak.

"Thank you to the Hollywood Foreign Press for this incredible honor." He pauses for a look at the slim marble pedestal with the golden globe on top and shakes his head as if in disbelief. "I'm really proud of the work we did on *Camouflage,* and I want to thank the injured servicemen and women at Walter Reed who were so gracious in sharing their stories with us." From memory, Flynn lists each of them by name and rank, drawing resounding applause. "I owe my sincere thanks to the entire team at Quantum as well as my personal team." The only names I recognize on the long list of people he mentions are Addie and his publicist, Liza. "I'd be remiss if I didn't express my profound thanks to Max

Godfrey and Estelle Flynn. I'd be nothing without them, and I love them and my annoying sisters with all my heart. Ian, India, Ivy, Connor, Mason and Garrett— Uncle Flynn loves you. Now go to bed. I want to thank Natalie for being here tonight and for changing my life so completely."

He blows me a kiss that brings new tears to my eyes.

"Finally, we're all deeply indebted to the servicemen and women and their families who sacrifice so much so the rest of us can live in peace and prosperity. Please don't ever miss a chance to thank them for all they do or to give a veteran a job. It's the least we can do for what they do for us. Thank you again for this amazing award."

We're on our feet again, cheering as he leaves the stage, and then Marlowe is hugging me and squealing with excitement. "I'm so damned happy for him. He is long overdue. You know what this means, don't you?"

"What?"

"He's the frontrunner for the Oscar now."

"Oh my God, that's crazy." I wonder how I'll ever stand the suspense of waiting to hear if he's nominated for an Oscar and then to know if he wins.

He's already told me he'll be gone awhile if he wins tonight, so Marlowe, Hayden and I settle back into our seats to enjoy the last few awards of the evening. Flynn returns to the stage a short time later and is joined by Marlowe and Hayden and the cast of *Camouflage* to accept the award for best motion picture, drama.

Hayden does the talking this time, thanking the Hollywood Foreign Press as well as the Quantum team and everyone involved in the making of the film. "Flynn, my oldest and dearest friend, you were beyond amazing in this film. You were our heart and soul, and I can't thank you enough for everything you did to keep me sane during the shoot."

Flynn pats his friend on the back. He's glowing with pleasure at seeing their hard work rewarded.

The show comes to an end, and I'm beginning to wonder what I should do, when Flynn comes for me, taking me by the hand and leading me backstage to be with him for the press interviews. Before we proceed to the pressroom, he takes me into a dark corner of the stage and hugs me.

I wrap my arms around him, overcome with the emotion of the moment—the thrill, the excitement, the pride.

He takes a deep breath that he releases slowly, and I suspect it may be his first deep breath of the day.

"I'm *so* happy for you."

"Thank you for being here with me." He punctuates his words with a sweet kiss that makes my head spin with the pleasure and connection I share with him.

"Let's get this press shit over with so we can party."

"I'm with you."

He tucks my hand into his arm. "Yes, you are."

Every reporter asks about me, but he deftly dodges the questions and keeps the focus on the film.

An hour later, we're finally free to leave for the parties, which are epic and packed with celebrities. Everywhere I look, I see another famous face. Flynn is an attentive date, introducing me to everyone, including Elton John, making sure my glass is never empty and that I get some food. Though the party we're currently at is insanely crowded, a table is made available for us so we can sit and have something to eat.

"What a night," I say to him when we're alone for the first time. My legs and feet are aching from standing so long in heels.

"It's so much better because you're here."

"I loved being here, and I couldn't be more excited if I'd won the award myself."

"We've got to make an appearance at two more parties, and then we're out of here. Okay?"

"Whatever you want. It's your night. I'm just along for the ride."

He smiles and kisses me right there in front of everyone.

I've never been happier in my life than I am in that moment.

CHAPTER 21

Flynn

What a night. Only now that I have the statue in hand can I admit to myself how badly I wanted it. And having Natalie with me to share in the magical evening only makes it that much sweeter. Liza has been texting me relentlessly, wanting to know more about Natalie, who made herself into a star with the kiss after Tina and Amy's good-natured ribbing.

Everyone wants to know who she is and what she means to me after I further "outed" us during my acceptance speech. But I stick to the script and decline to answer questions about her or us. I instruct Liza to do the same and tell her to stop texting me and go have a drink.

She's not amused.

We finally meet up with my parents at the third party, and they're thrilled with my big win. They greet Natalie with hugs and treat her like she's already a member of our family. I love them for that and a million other things. I love that I've made them proud, which has always been so important to me.

The four of us spend an hour together celebrating and getting drunk on champagne. I've never seen Natalie so excited and animated. She's loving every second of her big night in Hollywood, and it's thrilling to watch her reactions to every new person she meets.

I wanted to claw out Johnny Depp's bedroom eyes when he hugged my girl for a little too long before, a reaction I'm not proud of in hindsight. He's a friend and didn't do anything wrong. But I hate that Natalie finds him attractive. And yes, I know that's totally unreasonable because most women—including all three of my sisters—think he's irresistible.

As the clock strikes two a.m., my mother decides she's had enough. "Take me home, Max."

"As you wish, my love." He winks at me. "And that, right there, is the secret to a long and happy marriage."

They offer to drop us back at The Beverly Hilton, where I've booked a two-bedroom suite for the night. In light of my colorful dreams the last couple of nights, I plan to make use of that second room. I can't sleep next to her and not touch her. I'm not made of stone.

While we wait for my dad's driver to bring their car around, I discover I'm more than a little drunk and Natalie isn't in much better shape. She's leaning into me with a sort of reckless abandon that I find wildly attractive. Who am I kidding? Everything she does is wildly attractive to me.

And my parents are tuned in to the connection between us. I've noticed them watching us with barely restrained glee. They know this is different as much as I do.

Dad's driver pulls up to the main door of The Beverly Hilton. They get out to kiss us both good night.

"Proud of you, son," my dad says gruffly as he hugs me.

His praise brings tears to my eyes. "Thanks, Dad."

"And Natalie, you look positively gorgeous tonight," Max says when he hugs her. "I hope we see you again very soon."

"I hope so, too, Mr. Godfrey."

"Max. Please call me Max."

"Thank you, Max."

We hug and kiss my mom and wave them off as they leave. I take Natalie's hand and lead her into the lobby, which is still full of people even in the middle of the night. I'm waylaid by well-wishers and requests for autographs, which I take care of quickly so I can get Natalie upstairs.

We have the elevator to ourselves, so I sag against the back wall and she sags against me. I wrap my arms around her waist and nuzzle her neck.

"My feet are killing me. I haven't worn four-inch heels in, well, ever."

"I'll give you a foot rub."

She groans in anticipation, and that quickly, I'm rock hard.

"You were the most beautiful woman in that room tonight."

"Sure I was," she says with a laugh.

"You're the only one I noticed." I hold up the award that hasn't been out of my hands all night. "Hang on to this for me?"

"Sure…"

I love her gasp of surprise when I sweep her up into my arms and carry her down the long hallway to our suite.

"Flynn… What're you doing?"

"Your feet hurt. I'm just giving you a lift. Can you grab the keycard out of my shirt pocket?"

She roots around inside my suit coat until she finds the key, which she hands to me with a goofy smile.

"You're drunk."

"I'm not drunk. I'm pleasantly buzzed."

I put her down outside the door and use the keycard to gain entry. She goes in ahead of me, and I love her reaction to the elegant suite. "This is awesome!"

"I'm glad you like it. You'll find your bag in that room." I point to the larger of the two rooms, which I've designated as hers. Addie has seen to all the details, as always.

Natalie kicks off her shoes and groans again from the relief of being free of the shoes. That groan of hers is an incredible turn-on. "Will you unzip me?"

I cross the room to her, where she stands before the window that looks out over Beverly Hills and Hollywood in the distance. I find the zipper tab under her right arm and ease it down below her hip, nearly drooling at the sight of the silky, smooth skin that comes into view as the dress falls open.

I'm unable to resist temptation, which is how my right hand ends up encircling her ribs. Her head comes back to rest upon my shoulder. "Flynn…"

"What, sweetheart?"

"Take me to bed. Please?"

"You have rules, honey. Rules that are important to you."

"They were my protection. I don't need them with you."

"I don't want you to hate me after."

"I'll never hate you. I love you too much to ever hate you."

"What happened last night…"

She turns to me then, looking up at me with those expressive eyes that act as mirrors to her soul. "I'll be all right because it's you, and you love me."

Her faith humbles me. "Yes, I do. I love you so fucking much, it's not even funny." *I'm willing to change who I am for you*, I want to add, but I don't. I've said enough.

"Show me."

I push the dress off her shoulders, and it pools at her feet, leaving her in only a black strapless bra and matching thong. Taking her hand, I help her step out of the dress and then sweep her up again to carry her to the bedroom. She makes for a very sweet bundle, especially when she loops her arms around my neck and lays her head against my chest.

I set her down next to the bed and begin removing the studs that hold my shirt together.

Natalie pushes my hands aside and takes over. When she removes the last one, she drops them into my hand and then pushes my shirt apart, nuzzling her face into my chest hair. I'm dying for her. I'm on fire. But before I can give in to the desire that has overtaken us, practicalities must be seen to.

"Hold on just a second, sweetheart."

"What's wrong?"

"Not a thing. But we need protection. I'll be right back." I kiss her and hurry into the other bedroom. I've tucked an unopened box of condoms into my bag just in case we needed them. I didn't expect to need them tonight, though. I take one second—and only one second, because she's waiting for me—to summon the control I'll need to make this good for her. My biggest fear is sparking her greatest fears. I can't let that happen, not when she has entrusted me with something so precious.

I pull off my jacket, shirt and pants, leaving the tux in a pile on the floor in my haste to get back to her. In the other bedroom, I find her stretched out on the bed, her head propped up on her hand. She's lit candles on the bedside table that cast a warm romantic glow over the room. She pats the bed next to her, and I'm lost. Any remaining hesitation melts away in the face of her blatant invitation. I can only hope neither of us will regret this tomorrow.

"Are you sure you're not drunk?"

"Very sure."

"And you'll remember this in the morning?"

Her sexy, husky laugh goes straight to my cock. "I sure hope so."

She's fucking amazing, as if all the dreams I've ever had have come to life in one perfect woman who seems to love me as much as I love her. I push aside the nagging thoughts about what I'm giving up to be with her. There's no place for those thoughts in this room. Not now. Not tonight.

I crawl onto the bed and come down next to her. She reaches for me, and our lips find each other in a greedy, hungry kiss that sends my need straight into the red zone. The heat that's been building between us since the minute we met threatens to boil over as we cling to each other, our tongues battling fiercely.

She tastes like wine and honey and the sweetness so uniquely hers. I could drown in that sweetness, and I'd die happy. I've never wanted anything or anyone the way I want her. I want to possess her, own her, make her mine and love her so thoroughly, she'll never look at another man for the rest of her life.

Behind her back, I release the hooks that hold her bra together and push it out of my way, impatient to have her completely bared to me. The thong comes off next, and I take a moment to appreciate the spectacular sight of Natalie's naked body, stretched out on the stark-white comforter.

I can't decide what I want to touch first. Every inch of her appeals to me—from full luscious breasts with berry-red nipples to the hollow of her belly to the jut of hipbones, to long sexy legs and the sweet pussy that lies between them, beckoning me.

Kneeling between her legs, I begin at her feet with the promised massage that draws the sexiest moans from her lips. When both feet have been seen to, I pull her legs up and over mine, opening her to me. I want to tell her to put her hands over her head, to grasp the headboard and not let go, but tonight is not about domination. It's about love and respect. It's all about her.

I bend over her to take her nipple into my mouth, tugging and sucking until it stands up tall. Then I give her other breast the same attention.

Natalie writhes under me, her back arching, silently begging me for more. Hooking my arms under her legs, I lift them up and out, opening her to my tongue. If I live to be a hundred years old, I'll never forget the deep, needy sound she makes the first time my tongue connects with her clit.

All I hear is pure female satisfaction and a cry for more. I'm happy to deliver. With her legs now propped upon my shoulders, I open her to my tongue, licking her from front to back before settling in to suck on her clit. She comes immediately, writhing and crying out as I hold her in place, giving her my tongue over and over again until her thighs are quaking and she's hovering on the verge of another release.

I drive my fingers into her, taking her up and over again. "Ahh, God, Natalie. I want to feel that sweet pussy come all over my cock. I want to feel that so badly." I know a moment of panic when I wonder if I've offended her with my blunt language. "Sorry, I shouldn't have said it like that."

"I love how you tell me what you want. Will you always do that?"

I swallow hard, trying to rid myself of the guilt that struggles to the surface, reminding me there's a lot I haven't told her. "Yes, I promise. I'll always tell you." My hands are trembling as I roll on the condom. I want this to be so perfect for her—for both of us. It's been a long time since I've felt this kind of nervous anticipation about sex. But nothing has ever mattered as much as this does, as she does.

I'm out for perfection tonight. Nothing less will do. I come down on top of her, resting my hands on either side of her gorgeous face.

"How you doing?" I ask.

"Never better."

"You're really sure about this, Nat? We don't have to—"

She squeezes my lips with her fingers and raises her hips, letting me know exactly what she wants from me. I feel like I should've taken more time preparing her, but I can't wait any longer.

I take myself in hand and slide through the dampness between her legs. It's all I can do not to come when my cock connects with her hot wetness for the first time. I bite my bottom lip and pray for mercy as I begin to push into her, going slowly and watching her intently for any signs of distress.

But all I see in her is the pleasure. Her eyes widen and her lips part, and I push in deeper, wanting all of her. She's so tight and hot and wet. I'm in heaven.

"Talk to me, sweetheart. Tell me how it feels."

"So good," she says breathlessly. "Don't stop."

"I'm never going to stop loving you. Never." I hold back for as long as I can, giving her time to adjust and taking it as easy as I possibly can without losing my mind. I rock into her, slowly, insistently, still watching her for signs of flashbacks or pain of any kind.

Her hands slide down my back to cup my ass, and I'm lost. Absolutely gone. I break out in a cold sweat and pick up the pace, wanting to feel that tight pussy clamp down around my cock more than I want my next breath. Propping myself up on one arm, I reach between us and press my fingers to her clit, and I'm rewarded with a tight contraction that nearly finishes me off.

"Natalie... Christ, this feels so fucking good. I love you so much. Come for me, sweetheart." I continue to caress her clit until I feel her lift off, the tight squeeze of her internal muscles more than I can take after living on the razor's edge of desire for so many days.

She cries out as she comes, her fingers digging into my ass and pulling me deeper into her and taking me with her in an orgasm that seems to come from my bone marrow.

It feels like it lasts forever, the pleasure so intense and so profound, unlike anything else has ever been. I come out of it gasping for air, throbbing with aftershocks and surrounded by her sweet softness. In that moment, I begin to genuinely believe I can live without the other half of my sexuality. If this is all I ever get to have, it's more than enough. Or so I tell myself...

I'm almost afraid to raise my head, to look at her face, for fear of what I might see. Is she remembering the most painful moments of her life? Does she have regrets? Does she already wish we hadn't done this? Does she want to go back to when there were rules she was determined to live by? If I see any sign of that, I think I'll die inside. But I need to know.

Slowly, I lift my head off her chest to find her eyes closed and her lips curled into a small smile. The relief that hammers through me is so significant that I'm left light-headed. She's happy. She's satisfied. She's smiling.

I kiss that sweet smile, and her eyes open to gaze up at me. "Wow," she whispers.

"My sentiments exactly. How do you feel?"

"I feel very, very good. You?"

I kiss her neck and throat. "Same. Never better. Best night of my life, hands down. And in case you were wondering, this, right here, is the best part of the best night ever." I kiss her again. "Hands down."

Her smile warms and sustains me. It tells me everything will be all right. She's not going to regret this in the morning. Hell, it's already almost morning, and no signs of regret.

Her index finger traces the furrow between my brows. "What're you worried about?"

"That you'll regret this."

"Never. It was perfect. In fact, I can't wait to do it again."

"Just give me ten minutes to recover, and we'll do it again. We'll do it as many times as you want."

"Mmm." She yawns. "Ten minutes." She's out cold in less than five.

I withdraw from her carefully, my hand around the base of the condom so there will be no accidents. I leave her only long enough to dispose of the condom before I crawl back into bed with her. I've arranged for an afternoon flight back to New York, so we can sleep in as I promised her.

Curled up to her warm, naked body, I relive every second of this incredible evening. Winning a Golden Globe was fantastic, but making love to Natalie... That was life changing.

CHAPTER 22

Natalie

I wake to bright sunshine streaming in through windows left uncovered the night before. A drumbeat of pain in my temple reminds me of the large amount of champagne I consumed last night. And then I shift to find a more comfortable position and the dull ache between my legs reminds me of what else happened.

I had sex with Flynn Godfrey, and I loved every second of it.

He's asleep next to me, the hard angles of his face softened in repose. His jaw is sprinkled with whiskers that only add to his over-the-top sexiness. He's so beautiful, inside and out, and I'm completely addicted to him.

His big warm hand is flat upon my belly until it moves up to cup my breast and tweak my nipple. That's all it takes to make me want him again, despite the soreness.

"You're awake," I whisper.

"Mmm, barely. My head is pounding."

"Mine, too."

"Goddamned champagne." His voice is a low, gruff rumble. "Always tastes so good going down, but the hangovers are killer."

"It should come with a warning."

"Hang tight, sweetheart. I've got the cure." He drags himself out of bed, and I watch him move around the room, fascinated by his naked body. I want to memorize every detail so I'll never forget how he looks this morning. He leaves the room for a few minutes and comes back with a tall glass of orange juice and a bottle of pills.

When he returns, the first thing I notice is the huge erection that now extends past his belly button. I can't look away. I'm still staring when he sits on the bed next to me, offering me the OJ and some pain meds.

"See something you like?" he asks with a low chuckle.

"Most definitely."

"Are you sore down there, too?"

"Uh-huh."

"I'm sorry."

"I'm not." We share the glass of OJ, both of us taking pills for our headaches.

Flynn puts the glass on the bedside table where the candles from last night have burned down to stumps. Propping his hands on either side of my body, he looks down at me, his hair falling over his forehead.

I reach up to smooth it back.

He takes hold of my hand and presses a kiss to my palm. "Last night was incredible."

"For me, too."

"No regrets?"

"Not a single regret. I hope you know…" I feel shy all of a sudden, confessing my deepest thoughts to him. "I couldn't have done that with anyone but you."

"You'd better not be doing that with anyone but me."

"Flynn… You know what I mean."

He gathers me into his embrace as he gets back into bed. "I know what you mean, and I'm truly humbled to have been given such a priceless gift."

Empowered by my newfound confidence, I slide my hand down his chest to encircle his erection. "I fell asleep before we could do it again."

"Yes, you did."

"Are you busy right now?"

His laughter brings a smile to my face. I love making him laugh.

"You're sore, honey. We should take it easy today."

"I don't want to take it easy."

"You need to trust me on this. Unless you want a positively miserable day tomorrow, we should wait until you feel better before we do it again. And you'll need to rest up, because I plan to keep you very busy."

"Is that right?"

"Mmm-hmm." This is said against my neck as he kisses and licks and nibbles me. "I hate to say that we need to get up and get moving. I need to get you home for school tomorrow."

That makes me groan. Three days have never gone by so quickly. "Something tells me that winter in New York isn't going to look quite as magical to me after experiencing winter in southern California."

"You're the only one I know who'd call winter in New York 'magical.'"

"If you knew how hard I worked to get there, you'd think it was magical, too."

His phone rings, and he goes still.

"What?"

"That's Addie, and she wouldn't be calling me today unless she really needed me for something."

"How can you tell it's her?"

"She programmed in her own ringtone, so I'd always know when it's her."

"That's awesome. I love her."

"So do I, but I don't love her quite as much as usual this morning." He reaches for the phone. "Yes, ma'am?"

I can't hear what she's saying, but I can see his expression tighten and the pulse in his cheek kick in. Something's wrong.

"Have you spoken to the hotel? What did they say?" He runs his fingers through his hair until it's standing on end. "Yeah, that'll work. I'll call them when we're ready. Thanks, Addie."

"What's wrong?"

"The hotel is surrounded by press, and they all want to know more about you. Liza is being slammed with calls. *Fuck!*"

"Hey." I wait for him to look at me. "We knew this would happen, so don't stress. They'll lose interest in a day or two when we don't give them anything."

"I don't think they're going to lose interest that quickly. Addie said they're ravenous to know more about the gorgeous 'kiss girl' who has changed my life so completely. We're going to have to leave through the loading dock to avoid them."

"I know you're upset and worried about me, but please don't let this ruin what was the best night of my life. I'd do it again in a heartbeat. It was…"

"For me, too, sweetheart." He kisses me before we get up to take showers and get ready to leave.

When we're set to go, hotel security works efficiently to get us out of the building and into a waiting Cadillac Escalade that Addie arranged.

Flynn doesn't relax until we're safely on our way to LAX. He spends much of the ride on the phone with Addie, ensuring the security detail someone named Gabe hired for me is ready to meet us in New York. I'm hoping that will be a temporary thing, until the interest in us dies down.

I take the time to read texts from Leah, who says I looked A-MA-ZING, and Aileen, who loves that I kissed Flynn after Tina and Amy's comments about him. *Very well done*, Aileen proclaims. *You looked beautiful! (And so did he! Haha!).* Both of them ask me to convey their congratulations to Flynn on his big win.

We're on the plane before Flynn finally ends the call with Addie, satisfied for now, anyway, that everything is in place for our return to New York.

"Sorry about all that," he says when he stashes the phone in his pocket.

"It's not your fault."

"Well, it kind of is. I knew if I brought you last night, it would turn into a bit of a circus. But from what Addie said, it's an even bigger circus than we expected."

"I was warned, so no worries. I had the best time. It was well worth any aggravation we have to deal with now."

He laughs at my choice of words. "Aggravation is one word for it. I hope you'll understand if I'm a little overprotective where you're concerned."

I send a side-eye glance his way. "Are you planning to be my personal bodyguard?"

"You bet your ass I'm going to be guarding your sweet body."

The low growl that accompanies his words sends a shiver through me.

"You can start now if you'd like." I wonder who this new Natalie is, but I can't deny that I like her.

"I'd love to, but I'm not touching you until you have time to recover from last night. I can't bear the thought of hurting you in any way."

"You could never hurt me."

"It would hurt if we had sex today, so we're waiting, and that's nonnegotiable."

"You're not the boss of me," I say with a teasing smile.

"In this case, I am."

As the plane taxis toward the runway for the trip back to New York, I reach for his hand and hold on tight for takeoff.

"Thanks for the best weekend of my life."

He kisses my hand. "It was for me, too. Thanks for coming."

We move to the sofa as soon as we can, and after a few heated kisses, we end up sleeping for most of the flight. It's now safe to say I'm addicted to sleeping in his arms.

It's snowing in New York, and the approach to Teterboro is bumpy. Flynn holds my hand the whole way, and I breathe a sigh of relief when we touch down. The cold and snow are harsh reminders we're not in California anymore. I feel an overwhelming sense of letdown at realizing my big adventure has ended and it's back to reality.

My third-grade classroom is an awfully long way from Gucci Couture.

"This must be what Cinderella felt like when her coach turned into a pumpkin," I say to Flynn as we drive through sloppy wet snow and ice on our way into the city.

"Are you calling my Bugatti a pumpkin?"

"I would never insult the Bugatti. It was a metaphor for the weather and the end of a rather grand adventure."

"The first of many grand adventures we'll have together, sweetheart. You can count on that."

We arrive at my place a short time later. We're greeted by Fluff, who is so happy to see me, she barely registers that Flynn is with me. Leah isn't home, so we settle in to wait for the security detail to get there. Four huge men arrive an hour later, and all of them seem to know Flynn.

He introduces me to each of them and lets me know that at least one of them will be with me at all times going forward.

"What about when I'm in school?"

"We'll be outside the building to ensure that no one tries to gain access to you."

"They'd try to get into my school?" I ask, incredulous.

"We've learned to be prepared for any and all possibilities."

"They'll also drive you to and from school when I can't be here to do it," Flynn adds.

"Well, that won't suck in light of the current weather."

"One of us will be close by at all times," Dylan, the one in charge, says. He hands me a black object that has a big red button in the middle of it. "This is a panic button. If you need us, don't hesitate to push the button. We'll get to you within seconds."

I swallow hard at the thought of needing them that badly. "I will, thanks."

"We'll leave you to get some rest, and we'll see you in the morning for the ride to school. Your roommate is welcome to come, too. I understand she works at the same school."

"Yes, she does. Thank you. She'll appreciate that."

"Good night, then."

They nod respectfully on their way out.

"Are you okay with all this?" Flynn asks.

"I guess I have to be. It's weird, but I suppose I'll get used to it."

"I'm sorry that it's necessary, but I won't take any chances with your safety or security."

I go to him and put my arms around his waist.

He gathers me in close to him. "You want me to go so you can get ready for tomorrow?"

"No, I don't want you to go."

"Good answer."

We take Fluff out to pee and then work together to make a simple dinner of pasta with vegetables. He insists we turn in early since I have to get up at what he calls the "butt crack of dawn." Lovely. In bed, he holds me close but refuses to even kiss me so he won't be tempted to make love to me.

Nothing I do, and I try just about everything, convinces him to change his mind.

"Stop trying to break me," he mutters. "I can't be broken."

Fluff, who has worked her way in between us, growls at him.

"Good girl, Fluff." I stroke her ears. "You tell him if he's going to sleep in our bed, he has to follow our rules."

"Tomorrow night, you'll be in my bed following my rules, so you'd better watch your mouth."

Fluff growls again, making us both laugh. We consider it a major victory that she's allowed him into the bed in the first place.

The next thing I know, my alarm is going off, and Flynn is groaning in protest.

I lean over Fluff to kiss him. "Go back to sleep for a while. I'll let you know when I'm leaving."

"Wait, do you take Fluff out first thing?"

"Usually."

"Not today you aren't. I'll do it." He gets up slowly and reluctantly. "Five o'clock in the fucking morning? Seriously, Nat?"

"I have to ease my way into the day. It's my routine."

"Your routine is fucked up."

"And you're cranky in the morning."

"This isn't the morning! It's the middle of the fucking night."

I laugh at him as I gather up my clothes and head for the shower. "Fluff, be nice to Flynn. He's taking you out to pee. And isn't it cute that you both have names that start with FL? You're a match made in heaven."

"Do you have to be so fucking cheerful in the middle of the night?"

I'm still laughing when I step into the shower. I love that he's cranky in the morning and that his hair stands straight up and he looks nothing at all like a movie star. Rather, he looks exactly like the man I love with all my heart.

He's talking to Leah when I emerge from the bathroom, dressed and ready for work.

"Um, Nat, there's a movie star in our apartment," she says, smiling at me over a mug of coffee.

I wink at her. "Nah, that's just Flynn, and he's grumpy in the morning."

"It's not morning. It's the middle of the fucking night."

"I couldn't agree more," Leah says.

We all leave together, Flynn to head to his place while the security guys take Leah and me to work. She loves that we now have our own driver. Flynn kisses me good-bye on the sidewalk and waits until we drive off to head to his car.

After four days with him, I miss him already.

CHAPTER 23

Flynn

Watching Natalie drive off in the big SUV with her security detail, I experience a sense of unease. I hate that she needs security simply because she's dating me, but like I told her, I'm not taking any chances where she's concerned.

The seven hours until she gets out of school stretch out before me like an endless ordeal I have to endure so I can be with her again. Tonight, I'll take her to my place, and we'll pick up where we left off the other morning. I honestly can't wait to be inside her again. That's the closest to heaven I've ever been. But I can't think about that now or I'll be walking around with a hard-on all day.

I go home to shower and change before heading to the Quantum office to do some work. I've let everything slide over the last ten days, and it's time to get caught up. I've got a meeting at two thirty with Hayden to go over the plans for post-production on our new film, which has defied naming. That's one of many decisions that must be made soon. I keep the meeting short and sweet, because it's almost time to see Natalie. She has to tutor her student Myles right after school, but at four o'clock, she's all mine.

Hayden calls me right on time. "How's it going?" he asks.

"Great, you?"

"I'm still high from Sunday night. I can only imagine how you must feel."

I can't tell him that winning the Globe is the least of what happened Sunday night. "It was a good night."

"Natalie seemed to enjoy it."

"She did."

"Addie says the press is going wild over her, trying to get the skinny."

"Liza is dealing with them."

"You can't stonewall them forever, you know."

"I'll stonewall them for as long as I can."

"So it's serious with you two? What you said in your acceptance speech…"

"It's serious. I'm in love with her."

"Flynn… Jesus, you just met her. Don't you think you ought to take some time before you start talking about *love*?"

"You ought to know about taking some time."

"What the hell does that mean?"

"When are you going to admit that you're in love with Addie?"

He's silent for so long that I wonder if he's still there. "What the fuck are you talking about?"

"I have eyes, Hayden. Perfectly good working eyes, and I've known for some time that you're in love with her."

"You're out of your fucking mind! You fall in love and suddenly you see love everywhere?"

"It's not sudden. You've been into her for years now, but you're too damned afraid to do anything about it. So don't sit in judgment of me just because I choose to act on my feelings for Natalie."

"I don't even know what to say to you right now. We've got a ton of shit to deal with, and you're throwing this at me?"

"I'm just pointing out that people in glass houses shouldn't throw stones."

"Poetic, Flynn. Really."

My phone chimes with a text from Addie. *911.* Our code for call me right now no matter what you're doing. My stomach drops, and my first thought is of Natalie. "I've got to go. I'll call you back."

"Flynn, wait—"

I drop the desk phone into the cradle and call Addie on my cell.

"We've got a huge problem," she says.

"What? You're freaking me out."

"I don't even know how to tell you this, but *Hollywood Starz* is reporting that Natalie is actually a woman named April Genovese who accused the Nebraska governor of rape when she was fifteen. It went all the way to trial, where he was convicted and sentenced to twenty-five years to life in prison."

I'm going to be sick. "I'll call you back." I run for the bathroom that adjoins my office, where I'm violently ill. Oh my God, I've brought down the wrath of hell on my sweet Natalie. All I can think about is getting to her. Right now.

I wash my face, brush my teeth quickly and grab my coat and phone on the way out of the office. In the elevator to the parking garage, I feel like my skin is too tight to contain the rage and fear that I feel. She'll never forgive me for this. I'm certain that any chance I had of a life with her is gone now, but that doesn't mean I won't do everything within my power to try to make this right.

Driving the Range Rover, I emerge into a swarm of reporters staked outside the Quantum office who are screaming at me for a comment about Natalie. I press the accelerator, not caring in the least if I run them down. All that matters is getting to her.

Liza calls, and I take it even though she's about the last person I want to talk to. "Flynn, oh my goodness! Is it true?"

"There's no comment from us on this, you got me?"

"You have to say *something*."

"No, I don't. This is her personal business, and it has nothing to do with me or my career. It's off-limits."

"But—"

"Liza, if you wish to continue working for me, I want the full resources of your company on this. I want you to threaten lawsuits and anything else you can think of to make it stop."

"It's too late to stop it. It's already all over the Internet."

"I can't do this right now. I need to get to her. Do what you can to contain it."

"Is it true?"

"I don't even know, but that doesn't matter. This is going to hurt her, and I promised I'd never hurt her."

"You didn't do this. You had nothing to do with it."

"You know goddamned well I had *everything* to do with it." After a quick call to Dylan to put Natalie's security on alert, I throw the phone into the passenger seat and hit the gas. Getting to her is the only thing that matters.

Natalie

Stone-faced Mrs. Heffernan is waiting for me when I return to my classroom after seeing my students off at the end of another long day. "We have a problem, Ms. Bryant."

"What's that?"

"We have reporters at our door looking for you, and we're hearing from them that you aren't who you say you are."

I feel the earth shift under my feet, and for a brief terrifying second, I fear I'm going to pass out from the absolute shock that hits my system like a high-voltage bolt of electricity.

"Nothing to say?" She seems smug and satisfied, as if she's always known I'm no good.

"I… I'm exactly who I say I am."

"And you were never known by the name April Genovese?"

That name coming from Mrs. Heffernan is another high-voltage shock that rips through me. I can't seem to speak over the huge knot of fear that grips my chest. It's similar to the way I felt when I had the wind knocked out of me the day I met Flynn.

"The contract you signed is very clear, Ms. Bryant, or Ms. Genovese or whomever you are. Fraud of any kind will not be tolerated. I'm afraid your position here has been terminated. You're to clean out your personal effects and be out by five o'clock, or you'll be escorted from the premises by the NYPD."

I'm being fired, and there's nothing I can do about it. As a contract employee with a charter school, I don't benefit from the protection of a union. I'm completely on my own. And then I think about the children I've come to love in the months we've been together.

A sob erupts from my tightly clenched jaw. "You can't fire me. My legal name is Natalie Bryant. I haven't lied about anything."

"None of this appeared in your background check, which leads us to wonder what else you're hiding. We can't take chances with the safety and security of our students. The decision has been made, and your contract has been voided. Please clean out your classroom immediately."

She turns and walks out of the room, slamming the door behind her.

For the longest time after she leaves, I stand perfectly still, trying to process what she's told me. And then I begin to cry again, the sobs coming from deep inside me as eight years of hard work disappear in a wisp of smoke. After everything I've done to hide—changing my appearance, changing my name, changing my entire life—none of it protected me. My job, my classroom, my children, my new home, my new city... Everything has been taken from me, and there's not a damned thing I can do, because she's right. I did lie during my background check, but only to protect myself. Nothing I lied about put children at risk. I would never do that.

But what does it matter now?

Feeling like I'm hiking through quicksand, I find a box in the coatroom and take it to my desk, filling it with personal items that I'd brought to make my classroom homier for the children. I can barely see through the tears that blind me. I find the thank-you card that Logan gave me this morning, and it hits me like a punch to the gut.

Thank you, Miss Bryant, for making my mommy smile. You're the best teacher in the whole wide world and I love you. Logan.

I fall to my knees, racked with sobs. I can't bear the thought of never seeing him or any of my other children again. My heart is breaking into a million pieces.

Leah comes into the room, closing the door behind her. "Oh my God, Natalie! Did Stone Face really just *fire* you?"

I nod because I'm not capable of speech.

"She can't do that! None of this is your fault. She's a fucking bitch." Leah squats next to me and puts her arm around me. "Come on, let's get you out of here. I'll take care of getting your stuff tomorrow."

I shake my head. I need a few minutes to myself before I can think of leaving, of facing the reporters who've descended upon my school, wanting a piece of me. It reminds me too much of the hell I went through during the trial, when everyone wanted a piece of me until there was almost nothing left.

"It's okay, Leah." I wipe my face, but it's futile because the tears keep coming. "Go on home. I'll see you there."

"I can't leave you like this."

"Please... I'll be fine."

"Where's Flynn? Does he know about this?"

Flynn... I'm ashamed that I haven't thought of him once since Mrs. Heffernan stormed out. He must be out of his mind if he knows what's happened. The poor guy will blame himself, when it's my fault, not his.

The door flies open, and there he is, breathing hard, his gorgeous face stony with rage and fear and love. The love is so apparent, it's all I see.

"I'll take it from here, Leah."

Leah stands and walks toward the door, squeezing his arm as she goes past him.

"Natalie..." He comes to me, drops to the floor and gathers me into his strong arms. He holds me so tightly, I know there will be bruises, but I'm so numb I can barely feel a thing.

I cling to him because I don't know what else to do.

"Let's get you out of here."

"There're reporters."

"Let me worry about that." He stands and helps me up. "Let's get your coat on."

"She fired me, Flynn. Mrs. Heffernan fired me. My stuff..."

"Leah will get it." He grabs my purse and phone from my desk and hands them to me. Then he takes me by the arm and leads me out like he does it every day, taking me through the janitor's closet to an exit I didn't even know existed. My security team is waiting for us with two black SUVs with tinted windows.

I get into the backseat of the one Flynn directs me to. He gets in with me. He never lets go of my hand as we speed away from the school, my home away from home for the last five months.

"I need to know who could've done this to you, Natalie." I hear his rage in every word he says.

"There's only one person who could've done it," I say between sobs as it becomes clear to me that someone I trusted has betrayed me. "He's the only person in the world who knows me by both my names."

"Whoever he is, I'm going to tear his balls off, and then I'm going to fucking destroy him."

Other Titles by Marie Force

Other Titles by M.S. Force
The Quantum Trilogy
Book 1: Virtuous

Book 2: Valorous

Book 3: Victorious

Contemporary Romances Available from Marie Force
The Treading Water Series
Book 1: Treading Water

Book 2: Marking Time

Book 3: Starting Over

Book 4: Coming Home

The Gansett Island Series
McCarthys of Gansett Island Boxed Set, Books 1-3

McCarthys of Gansett Island Boxed Set, Books 4-6

Book 1: Maid for Love

Book 2: Fool for Love

Book 3: Ready for Love

Book 4: Falling for Love

Book 5: Hoping for Love

Book 6: Season for Love

Book 7: Longing for Love

Book 8: Waiting for Love

Book 9: Time for Love

Book 10: Meant for Love

Book 10.5: Chance for Love,
A Gansett Island Novella

Book 11: Gansett After Dark

Book 12: Kisses After Dark

The Green Mountain Series

Book 1: All You Need Is Love

Book 2: I Want to Hold Your Hand

Book 3: I Saw Her Standing There

Book 4: And I Love Her

Novella: *You'll Be Mine* in the *Ask Me Why* Anthology

Book 5: It's Only Love (November 2015)

Single Titles

The Singles Titles Boxed Set

Georgia on My Mind

True North

The Fall

Everyone Loves a Hero

Love at First Flight

Line of Scrimmage

ABOUT THE AUTHOR

M.S. Force is the erotic alter-ego of *New York Times* bestselling author Marie Force. The Quantum Trilogy is M.S. Force's first foray into erotic romance, but it won't be the last!

With more than 3.5 million books sold, Marie Force is the *New York Times*, *USA Today* and *Wall Street Journal* bestselling, award-winning author of 40 contemporary romances. Her New York Times bestselling self-published McCarthys of Gansett Island Series has sold more than 1.8 million e-books since *Maid for Love* was released in 2011. She is also the author of the *New York Times* bestselling Fatal Series from Harlequin's Carina Press, as well as the *New York Times* bestselling Green Mountain Series from Berkley Sensation, among other books and series, including the new Quantum Trilogy, written as M.S. Force.

While her husband was in the Navy, Marie lived in Spain, Maryland and Florida, and she is now settled in her home state of Rhode Island. She is the mother of two teenagers and two feisty dogs, Brandy and Louie.

Join Marie's mailing list for news about new books and possible appearances in your area. Join one of Marie's many reader groups at marieforce.com/connect. Contact Marie at *marie@marieforce.com*.

Follow her on Facebook at Facebook.com/MarieForceAuthor, on Twitter @ marieforce and Instagram at marieforceauthor.

CPSIA information can be obtained at www.ICGtesting.com
Printed in the USA
LVOW07s2138130915

453874LV00002B/79/P